THE BURGLAR WHO MET FREDRIC BROWN

More by Lawrence Block

THE BERNIE RHODENBARR MYSTERIES

BURGLARS CAN'T BE CHOOSERS • THE BURGLAR IN THE CLOSET • THE BURGLAR WHO LIKED TO QUOTE KIPLING • THE BURGLAR WHO STUDIED SPINOZA • THE BURGLAR WHO PAINTED LIKE MONDRIAN • THE BURGLAR WHO TRADED TED WILLIAMS • THE BURGLAR WHO THOUGHT HE WAS BOGART • THE BURGLAR IN THE LIBRARY • THE BURGLAR IN THE RYE • THE BURGLAR ON THE PROWL • THE BURGLAR WHO COUNTED THE SPOONS • THE BURGLAR IN SHORT ORDER • THE BURGLAR WHO MET FREDRIC BROWN

THE MATTHEW SCUDDER NOVELS

THE SINS OF THE FATHERS • TIME TO MURDER AND CREATE • IN THE MIDST OF DEATH • A STAB IN THE DARK • EIGHT MILLION WAYS TO DIE • WHEN THE SACRED GINMILL CLOSES • OUT ON THE CUTTING EDGE • A TICKET TO THE BONEYARD • A DANCE AT THE SLAUGHTERHOUSE • A WALK AMONG THE TOMBSTONES • THE DEVIL KNOWS YOU'RE DEAD • A LONG LINE OF DEAD MEN • EVEN THE WICKED • EVERYBODY DIES • HOPE TO DIE • ALL THE FLOWERS ARE DYING • A DROP OF THE HARD STUFF • THE NIGHT AND THE MUSIC • A TIME TO SCATTER STONES

KELLER'S GREATEST HITS

HIT MAN • HIT LIST • HIT PARADE • HIT & RUN • HIT ME • KELLER'S FEDORA

THE ADVENTURES OF EVAN TANNER

THE THIEF WHO COULDN'T SLEEP • THE CANCELED CZECH • TANNER'S TWELVE SWINGERS • TWO FOR TANNER • TANNER'S TIGER • HERE COMES A HERO • ME TANNER, YOU JANE • TANNER ON ICE

THE AFFAIRS OF CHIP HARRISON

NO SCORE • CHIP HARRISON SCORES AGAIN • MAKE OUT WITH MURDER • THE TOPLESS TULIP CAPER

NOVELS

A DIET OF TREACLE • AFTER THE FIRST DEATH • ARIEL •

BORDERLINE • BROADWAY CAN BE MURDER • CAMPUS TRAMP • CINDERELLA SIMS • COWARD'S KISS • DEAD GIRL BLUES • DEADLY HONEYMOON • FOUR LIVES AT THE CROSSROADS • GETTING OFF • THE GIRL WITH THE DEEP BLUE EYES • THE GIRL WITH THE LONG GREEN HEART • GRIFTER'S GAME • KILLING CASTRO • LUCKY AT CARDS • NOT COMIN' HOME TO YOU • RANDOM WALK • RONALD RABBIT IS A DIRTY OLD MAN • SINNER MAN • SMALL TOWN • THE SPECIALISTS • SUCH MEN ARE DANGEROUS • THE TRIUMPH OF EVIL • YOU COULD CALL IT MURDER

COLLECTED SHORT STORIES

SOMETIMES THEY BITE • LIKE A LAMB TO SLAUGHTER • SOME DAYS YOU GET THE BEAR • ONE NIGHT STANDS AND LOST WEEKENDS • ENOUGH ROPE • CATCH AND RELEASE • DEFENDER OF THE INNOCENT • RESUME SPEED AND OTHER STORIES

NON-FICTION

STEP BY STEP • GENERALLY SPEAKING • THE CRIME OF OUR LIVES • HUNTING BUFFALO WITH BENT NAILS • AFTERTHOUGHTS 2.0 • A WRITER PREPARES

BOOKS FOR WRITERS

WRITING THE NOVEL FROM PLOT TO PRINT TO PIXEL • TELLING LIES FOR FUN & PROFIT • SPIDER, SPIN ME A WEB • WRITE FOR YOUR LIFE • THE LIAR'S BIBLE • THE LIAR'S COMPANION

WRITTEN FOR PERFORMANCE

TILT! (EPISODIC TELEVISION) • HOW FAR? (ONE-ACT PLAY) • MY BLUEBERRY NIGHTS (FILM)

ANTHOLOGIES EDITED

DEATH CRUISE • MASTER'S CHOICE • OPENING SHOTS • MASTER'S CHOICE 2 • SPEAKING OF LUST • OPENING SHOTS 2 • SPEAKING OF GREED • BLOOD ON THEIR HANDS • GANGSTERS, SWINDLERS, KILLERS, & THIEVES • MANHATTAN NOIR • MANHATTAN NOIR 2 • DARK CITY LIGHTS • IN SUNLIGHT OR IN SHADOW • ALIVE IN SHAPE AND COLOR • AT HOME IN THE DARK • FROM SEA TO STORMY SEA • THE DARKLING HALLS OF IVY • COLLECTIBLES • PLAYING GAMES

THE BURGLAR WHO MET FREDRIC BROWN

LAWRENCE BLOCK

For

ROBERT SILVERBERG

The Burglar Who Met Fredric Brown

ISBN: 978-1-954762-20-6

Cover by Jeff Wong
Production by JW Manus

A LAWRENCE BLOCK PRODUCTION

The Bernie Rhodenbarr Series

#1 *Burglars Can't Be Choosers*
#2 *The Burglar in the Closet*
#3 *The Burglar Who Liked to Quote Kipling*
#4 *The Burglar Who Studied Spinoza*
#5 *The Burglar Who Painted Like Mondrian*
#6 *The Burglar Who Traded Ted Williams*
#7 *The Burglar Who Thought He Was Bogart*
#8 *The Burglar in the Library*
#9 *The Burglar in the Rye*
#10 *The Burglar on the Prowl*
#11 *The Burglar Who Counted the Spoons*
#12 *The Burglar in Short Order*
#13 *The Burglar Who Met Fredric Brown*

1

It was around a quarter to five on a Wednesday afternoon in October when I marked my place in the Fredric Brown paperback I'd spent much of the day reading. I tucked it in my back pocket, then went outside and retrieved my table of bargain books from the sidewalk. This was a good fifteen minutes earlier than usual, but when you're the store owner you can do this sort of thing on a whim. That's one of the nice things about being an independent antiquarian bookseller, and there are days when it seems like the only nice thing.

This was one of them.

I typically start to shut down for the day around five, and usually manage to clear the last customer from the premises by five-thirty. Then I do what tidying up needs to be done, freshen Raffles's water dish and put some dry food in his bowl, draw the steel window gates shut, and lock up. The Bum Rap, where Carolyn and I have a standing appointment with a bottle of scotch, is just around the corner at Broadway and East Tenth Street. It's a five-minute walk, and I generally cross the threshold within a few minutes of six o'clock.

I have to pass Carolyn's establishment, the Poodle Factory, in order to get to the Bum Rap; it's almost always closed when I do, and she's almost always at our usual table by the time I arrive.

But not today, because I was out the door at Barnegat Books by twenty-eight minutes after five. (I don't know why I checked the time, or why I still remember it. But I did and I do.) The Poodle Factory is two doors east of the bookshop, and Carolyn Kaiser was sweeping dog hair out the door when I got there.

"Bernie," she said. "Oh, don't tell me. You haven't got time for a drink tonight."

"Why would I tell you that?"

"Well, I don't know," she said. "Personally, I always have time for a drink, but something could have come up. A chance to examine and possibly buy a promising collection of books. The opportunity to have drinks and dinner with a personable and attractive woman."

"You're a personable and attractive woman," I pointed out, "and I'm about to have drinks with you. I don't know about dinner, but it's certainly a possibility."

"A woman," she said, "with whom the possibility exists of a romantic encounter. You know what I mean, Bern."

"At the moment," I said, "you're the only woman in my life."

"Then I don't know what it would be. A dental emergency?"

"A dental emergency?"

"Well, people have them, though mine are always on weekends. The last toothache I had hit me on a Friday an hour after my dentist went home to Mamaroneck, and all I could do was stay drunk until Monday morning."

"The sacrifices we're called upon to make."

"Don't I know it? But you're not canceling our date, so why am I trying to figure out the reason?" She'd been running through her usual chores, and now she drew the door shut and turned the key in the lock. "Next stop," she said, "the Bum Rap."

"Not yet."

"Oh?"

"That's why I wanted to catch you before you got out the door," I said. "There's someplace I'd like to go first. It's maybe four or five blocks from here, and I thought we could walk over there together."

"Four or five blocks? I don't see why not. It's not like I'm wearing high heels."

"No."

"I mean, even when I was seeing that woman who tried to turn me into a lipstick lesbian, I never even thought about heels."

Carolyn occasionally claims to be five-foot-two, although she'd have to be standing on something for that to be true. Or, say, wearing three-inch heels. She is, however, my best friend in the whole world, and I kept the thought to myself.

"There," I said.

We'd walked the half block to Broadway, turned to the right and headed downtown. We passed Two Guys from Luang Prabang, the restaurant that had supplied the excellent Laotian food we'd lunched on a few hours earlier, and we passed the Bum Rap, and we walked another block to Ninth Street and turned left. Two more blocks and we were standing across the street from a very tall and very narrow building that was all steel and glass.

"Damn," Carolyn said. "What's that doing there?"

"Occupying space," I said, "though not very much of it in terms of its footprint. Given the size of the lot, it ought to be seven stories tall, maybe twelve at the most."

"I could count windows," she said, "but looking straight up gives me an ice cream headache. How tall is it?"

"Forty-two stories."

"I read something about buildings like this, Bern. They call them splinters."

"I think it's slivers."

"Same difference. Either way they get under your skin. What the developers do, they buy a building, maybe two buildings, and evict all the rent-controlled tenants and knock everything down. What do you figure happened to the people who used to live here?"

"Maybe they're at Bowl-Mor," I said, "bowling a few frames and knocking back a couple of beers. Oh, wait a minute. They can't be there, can they? Because the glass-and-steel people knocked down that building, too."

Bowl-Mor, which it won't surprise you to learn was a bowling alley, had been a going concern for years before I became the owner of Barnegat Books. It was part of the local landscape, and I passed it every morning when I walked the few blocks from the Union Square subway station to the bookstore. That changed a year or so ago when developers acquired the building that housed it and replaced it with an oversized office building designed to house software developers and others of their ilk.

That's been standard operating procedure on the island of Manhattan ever since the Canarsie Indians sold the place for twenty-four dollars and walked away congratulating themselves on their cunning. Buildings come and go, but the move to create Silicon Alley ran into opposition from the strong Greenwich Village preservationist movement. While those blocks of University Place lie outside the official Greenwich

Village Historic District, you could argue that they were very much a part of the Village, and more than sufficiently historic to remain untouched.

And so it was argued, by some very earnest and public-spirited people, and financial considerations tipped the scales, as they do most of the time. And that was the end of Bowl-Mor.

"It still bothers you," Carolyn said. "I mean, I sort of get it, Bern, but when did you ever do more at Bowl-Mor than give it a nod as you walked on by?"

"We went bowling," I said. "Don't tell me you don't remember."

"I remember. It was fun."

"Right."

"At first I couldn't keep the ball out of the gutter, but then I started to get the hang of it. I can even see where it could become a lesbian thing, like softball. And maybe it is, for all I know. In Cleveland, say."

"If they have lesbians in Cleveland."

"We are everywhere, my friend." She sighed. "Bowling. You and I bowled once and we never went back."

"But we could have."

"And now we can't."

"Exactly. And many's the time after lunch when I thought about letting the store stay closed for an hour while I bowled a couple of frames. And no, I never actually did this, but the point is I thought about it, and it was something I could have done."

"Coulda woulda shoulda, and now you can't, and here we are standing in front of a sliver or a splinter or whatever the hell it is. They kicked the tenants out and then they bought air rights from everybody on the block and built something that reaches halfway to the moon. I didn't know there were any slivers in this part of town."

"I think the Innisfree is the first."

"Is that what they call it? Who lives here, Bern?"

"Hardly anybody."

"They couldn't sell the apartments?"

"Oh, they didn't have any trouble selling them," I told her. "They were all sold before the building was completed. But most of them are empty."

She thought for a moment. "Foreign buyers," she said.

"Mostly, yes."

"Looking to launder money and have a secure investment in New York when things go to hell in Moscow or Minsk or Budapest or Istanbul, wherever they were playing King of the Hill. Oligarchs, Bern? Is that the word I'm looking for?"

"It's a word you hear a lot these days," I allowed, "but I don't know the exact definition, or how many of the buyers fit it. I think there's a better term."

"Oh?"

"Rich bastards," I said. "That pretty much covers it, and it's not limited to foreigners. Because there's at least one Innisfree resident who's about as foreign as apple pie. He was born right here in the USA."

"Who's that?"

Something kept me from uttering the name. "If it wouldn't give you an ice cream headache," I said, "I'd suggest you tilt your head back and look up at the very top floor. Not that you could see much of anything from this angle, but if you could, and if you were equipped with Superman's x-ray vision, you'd see something pretty remarkable."

"A rich bastard?"

"That too," I said, "if he happens to be home now. But you'd also see the Kloppmann Diamond."

"The Kloppmann Diamond," she said. "It's here, Bern? On top of the Innisfree?"

"That would put it on the roof. But it's a few feet down from there, in the penthouse."

"I remember when the Museum of Natural History announced they were planning on selling it. They used a different word."

"Deaccessioning. They made the difficult but essential decision to deaccession their most valuable gem."

"I remember a lot of people got upset."

"There was a flap," I said. "You'd have thought the Louvre was putting the Mona Lisa on the auction block."

"Smile and all. I remember somebody on New York One suggesting that Mike Bloomberg and Jeff Bezos and Elon Musk and Bill Gates should each kick in an eight-figure sum, outbid all comers, and give the diamond back to the museum. But that idea never seemed to get anywhere."

"Gee, I wonder why."

"Maybe because the four billionaires had the same thought I did, which was that the museum would say 'Thank you very much,' and wait a few years and then put it up for sale again. But they went through with it and sold it?"

"At Sotheby's," I said. "The week before last."

I raised my eyes forty-two stories, but I didn't keep them there long. There was nothing to see, just glass and steel, and the sense of vertigo I experienced made even that a blur. I lowered my gaze, all the way down to street level, and noted once again the security cameras mounted on the front of the building, and on the smaller and far less prepossessing buildings on either side.

And, indeed, on almost every building on the block, which made this a block like any other block in the city I call home.

Carolyn was asking about the sale, and the hammer price, and the identity of the winning bidder. "And you said he's an American, Bern?"

"I did, didn't I?"

"Like apple pie."

"More like school shootings," I said. "Or lynching."

"As American as lynching. But who is he?"

Something kept me from supplying the name. "I'd say he was the worst man in the world," I said, "but that covers a lot of ground, and there's no end of predatory pedophiles and serial killers who might very well argue the point. But I get the feeling we're going to get a glimpse of him right now."

A gleaming silver limousine, long enough to accommodate an entire high school cheerleading squad on prom night, was pulling to a stop in front of the Innisfree.

A door opened. A man emerged, his pink head the size and shape of a bowling ball, and every bit as unencumbered with hair. He was wearing a suit he'd bought from the Big & Tall Shoppe, but he'd done some squats and pushups since his final fitting, and he looked as though he might burst out of it.

"Is that him, Bern? What's a guy like that going to do with the Kloppmann Diamond? Wear it for a pinky ring?"

Another of the limo's doors opened, and another man got out, and if he wasn't a twin of the first hulk he was at the very least a brother from another mother. Same size, same gleaming skull, same suit that had failed to keep up with the hypertrophy of his massive upper body.

"There's two of him," Carolyn said. "You'd think one would be enough."

"More than enough," I agreed, "but neither one looks like the man who bought the Kloppmann. My guess is they're his bodyguards, and the body they're guarding is in the rear seat of the limo, waiting for one of them to open the door for him."

That was what happened, but from our point of view it was anticlimactic, because one of the bodyguards opened the rear-most curbside door, and the limo blocked our view of the man who got out of it. He was halfway to the Innisfree's entrance by the time it drove off, and we caught a glimpse of him from the back, flanked by his two guardians, even as the liveried ostiary made a show of throwing open the door for him.

In no time at all he was through it, and it had swung shut behind him. "So much for Orrin Vandenbrinck," I said. "Let's get out of here. I need a drink."

2

By the time we got to the Bum Rap, someone was sitting at our usual table. Some two, I should say, the pair consisting of a man around forty with a tweed flat cap on his head and a woman who'd been badly served by her hairdresser, and whose expression showed that she was aware of this, and would not soon forgive or forget. And that's all you have to know about them, because we never saw either of them again, and I only mention them because there they were, sitting at our table.

Not that it mattered, because one table at the Bum Rap is every bit as good as another. The only reason we sit at the same table each time is because it saves deciding where to sit. And if the table's taken, as it sometimes is, we find another.

What's important isn't the table. It's what's on the jukebox, and what's in one's glass. Kris Kristofferson was on the jukebox, looking for his cleanest dirty shirt, and that's always a plus, but I still needed a drink.

When we walked in, Maxine was delivering a glass of beer to a man on the far side of the room, but it didn't take her long to get to our side. "Thank God you're here," Carolyn said. "I'll have my usual scotch on the rocks, and Bernie'll have the same, except he may want it with water. Or even soda."

"Why don't we ask him?" I suggested. "If we do, we might find out he doesn't want scotch at all."

I looked at the ceiling. It's one of those old-fashioned stamped tin ceilings, and if you're going to look at a ceiling you could do a lot worse, but I was just pretending to give the matter some consideration. "A martini," I pronounced. "Very dry, very cold, and very soon."

Carolyn: "Gin or vodka?"

"Gin," Maxine said, "because if it was vodka you'd say 'Vodka martini.' But nobody says 'gin martini.' That'd be what-chamacallit."

"Huh?"

"Oh, you know. Like baby puppy or crooked politician. There's a word for it."

"Redundant," I said.

"There you go. Any particular kind of gin?"

I shook my head and she went off to fetch it, and brought it in a stemmed glass with an olive for garnish. "I figured straight up," she said, "because if you wanted it on the rocks you'd have said so."

"Good thinking."

"Same thing if you wanted a twist instead of an olive. Like gin and straight up and olive are the default mode, you know?"

"Exactly," I said, and she went away beaming, having set our respective drinks before us, and we raised our respective glasses but didn't bother clinking them together, or trying to think of something to toast. Carolyn had a swig of scotch and I hesitated for perhaps a hemisemidemiquaver of a moment, then took a long drink of cold gin. I don't know if it had been shaken or stirred, and why on earth would anyone care?

Carolyn was holding her breath, watching me, and let it out when she saw me swallow.

I asked her what was wrong.

"Wrong? We're in the Bum Rap, winding down after a long day of washing dogs and selling books—"

"Mostly not selling books," I said.

"Selling, not selling, whatever. We're here, and there's booze in our glasses and we've just transferred some of it to our tummies, and what's that line you like about malt and Milton Berle?"

I had to unpack that one. "Not Milton Berle," I said. "John Milton, the poet."

"That's who I meant, and what's the line he wrote?"

"He wrote *Paradise Lost,*" I said, "among other things, but it was A. E. Housman who wrote the line you're thinking of. 'Malt can do more than Milton can / To Justify God's Ways to man.'"

"That's it. And whatever malt can do, Bern, scotch can do it quicker." She took another sip. "I feel better already. How about you?"

"I feel fine," I said, and drank some more of my martini. The last martini I could recall was one I'd had before lunch with Marty Gilmartin at his club, The Pretenders. That had been in the spring, I seemed to remember. Call it April, and now it was October, so that was what, six months?

Unless it was an earlier April, which seemed equally possible, in which case it was a year and a half. Either way, it seems fair to say it was a long time between martinis.

"I took a sip of my drink," I said, "and you were the one who relaxed. Visibly."

"So? We're close, Bern. Like Corsican brothers. You take a drink and I relax."

I looked at her.

"Okay," she said. "What happened is you said you didn't

want scotch, and that worried me. I was afraid you were going to order Perrier instead, and we both know what that means."

What it used to mean, back in the good and bad old days, was that I wanted to maintain a crystal clear head for an evening of breaking and entering. But I hadn't done any of that since well before my last martini, whether it was six months or a year and a half ago.

I thought about it. "I walked you over to the Innisfree," I said, "and told you about the Kloppmann Diamond, and pointed out Orrin Vandenbrinck—"

"And I could feel how much you wanted to steal it, Bern."

"Well, sure," I said. "I'm a born thief and I love to steal. It's a character defect, I've never denied it, but it's not a phase I'm going through. It's part of who I am."

"Right."

"And the Kloppmann Diamond is about as good as it gets in the world of precious stones, and the man who owns it is one of the most contemptible human beings on the planet. And instead of stashing it in a vault, as anyone with half a brain would do, he's announced to all the world that he's keeping it in his apartment, an apartment that's a very short walk from where we're sitting right this minute."

"Jesus, Bern. You still want to steal it, don't you?"

"Of course I do. But it's not going to happen. I may be crazy but I'm not stupid. Look, I haven't picked a lock or climbed through a window in ages, and it's not because I've reformed. I've been rendered obsolete."

"Obsolete."

"Well, what else would you call it? You saw the security cameras at the Innisfree. And you saw the ones we passed on our way here."

"Only because you pointed them out to me, Bern. 'Look, there's another one! Smile, Carolyn—you're on *Candid Camera!*'"

"And those were just the ones I spotted. There were probably just as many I never noticed. I understand the UK's even worse, and that if a Londoner's not inside a private dwelling he's almost certain to be in front of a camera. And New York's not far behind."

"Commit a crime," she said, "and the world is made of glass."

"He didn't know the half of it."

"Who's that, Bern?"

"Ralph Waldo Emerson," I said. "That's who you were just quoting. The world is made of glass, all right, and the glass is a camera lens. And it's not just the cameras, either. You remember when that one manufacturer was crowing about his pickproof lock?"

She did. "And you bought one," she said, "purely for research purposes, and you sat down with it, and how long did it take you to get through it? Two minutes?"

"A little longer than that, but the word *pickproof* turned out to be false advertising. But that was then. Now they've got electronic locks that I wouldn't stand a chance against. I wouldn't even know where to begin."

I brought my glass to my lips, only to find that I'd somehow contrived to finish it. I looked up, caught Maxine's eye right away, noted that Carolyn's glass was as empty as my own, and made the circular motion one makes to indicate that we could do with another round.

While we waited for it, I expanded my rant. I had two vocations, I said, and that was the right term for them because they weren't just how I made my living, they were each a genuine calling. Burglary and bookselling, not that far apart in the dictionary, and both of them proper Twentieth Century occupations that had withered and died in the new millennium.

People didn't browse a bookshop anymore, unless they were looking for a preview of something they could subsequently order online. They weren't crazy, it wasn't part of a plot; the world had changed, and it was infinitely easier and more efficient, not to mention cheaper, to do your book hunting at your computer.

"That's fine for everybody—except those of us who own bookshops. And I have to admit it's even worked out well for some of my fellow booksellers; they set up web sites, list their entire inventory, and spend their days packing up books and filling orders. More often than not they close their stores, because why pay rent when you can work out of your house and stow your wares in a storage locker? Your whole operation is easier and less expensive to run, and you never have to talk to a customer."

"I thought you liked talking to customers, Bern."

That was something I'd had in mind when I bought Barnegat Books from old Mr. Litzauer—bright literate conversations with bright literate customers, and there'd been many of them over the years, some of them of the female persuasion. Now what I mostly get are the ones who can't understand why I don't want to buy their mother's collection of Reader's Digest Condensed Books.

"And a modern up-to-date burglar," I went on, "wouldn't sit around bemoaning all the locks he could no longer pick. He'd give his burglar tools a decent burial and pay the kind of attention to computers that I paid to locks. He'd teach himself how to hack his way past filters and firewalls and into back doors and rabbit holes, and don't ask me what those words mean, because if I knew more than a handful of buzzwords I'd be a rich man working ten days a year. I'd know the ins and outs of computer security, and I'd cobble up some ransomware and hold some city hostage. 'Listen up, Portland. I just shut you down, your cops, your fire department, your hospitals, your schools. All your traffic lights are green in both directions and your motorists are playing the world's wildest game of bumper cars. You've been cyber-poisoned, and if you want the antidote all you have to do is transfer a million dollars' worth of some incomprehensible cryptocurrency into my numbered account.'"

"Which Portland, Bern? Maine or Oregon?"

"They can take turns," I said. "But I never wanted to be that kind of a thief. I didn't start letting myself into other people's houses because I wanted to increase my net worth dramatically. If that's what I wanted I'd have gone to work for Goldman Sachs. I get a thrill out of burglary, Carolyn. You want it to be profitable, same as I want to sell a book for more than I paid for it, but when you come right down to it the money's just a way of keeping score."

There was more to the rant, there always is, but it was nothing I hadn't said before and nothing she hadn't heard before, and eventually I'd let off enough steam to give it a rest. I looked at my glass and saw that the second martini had gone the way of the first.

"You want another, Bern? I'll keep you company if you do."

"I do," I said, "and I don't, and don't is gonna win this one. A third martini would undo the good work of the first two."

"You'd drink yourself sober? I've heard of that, but I've never seen it happen in real life."

I shook my head. "You were right," I said.

"I was? That's good news. What was I right about?"

"The martini," I said. "The first one. I ordered it because I figured it would hit me harder than my usual scotch and water."

"And did it?"

"Of course," I said. "And that's what I wanted, partly because of the kind of day it had been, but also because so much of me wanted nothing more than to go back to that inexcusable waste of glass and steel and find a way into the penthouse."

"You wanted the Kloppmann Diamond."

"I wanted to take my best shot at it. And I knew I was being crazy, and I knew I had to keep myself from what would clearly be self-destructive behavior, and I wasn't sure scotch would do it. I could have a glass of scotch, or even two of them, and walk away telling myself I was still clearheaded enough to risk life and limb at the Innisfree. I'd be wrong about that, but that's what I'd tell myself, and I might be addled enough to think I was making sense."

"But with one or two martinis—"

"It'd be a different story. And I've had my two martinis, and I have to say they've done the job. I'm not slurring my words, at least I don't think I am—"

"You're not, Bern."

"—and I'm pretty sure I could walk a straight line, although I don't know that I could pass a field sobriety test."

"Since you don't own a car," she said, "you probably won't have to."

"All in all," I said, "I feel the way a person would want to feel after drinking a pair of martinis. A little looser, a little less wired. But if I had a third martini—"

"You'd be drunk?"

"I'd be at risk of losing the certainty I feel right now that this is no night to return to a life of crime. The third martini could all too easily unlock the oh-what-the-hell factor."

"Oh what the hell," she said. "'Oh what the hell, I know she's straight, but why not put the moves on her anyway? Oh what the hell, so who cares if she's married? How much of a problem could that possibly be?'"

"There you go."

"There I've gone, Bern, all too often, and I've almost always regretted it. No third martini for you."

"Absolutely not. I don't even want one, truth to tell. In fact—"

"You want to call it a night."

"I think so. I think I'll treat myself to a cab, and I think I'll get in bed with my book and read myself to sleep."

"You were talking about the book at lunch," she recalled. "Fredric Brown?"

I took it from my pocket.

"*What Mad Universe.* It's science fiction? I've only read his mysteries. *Night of the Jabberwock, The Wench is Dead.*"

"Fine books."

"*The Awesome Clipjoint.* No, that's wrong."

"Fabulous," I said.

"Of course, *The Fabulous Clipjoint.* When did he write it, back in the Fifties?"

"1947."

"Well, that was well before awesome. People who say *awesome* now wouldn't be born for another thirty years. What's it about, Bern? Colonies on Alpha Centauri? Space ships shooting at each other with lasers?"

"It's about alternative universes," I said, and explained as best I could after having had that second martini. "You remember Voltaire's line in *Candide*? About this being the best of all possible worlds? Well, Brown's premise in *What Mad Universe* is that all possible worlds exist, all possible universes, and you and I happen to be in this particular universe, sitting at a table in what some people would call a dive bar—"

"But for us it's a home away from home."

"Whatever. But if something gave us the right sort of nudge, we could be in a different universe. I'd still be me and you'd still be you, and the Bum Rap might still be here, but it would be a different universe and we'd be leading slightly different lives. You'd still have a Roosevelt dime in your pocket, but FDR would be facing in the opposite direction."

"What difference would that make?"

"Maybe none."

She thought it over, shook her head. "I get the feeling it's too deep for me, Bern."

"No, if you were to read the book it would make perfect sense to you, Carolyn. Or if I could explain it better, but that'll have to wait until another day. All I want to do now is go home."

"I could go home myself," she said, "and eventually I probably will. But first I'll head for the Cubby Hole, in the hope of finding some dishy dame who's neither straight nor married. And, if this is really the best of all possible worlds, I might get lucky."

3

I got lucky. I walked out the door, headed for the curb, held up a hand, and a cab stopped. I told the driver I wanted West End Avenue and Seventieth Street. Whatever he may have wanted, he was circumspect enough to keep it to himself.

Traffic was what you'd expect at that hour, but the gin had done a commendable job of editing my perceptions of the world. The horns some drivers honked didn't sound all that angry, and indeed there was something melodious about them, something pleasantly harmonic in their interplay. If the trip took longer than it should have, well, might not one view its duration as serving a purpose, easing the transition between the social buzz of the Bum Rap and the virtual isolation of my apartment? Wasn't it all part of the natural order of things in this, the best of all possible worlds?

Truth to tell, I may not have been a hundred percent awake in the back seat of that cab.

And, whatever purpose the ride did or didn't serve, it transported me to my home; by the time I got there the gentle embrace of the martinis had largely dissipated, and I paid the driver and tipped him with the restrained generosity of a grateful but sober gentleman. My doorman was doing a crossword puzzle and paying no attention to the CCTV monitor; it showed what our four security cameras had to report, and a glance let me know he wasn't missing anything. I wished him a pleasant evening, and I went up to my apartment.

If I'd still been at the full affect of the gin, I might have showed off and let myself in without using my key. Instead I opened the door in the conventional manner and thought about fixing myself something to eat.

A sandwich? No, a can of chili. As it cooked I stirred in some grated cheddar, then tarted it up with some hot sauce. I opened the fridge, considered a can of beer, chose a can of ginger ale instead, and drank it with my meal, even as I found my place and returned to Fredric Brown and *What Mad Universe.*

The best of all possible worlds?

Well, that covered a lot of ground. But, with a bowl of chili and a glass of ginger ale and a good book in hand, it wasn't so bad, was it?

The day it followed upon, on the other hand, was a rat bastard.

Or was it? Lunch had been pleasant enough. It was my turn to host and Carolyn's turn to bring the food, and she brought Laotian take-out from Two Guys from Luang Prabang. We weren't sure what we were eating, but agreed it was tasty, and that the restaurant's current incarnation was its best since Two Guys from Taichung.

"Juneau Lock," she said, remembering. "Have you been in touch with her, Bern?"

She meant Katie Huang, who'd very deliberately mangled the English language during her shifts behind the counter at the Taiwanese version of Two Guys; then she'd shower and change and hurry uptown to Juilliard, where she was their most promising flautist. *Juneau Lock* was what she'd say when I'd point to a dish at Two Guys, and it was how she chose to pronounce *You no like,* but she'd sell it to me anyway, and we always liked it.

Eventually she'd dropped the act and she and I got to know each other, and we became as much of an item was we could, given the hectic nature of her schedule. And now the restaurant was just a memory, albeit a happy one, and she was in New York a little more frequently than Halley's Comet, but not by much.

"She was in town in the early spring," I remembered, "performing with a chamber orchestra at Weill Recital Hall. We managed to fit in coffee afterward, but then she had to go straight to the airport."

"So there was no opportunity for, um, romance."

"We managed a hug and a couple of kisses," I said, "but when you've spent an hour or two watching a beautiful woman playing the flute—"

"I guess it raises your expectations," she said, and I agreed that it did.

Aside from that interlude, the day had been like most of them lately. A man with a bright blue bowtie brought in three books he'd found on my bargain table and paid ten dollars for them. I always appreciate that out of proportion to the dollars involved, as he could have saved time and money by simply walking off with them. (And that, I've long suspected, is what most people do, and I can't say it breaks my heart. If anything, it lightens the load when I bring the table inside at day's end.)

He was my only pre-lunch cash customer, but he wasn't the only person to cross my threshold. A young woman, thin as your average rail, planted herself in the self-help section and spent close to an hour reading a quick-weight-loss diet book that had topped the bestseller lists thirty years ago. I don't know why she thought she needed it, but her need evidently stopped short of the commitment of ownership.

I lost track of her, and then looked up from my book when she cleared her throat to get my attention. "Your cat," she said. "Is she a Manx?"

"He," I said.

"I'm sorry."

"Don't be," I said. "He's not the man he used to be, thanks to a vet's intervention."

"I couldn't help noticing that he doesn't have a tail."

"It sticks out, doesn't it? Or would, if he had one. I don't know that he's an actual Manx. He may have lost the tail in a roomful of rocking chairs, and I suppose that would make him a Manx manqué."

I should tell you that I was not uttering these words for the first time. One develops a line of patter and trots it out when it seems appropriate. A bit of bubbly conversation can break the ice, and a break in the ice can leave a visitor feeling that the only sporting thing to do is buy a book. And even if it doesn't, doesn't a spot of chat make for a nicer day?

Not always. Her eyes glazed over, suggesting that perhaps *manqué* was not part of her working vocabulary, and she forced a smile and took her leave. The little bell attached to the door tinkled when she opened it, and tinkled again when it swung shut. I never even got to introduce Raffles by name.

And of course there were two or three people who came in, looked around for a few minutes, and then went on their way. One of them took a moment to jot down a couple of book titles, and I knew where that would lead. There's a hand-lettered sign on my wall, *Please wait until you have exited the premises before ordering the book from Amazon.* I probably ought to take it down, if anything it's likely to be counterproductive, but it's an unobtrusive sign and not that many people notice it, and I have to admit I like having it there.

After lunch, I made my second sale of the day. It was a cash sale, and came in the form of five twenty-dollar bills, in return for which I handed my customer two dollars in change.

You'd think that would have pleased me, wouldn't you?

You'd be wrong.

The customer was a young man named Mowgli, who's been a frequent visitor to Barnegat Books for years. He was a high school kid when he first started showing up, although I don't think his teachers ever got to see very much of him. In no time at all he found a niche for himself as a book scout, dropping in regularly with a tote bag full of volumes he'd acquired in jumble shops and rummage sales. He knew what was good and what wasn't, and more often than not the books he brought to me were ones I was happy to put on my shelves. I'd name a price for the ones I wanted and he always took it without argument, and every transaction was a win for both of us.

Then eBay.

And, virtually overnight, Mowgli morphed from supplier to customer. There was a day when he came in with his tote bags and sold me a dozen books, and there was the day a week or so later when he came in with an empty tote bag that had a dozen books in it when he left. "There's this thing I've been trying," he said. "Selling books online. It's kind of a pain in the ass, packing them up and standing in line at the post office, but what you're doing is running an auction, and sometimes the bidders get carried away."

He never sold me another book, and ever since then he's dropped in every week or two to cherry-pick my stock. He never haggles, never asks for a discount, always pays whatever price I've marked on the flyleaf—and some of the books he's bought from me are ones he sold me in the first place.

I shouldn't resent this. He's the same decent kid he's always been, and just as it was profitable for me to buy books from him, so is it profitable now when he buys them from me. It should brighten my day to see his face in the doorway, but I have to force a smile at the sight of him.

"You ought to try this, Bernie," he has told me more than once. "Just get some geeky kid to build you an eBay store and list all your stock. Instead of offering your books to the handful of people who happen to be walking down East Eleventh Street, you're putting everything in the store in front of millions of eyeballs all over the world. Just the other day I sold a small-press edition of a Dawn Powell novel to a customer in Lesotho. I had to look it up. Lesotho, not Dawn Powell."

"Right."

"Lots of booksellers are doing this. They're making money—plus they're saving money on rent, because what do you need with an expensive street-level storefront when your customers never come anywhere near the store?"

And so on.

The thing is, I knew what he was saying was true. I'm by no means a computer whiz, but I know my way around the internet, and I could learn anything else I needed to know. I could hire someone to do the packing and shipping, and without too much effort I could probably increase my gross sales by a factor of ten. I'd keep the store where it is—the rent's not a problem, since I own the building—and I'd be more proactive in seeking out accumulations and personal libraries to buy.

See, I've given this a lot of thought. I know what I'd do, and how I'd do it.

And I don't want to.

Because what it comes down to is that I didn't buy Barnegat Books in order to get into the mail-order business, or some Twenty-first Century cyber-equivalent thereof. I didn't want to spend my days sitting at the computer. I wanted to spend them sitting behind the counter, having live real-time conversations about books with literate and personable men and women.

Never mind. I had a shower and I made myself a cup of chamomile tea, and by nine-thirty I was in bed with my book.

It was science fiction, of course, but it was also set in the arcane world of the genre and its readers; the protagonist edited a science-fiction magazine, and there was a sort of Inside Baseball element to the way 1940s SF fandom played a role in the story. I suppose that dated the book, but it didn't seem to matter. Brown's narration and dialogue flowed so smoothly that I had no trouble entering the book's fictional reality and remaining there in comfort.

I would set the book down from time to time for a sip of tea, and I'd let my mind wander down some train of thought the book had inspired. Multiple alternative universes, as infinite in number as the stars—it was a lovely notion, and a fine premise for a novel, even though it was essentially preposterous.

I thought of the classic definition of a Unitarian: Someone who believes in one God at the most. Surely one universe was all anybody could ask for, and weren't we lucky it had been provided for us?

The best of all possible worlds, I thought. And turned the page.

4

I stayed up long enough to finish the book, turned off my light, and woke up eight hours later with the sense of having slept through a full night's worth of vivid dreams without remembering any of them. Whatever they may have been, they'd left me well rested, so I couldn't see that I had any cause for complaint.

Shower, shave, etc. I put on my usual costume—chinos, a blue button-down shirt, and a navy blazer. I thought about a tie, as I occasionally do, and I decided against it, as I almost always do. It's my store, as I've said, and in the spirit of our casual age I could wear jeans and a Mötley Crüe T-shirt, and a year or two ago I went through a month or two of doing just that.

But what I discovered was that when I went for casual comfort, people tended to relate to me as to a clerk earning hourly wages; when I wore the blazer, they assumed I owned the place. Since the pride of proprietorship was about the only thing I get out of Barnegat Books, I figured I'd dress accordingly.

I didn't recognize the fellow behind the desk, but that's not unusual. Our doormen come and go, often departing before I manage to learn their names. I wished this one a good morning, and he looked up from his Spanish-language newspaper and gave me an uncertain smile.

"No CCTV," I said, pointing to the spot on the wall usually occupied by the monitor. "Did it break down again?"

The smile faded a degree or two, but his expression remained uncertain. There didn't seem too much point in trying to prolong our conversation, such as it was, so I walked out into a perfectly satisfactory October morning.

I had my usual breakfast at the diner around the corner on Seventy-second Street, skipped a second cup of coffee, and entered the subway station at Seventy-second and Broadway, and that's when I got the first clue that this was going to be an unusual day.

I couldn't find my Metrocard.

I keep it in a compartment in my wallet, and I always put it back in the same place, because it's something I use at least once and more often twice a day, so I don't want to have to hunt for it. Reach into pocket, remove wallet, take card from usual spot, swipe it at the turnstile, and put it back—it doesn't take long for this to become automatic, and I did it now as automatically as ever, except my Metrocard had unaccountably gone missing.

I'd used it last the previous morning, and would have used it again to return home, but for that second martini that had made advisable the small luxury of a taxi. I was sure I'd put it back after use, but I'd drawn my wallet from my pocket any number of times since then, and I might have been careless enough for something to slip out and disappear.

In the cab, say, when I'd fumbled for the right bills so I could be as generous as I wanted to be, without doing an imitation of drunken sailor.

These things happen, and a Metrocard with less than $20 of stored credit is a far less upsetting loss than my American Express card, say, or my driver's license, both of which a quick search showed I still had. (On the other hand, if I had to lose something, why couldn't it have been the card an earnest customer had pressed upon me, the overly elaborate business card of a psychic healer who was said to work wonders? For that matter, why hadn't I ditched the card as soon as that particular customer was out the door?)

Never mind. There's a clutch of vending machines where you can add additional funds to your Metrocard—or, if you've lost the thing, purchase a replacement. I looked for it, but they'd apparently moved it, and I couldn't seem to find where they'd relocated it.

I went to the booth and told the attendant I needed a new Metrocard.

She smiled pleasantly. "A SubwayCard," she said.

"A card to get on the subway," I said, and made a swiping motion to get the point across. "A Metrocard."

Another smile. "Where are you from? I hope you're enjoying New York."

"I'm from West End Avenue," I said, "and I like it here just fine. But I'd really like to get downtown to open my store, and I lost my Metrocard and I need to replace it."

Her expression changed. She'd been giving me the smile one offers to a hapless tourist, and now what I was getting was the tentative look extended to the ambulatory psychotic. I probably wasn't dangerous, her expression suggested, but better safe than sorry.

"I'm sure many people call them that," she said carefully,

"but here's what we have." And she held up a wallet-sized plastic rectangle. It had the same black strip across its bottom that you'd find on a Metrocard, but instead of slanting blue letters on an orange background it sported white block caps on a forest green field, and what they spelled out was not Metrocard but SubwayCard.

I felt the way a pinball machine must feel when the player jostles it overmuch.

Tilt!

She went on talking, telling me how I could acquire a SubwayCard of my very own, but the words had stopped registering. I walked away in the middle of a sentence, and while that wasn't very polite, I have a feeling she was relieved to see me go. I walked to a spot that was out of pedestrian traffic and went through my wallet again, still looking for my Metrocard but on the lookout for something else as well, something green with white lettering.

And there it was. My very own SubwayCard, with the subtle silhouette of a train behind those white letters, and the same MTA logo in the same spot that you'd find on a Metrocard.

I walked over to the nearest bank of turnstiles. I swiped my SubwayCard, and when I pushed the turnstile it yielded just as it had always yielded to my trusty old Metrocard, and I walked on through.

I put the SubwayCard back in my wallet, in the compartment where I'd always kept my Metrocard.

Then I headed for the platform to catch my train.

* * *

Now and then, when the weather's nice enough, I'll take one train all the way to Seventh Avenue and Fourteenth Street and walk across town to my store. But more often than not I'll change at Times Square to a different line that drops me at Union Square. This was a nice enough day for the walk, but I felt the need to make things as ordinary as possible.

Both trains were standing room only, hardly unusual during the morning rush hour, and I held on to a metal post even as I tried to keep a grip on reality. I was positive I'd never seen a SubwayCard before, or even heard of it, and yet I had one in my wallet. I tried to make sense of this, and no matter how I looked at it, I could only draw one conclusion.

I was losing it.

I'd lived in the same apartment building long enough to watch some of my fellow residents succumb to dementia. A woman who'd lived on the ninth floor for longer than I'd been a tenant had taken to spending her evenings in the lobby, perched on the wing chair for hours on end with her hands folded neatly in her lap. Sometimes she talked to people, and sometimes she talked to herself, but much of the time she just sat there.

And then she started coming downstairs in her nightgown, and the tenants and management tried to figure out how to respond, and then one evening she evidently found the lobby overly warm, and took off the nightgown. And not long after that she was taken off somewhere, to what gets called assisted living, as it was pretty clear she required assistance of some sort.

And nobody ever saw her again.

Metrocard, SubwayCard. Was that the way it started?

By the time I changed trains at Times Square, I had bolstered myself with the realization that I was way too young for age-related dementia. And by the time I emerged from the depths at Union Square, I found myself meditating upon another phrase.

Early-onset dementia.

Was that a possibility? I mean, how early is too early?

It was still a beautiful October morning. And as I headed south on University Place, I realized I had a tool available to me that would enable me to deal with whatever I was facing, the one coping mechanism that gets most of us through the days and weeks and months.

Denial. Really, what would we do without it?

I'm fine, I told myself, striding along briskly and confidently. Life in the Twenty-first Century is overflowing with things that don't make sense, and most of them don't have to. I'd got along fine with my Metrocard ever since the MTA decided to phase out tokens, and now I could get along fine with my SubwayCard since they'd evidently phased out Metrocards. I'd managed to get on the train, hadn't I?

Nothing to worry about. I was perfectly fine.

And, as I walked, the sight of the familiar was reassuring. I walked on past this newsstand and that stationery store, read the familiar signage, nodded at the occasional familiar face. When I'd crossed Twelfth Street I looked to my right and saw the sushi joint that had moved in when the Cuban restaurant moved out. It had been there long enough for me to have forgotten the name of its predecessor, although it would probably come to me if I worked at it, but the Japanese place called itself the Cho-Cho, and the one meal Carolyn and I had had there led us to rename it the So-So.

But it was still there, and the sight of it this morning was somehow comforting, even if nothing would persuade me to walk in and order something.

Beside it, Bowl-Mor was off to an early start. Did people actually go bowling at nine in the morning? Evidently, as one burly fellow was holding the door for another, who might have been his brother. Each was carrying a bag that held a bowling ball—unless what one or both of them contained was actually a human head.

Bowling balls did seem more likely. Occam's razor and all that.

I walked on, turned left at Eleventh Street. The storefronts run mostly to antique shops, just as they did when I bought Barnegat Books; they're a little fancier now, like everything else, but not so much so that an antiquarian bookshop or a dog grooming salon look out of place.

Sometimes as I walk the half block from University Place to my store I'll amuse myself by seeing how many security cameras I can spot on the south side of the street. But this was a sunny morning, and the way the sun was bouncing off the windows and roofs took the joy out of that particular way of passing the time. Since I wasn't able to make out a single camera, I contented myself with making faces at the cameras I knew were there, and that kept me busy all the way to the bookshop.

I opened the window gates, unlocked the door, turned the sign from *Sorry—We're Closed!* to *Open—Come On In!* I flicked on the overhead light, and by then Raffles was threading his way between my feet in the manner of his species. *I'm here,* he was telling me, *and I'm hungry, and even though you've never failed to feed me first thing every morning, I still feel it's necessary to remind you of my presence. Because why leave something so important to chance?*

5

So it was a typical morning at Barnegat Books, except that the level of in-store activity was atypically high. With Raffles fed and his water dish freshened, I lugged the bargain table outside and had barely managed to settle myself behind the counter before an older gentleman came in from the street with three of the books from that very table.

"I've been looking far and wide for this one," he said, and I wondered why. It was the Lonely Planet guidebook for Indonesia, and I'm sure it had once been useful and definitive and up-to-date, but that would have been in 1984, the publication date clearly visible on the cover. An out-of-date travel guide is about as useful as a take-out menu from a restaurant that's gone out of business, and about as much in demand. Such items come into my hands from time to time as part of a larger lot, and more often than not they go directly into the trash, but sometimes one winds up on the bargain table, and sometimes somebody decides it's just what he has to have.

It's a nice way to start the day. That was ten dollars I hadn't had before, and three books I hadn't wanted in the first place, and he was no sooner out the door with his treasures than a woman came in, and before the door could swing shut, a man came in wearing a suit and carrying a Coach briefcase.

He wanted to know where the Russian novelists were, and

I refrained from replying that most of them were dead or in the Gulag. I told him instead that, while mysteries and science fiction had their own sections, all the rest of the store's fiction was in a single section, to which I pointed him.

"The books are shelved alphabetically by author," I said. "Is there any particular one you're looking for?"

"I'm actually looking for a translator," he said. "Constance Garnett."

"She translated most of them, didn't she? Dostoyevsky, Chekhov, Tolstoy, Turgenev—"

"And Gogol. And Goncharov, and Ostrovsky, and one other writer I can't think of."

"Ah," I said.

"Herzen," he said, thinking of him after all. "Alexander Herzen. How could I forget him?"

I could forget him with no trouble at all, I thought, and in fact couldn't be sure I'd ever heard of him in the first place. "I don't think I have anything by Herzen at the moment," I said. "There's some of most of the others, especially Dostoyevsky and Tolstoy, though I'm afraid I shelved the books without bothering to take note of the translator. But why don't you look for yourself?"

While he was doing so, I went over to the mystery section to look for something to read. I'd finished *What Mad Universe* before I'd gone to sleep, and among other things it had reminded me how much I liked Fredric Brown. I had half a dozen of his mysteries, none of them first editions, although *Thirty Corpses Every Thursday*, one of the volumes Dennis McMillan had published of Brown's stories from the detective pulps, was certainly collectible if not very pricey. I looked it over, decided I wanted a novel rather than a batch of short stories, and decided too that it didn't matter if it was a book I'd already read.

I chose a paperback of *The Screaming Mimi,* which I remembered fondly if dimly, and settled on my stool behind the counter. I hadn't got past the first page when a woman approached carrying a copy of a late Philip Roth novel, *The Plot Against America.* "I think this is the one I want," she said. "The one where Lindbergh is the bad guy. I guess after his kid was kidnapped you couldn't blame him for having a short fuse."

"Um," I said. She was, one might say, a woman of an uncertain age, and whether or not she was age-appropriate for the proprietor of an antiquarian bookshop was an open question. She was certainly attractive enough to make the cut, with her honey-colored hair and her hazel eyes.

"But what I wondered," she said, "is whether this is the one where he talks about his stamp collection."

"Lindbergh?"

"Was Lindbergh a stamp collector? No, the narrator." She pointed to the center of the book's front cover, where an American stamp reposed, overprinted with an uncompromising swastika.

"It's a stamp from the National Parks series," she said. "It says Yosemite on it."

"I'll take your word for it. May I ask why this matters?"

"It's my brother," she said. "He's a stamp collector. In, like, an obsessive way."

"I suppose that's the best way to collect anything."

"Well, Gregory's on the spectrum," she said, "but at the high-functioning end of it. And I think he'd really like Philip Roth, but it's hard to get him to read anything that isn't about fellatio."

"Um."

"Philately," she said. "Oh my God, I can't believe I said that."

"Um."

"I swear I don't know where that came from," she said, and licked her lips, and blushed deeply when she realized what she'd just done.

"Stamp collecting," I said, because somebody really had to say something.

"My brother," she said, nodding gratefully.

"He collect stamps."

"Passionately," she said, and her blush deepened. "So I wondered, I thought you might know—"

"If the narrator of *The Plot Against America,* who like the author is conveniently named Philip Roth—"

"Really?"

"—also collects stamps. He does."

"You read the book?"

"I did, and it's not as though the plot hinges on young Philip's stamp collection, but he does talk about it."

"Oh, that's great! In that case—"

"But you don't have to take my word for it," I said. "You can check the book description when you order it from Amazon."

Now that was a snarky thing to say, and I couldn't tell you what prompted me to say it. Whatever it was, her reaction wasn't what I'd have expected. She didn't appear to be insulted or offended. She just looked puzzled.

She said, "Amazon? You mean like the river?"

"The river that drains a continent."

"In, like, South America? What's that got to do with anything?"

"Um—"

"Or am I turning into an Amazon myself?" She flexed a bicep. "Like, you know, putting in too many hours at the gym?"

"Um."

"I'd like to buy this," she said, brandishing the book. "How much is it, anyway?" She checked the publisher's price on the cover. "Twenty-six dollars?"

"That's what Houghton Mifflin got for it," I said, "when it was fresh off the press." I took the book from her, checked the flyleaf. "Fifteen dollars," I said.

That was perfect, she told me. Could I take American Express? I could take it or leave it, I said, but yes, I assured her, I took all major credit cards. She handed me her card, and I did what one does, and so did she, and I bagged the book and handed it to her, along with her receipt.

I said I hoped her brother liked the book.

"Well, it's a crap shoot," she said. "Either he'll read five pages and then never pick it up again, or he'll read it over and over again until there's no ink left on the pages. I, uh, wrote my phone number on the receipt. In case, you know, American Express wants it."

"Um."

"Or, you know, whatever."

When the door closed behind her, I checked the slip she'd signed. Her name was there, Mallory Eckhart, along with a number that began with 917, indicating that it was a cell phone.

I copied the name and the number into my own phone. Would I ever dial it? If I did, what on earth would I say?

I ran various awkward conversations through my mind.

Then I stopped, because my door opened and there was Mowgli, toting a World Wildlife Fund tote bag.

"Hey, Bernie," he said, and took a minute to note the presence of customers in my store. There were three or four of them at that point, and that's three or four more than you'll usually find at that hour of a Thursday morning.

"Hey, Mowgli."

"You got a minute? Or should I take a number and wait?"

There were indeed people in the store, but nobody looked to be in need of my attention. "Now's as good a time as any," I said, "but I haven't added any stock since yesterday, so I don't know what there is to interest you."

He looked puzzled. I seemed to be having that effect on people this morning. Then he shrugged and began unloading his WWF bag onto my counter. "I scored," he said, "and it was at the Sally Ann in Chelsea. The one on Eighth Avenue? I just happened to be on that block, and I was gonna walk right on by because I never find anything there. Enough other book pickers work that place on a regular basis, so that all that's left whenever I show up are book club editions of Dan Brown and James Patterson, and maybe a beat-up copy of *The Boca Raton Diet,* and doesn't that just get your heart racing?"

"But today was different?"

"What happened," he said, "is I got an earworm. You know what that is? A song that wanders into your mind and can't find the exit? This was just one phrase, over and over. '*If you turn me down once more I'll join the Salvation Army . . .*'"

"Is that how it goes, Mowgli?"

"No, of course not," he said. "It's supposed to be the French Foreign Legion, but if you make it the Sally it really rocks. You can leave all the other lyrics alone. '*If you think I won't find romance in the Salvation Army / Think about that uniform and all its charm.*' Well, I didn't find romance, but what I found was plenty. See?"

I saw. The books were mostly mystery and suspense, solid authors like Sandford and Connelly and Paretsky and Deaver and Burke. No paperbacks, no book club editions, all original publishers' hardcovers, with the dust jackets in excellent shape.

"The two Andrew Vachss novels are signed," he said. "You know he died."

"I know."

"I wish he hadn't," he said with feeling. "It's not just the books, it's what he did in the world." He averted his eyes. "For, you know, abused kids."

Who knew? I didn't say anything and neither did he, and then he shrugged and said, "You know, I came out of it okay, but not everybody does. They're first editions, the two Vachss novels."

"*Strega* and *Hard Candy*."

"Right."

"Well," I said. "You should do very well with these, Mowgli."

"Huh?"

"They ought to bring a decent price on eBay."

"What's that, Pig Latin? I'm a little bit lost here, Bernie. Are you telling me you can't use them?"

Tilt!

"I didn't realize you were offering them to me," I said.

"Are you kidding? Why else would I schlep them all the way over here?"

Why indeed? To gloat? But he hadn't been gloating. He'd been pitching his wares.

"Of course I can use them," I said, and grabbed a pencil and began figuring out a price.

By the time Mowgli and I had concluded our business, all his books were back in the tote bag with the panda on it. "You can keep this," he'd said. "You wouldn't believe how many tote bags I've got around the house. I swear they breed."

"Like wire coat hangers?"

"I never thought of it that way," he said, "but you're right. Every closet has its own population explosion. A pleasure doing business with you, Bernie."

Raffles was sleeping, not for the first time, in a patch of sunlight in the front window. On his way out, Mowgli stopped to give him a scratch behind the ear. Raffles likes that, but only from people he trusts. He was fine with Mowgli, and even extended his forepaws in a stretch to indicate his general contentment.

I felt the same way myself, and so evidently did Mowgli, who was whistling as he crossed the threshold. The tune was that of the French Foreign Legion song—or, now and forevermore, the Salvation Army song. "*Just one more time, are you gonna be mine, or au revoir cheri / It's the Salvation Army for me.*"

6

Pricing the books I'd brought from Mowgli could wait until I had the computer's help to determine what prices other sellers were asking. With most books I'm willing to wing it, relying on my experience and general feel for the business, but collectible crime fiction is one of the more volatile areas, and I was in no mad rush to get the books on my shelves.

The first step was to transfer the tote bag to my back room, and even that had to wait because of the way customers kept demanding my attention. One, an older woman with a haunted look about her, bought three Jeffrey Farnol novels that had been on my shelf as long as I'd owned the store. Farnol was an English writer who produced a period romance novel annually for over forty years until his death in 1952. If Georgette Heyer was the mother of the Regency Romance, he could claim to have fathered it—but I can't keep Heyer in stock, while I'd acquired four Farnol novels along with the keys to Barnegat Books, and in all the intervening years I'd sold just one.

"*Adam Penfeather, Buccaneer,*" I said, as I took my customer's money and counted out her change. "And don't ask me why I remember the title."

She didn't. "A wonderful book," she said with feeling. "Donkey's years since I've read it. Now that you've mentioned it, I think it may be time for me to read it again." She smiled, patted the bag of books she'd just bought. "But first . . ."

I wished her happy reading. Oh, it would be exactly that, she said, beaming.

Her place at the counter was quickly taken by a man who'd somehow managed to find six books on my bargain table that he wanted to own. I took a twenty-dollar bill from him and wished him well, and then a young man with a gold and green John Deere baseball cap noticed *The Screaming Mimi* paperback on my counter and asked if I had a hardcover copy, and I said I didn't but pointed him to the other Fredric Brown novels, and, well, eventually there was enough of a lull so that I got away from the counter, Mowgli's books in tow, and stowed them in the back room.

And then my John Deere fan was back. He hadn't found anything he needed by Brown, but he'd noticed a couple of books by Dennis Lehane, and they weren't ones he needed, but did I happen to have *Darkness, Take My Hand?* That was Lehane's second book, and of course he'd read it, and it wasn't supposed to be as scarce as *A Drink Before the War,* but God knows he'd searched hard and couldn't find it, and—

"Wait right here," I said, and made a quick trip to my back room. "It just came in," I said, "and I haven't had time to price it. I'll probably do that tonight, if you wanted to come back tomorrow. Or if you want it now, how's fifty dollars?"

I guess my price must have been low. He had his Visa card out of his wallet before I'd finished my sentence.

I'd look it up afterward, I thought, and find out just how far below market I was. But what did it matter? When I'd calculated what to pay Mowgli, the Lehane was one of a batch I'd pegged at five dollars apiece, and I'd turned it over in less than an hour for ten times that.

And what had Mowgli paid for it? Fifty cents? A dollar? He'd picked it up from the Salvation Army at a thrift-shop price, so he was well ahead of the game, and they got it and everything else for nothing, as a donation, so this looked to me like a win all around.

"*If you think I won't find romance in the Salvation Army . . .*"

But why, I wondered, had my customer had so much trouble finding the book? Was he spending too much time on his tractor? Had he lost track of one of the miracles of the modern age, that anyone could find any book in no time at all?

If a book existed, you could turn up a copy in five minutes. And if it didn't exist, well, then it might take you all of ten. Dreaming of one of the famous books forever lost to time, like Homer's *Margites* or Shakespeare's *Cardenio?* How about *The Isle of the Cross,* by Herman Melville, or maybe Thomas Hardy's *The Poor Man and the Lady?* Boot up your computer, get online, check ABE Books. No luck there? Well, don't stop now. Check eBay, why don't you?

"*What's that, Bernie? Pig Latin?*"

7

At noon I did something I'm rarely called upon to do. I actually shooed customers out of the store, promising them I'd be open again in an hour or so. Then I stopped in my back room for a few minutes, but this time I left Mowgli's books unexamined.

It was close to twelve-thirty by the time I got to the Poodle Factory, lunch in hand, and Carolyn made a show of looking at her watch and clearing her throat.

"If you hear something growling," she said, "it's not that sweet Sussex Spaniel in the cage on the left, Bern. It's my tummy."

"Sorry. It was an unusual morning."

"Well, it's an unusual world," she said. "Bernie, I Googled Orrin Vandenbrinck. I thought you were exaggerating when you said he was one of the world's worst human beings."

"I wasn't."

"No, you weren't. He did a hostile takeover of this up-and-coming pharmaceutical firm, Gantrex, when they developed a drug with a name I can't remember that does something I don't understand, but it turns out millions of people need it."

"Right."

"And if you need it that means you have to take it for life, and the manufacturer was retailing a month's supply for just under a thousand dollars, which most people could find a way to afford if they gave up everything they enjoyed in life. And, since the production cost of a month's supply was maybe a buck ninety-eight, the little company was in good shape."

"Right again."

"Making a hefty profit, most of which was supposed to go right back into research and development, so that maybe they could get lucky again and come up with another wonder drug."

"There you go."

"So the first thing Vandenbrinck did was boost the price a little, and all of a sudden a month's supply of this crap, and why can't I remember the name of it?"

"Nobody can."

"I bet *he* can," she said. "Orrin Vandenbrinck, and I'm pretty sure he can remember the price, too, because even I can remember it. He made it easy to remember, Bern."

"Twelve thousand, three hundred and forty-five dollars," I said.

"And sixty-seven cents. One two three four five," she said, counting on her fingers, "and six and seven. 'How did you set the price, Mr. Vandenbrinck?' 'I was counting out loud one morning, Senator, and I liked the way it sounded.'"

"Senator?"

"There was an investigation. Nothing came of it. Because this is a free country, Bern, and if I own something I can charge whatever I want for it." She rolled her eyes. "Besides, a company like Gantrex needs to make what look like excessive profits on its successful drugs in order to finance the ongoing research required to come up with the next medical miracle."

"That does sound logical," I admitted.

"What it sounds like to me," she said, "is Michael Douglas in that movie, explaining that greed is good. But what it turned out to be was flat-out crap, because instead of plowing back his profits, Vandenbrinck fired a few dozen people and shut down his entire research and development department. Guess why, Bern."

"So that Gantrex could concentrate all its resources on producing its one successful drug and saving human lives?"

"You must have read the same article I did. But isn't it comforting that he found a use for his runaway profits? He bought a home in the Hamptons and another on the French Riviera, and then he decided he needed a pied-a-terre in New York and bought the penthouse at the Innisfree. He tried to buy a football team, but all of the NFL owners banded together to block the sale."

"I guess they must have their standards," I said. "Who knew?"

"So the next thing he bought was the Kloppmann Diamond. You know what he paid for that?"

I did: Sixty million dollars, plus Sotheby's ten percent bidder's premium. But I let her go on, powered by indignation, and she kept it up even as she was dishing out the food I'd brought.

The food won. "This smells terrific," she said, abandoning Orrin Vandenbrinck and all his offenses. "Where's it from, Bern?"

"Two Guys."

"This is Laotian? It looks and smells completely different from anything we ever had from there."

"That's because it's Tajiki."

"Tajiki?"

"As in Tajikistan."

"Why would a Laotian restaurant start serving—say the word again, Bern?"

"Tajiki."

"Why would they start serving Tajiki food?"

"Because they're not a Laotian restaurant anymore," I said. "Two Guys From Luang Prabang is history. Hey, we knew it wouldn't be there forever. It's the restaurant's karma, for heaven's sake. Great ethnic food, reasonable prices, service with a smile unless they're from a country where smiling is impolite, and then in six months or a year or two years at the outside they're gone, and whoever takes their place repaints the sign and changes the menu and takes one more shot at the American Dream."

"And the sign's been repainted again?"

"Just the part that used to say *Luang Prabang*."

"What does it say now? Tajikistan?"

"Dushanbe," I said.

"Dushanbe?"

"That's the capital of Tajikistan."

"So it's Two Guys From Dushanbe?"

"That's what it says. Right there on the sign."

"I have to admit this is delicious. Lamb?"

"Probably. Unless it's goat."

"Or some other animal I'd just as soon not know about." She frowned, and not because she didn't like what she was eating. "Bern, the Luang Prabangers were there yesterday. I know that for a fact, because I bought lunch yesterday, and—"

"I know."

She thought about this, and I could tell she was trying to make the pieces fit, and finding out that they wouldn't.

"They were there *yesterday*."

"Right."

"I couldn't begin to guess how many versions of Two Guys

we've seen. Fast turnover is the rule. Whether the two guys are from Abidjan or Managua or Antananarivo—"

"Antananarivo," I remembered. "Madagascan cuisine. Tasty, but they didn't last long, did they?"

"Too many syllables, Bern."

"I guess."

"Anyway, the story at Two Guys is here today and gone tomorrow. And the turnover's quick, but it's not instantaneous. They're always closed for a month between incarnations, but the Laotians were there yesterday and the Tajiks are there today, and how can that be?"

"Carolyn," I said, "let me ask you a question. Do you have a Metrocard?"

"What's that got to do with anything?"

"Do you?"

"A Metrocard? Like to get on a bus or subway? Well, of course I do. Doesn't everybody?"

"Do you have it with you?"

"It lives in my purse," she said, "and I hope it doesn't get lonesome, because God knows I don't use it all that much. My world's nice and small, Bern. The Poodle Factory, my apartment, Henrietta Hudson's, and the Cubby Hole. Everything's pretty much within walking distance of everything else, and walking's the only exercise I get, so I walk everywhere. Unless it's raining when I leave the apartment to come here, though even then I'll usually grab an umbrella and take my chances."

"Right."

"But if it's too windy for an umbrella I'll sometimes walk two blocks and take the Tenth Street crosstown bus. Except unless the bus turns up right away, which it never does, I give up and hail a cab. To tell you the truth, I can't remember the last time I actually used my Metrocard."

"Well," I said, "check and see if you've still got it, will you?"

"Why wouldn't I still have it?"

"Just check, okay? Humor me."

"A SubwayCard," she said, turning the thing this way and that. "How did it get in my bag, and what did it do with my Metrocard, and just what the hell is a SubwayCard anyway?"

"Think of it as the MTA's equivalent of Two Guys From Dushanbe."

"Huh?"

"Sit down," I said. "Relax. And let me tell you about my morning."

8

I talked for a long time, and I don't think I left much of anything out. At first Carolyn had questions, but it didn't take her long to stop asking them. I wound up telling her how when I'd left the bookstore I'd thought about something from the deli or the Thai place, and then decided that just because we'd had Laotian food yesterday was no reason not to have it again today.

"So I went to Two Guys," I said, "and it was a different Two Guys, with two different guys behind the counter, and I don't know how to explain this, but I was surprised but not shocked. Because if the world had turned upside-down, why shouldn't Luang Prabang turn into Dushanbe?"

"Bowl-Mor is honest to God back on University Place?"

"Right where it's always been. You want to walk over there and see?"

"Not right now." She thought for a moment, then hauled off and slapped herself across the face.

I stared at her.

"In case it was all a dream," she said, "but it's not, is it? You want me to slap you, Bern?"

"Not unless I've said something offensive."

"None of this is offensive," she said, "but that doesn't mean

I can get my mind around it. I mean, it's not enough to say it's weird. What it is, it's impossible."

"I know."

"Like, literally impossible. As in there's no way on earth that what's happening could be happening."

"I know."

"It's flat-out unbelievable," she said, "but as sure as I've just scarfed down a plateful of Tajik food, which I didn't even know they had any of, so how could I dream it?"

"Good point."

"I mean, my Metrocard's gone and instead I've got a green and white SubwayCard, so how can I refuse to believe it? You know what I'm gonna do right this minute, Bern? I'm gonna get on the computer and see if Amazon has a book on the cuisine of Tajikistan."

"Sounds like a plan."

She was back a few minutes later. "Just as you said," she reported. "There's no Amazon and there's no eBay. You Google Amazon and all you get is the river."

"Well, it's a pretty important river."

"It was a pretty important company. How could it disappear? And it's not like it went bankrupt, because then there'd be a million articles about it. Instead it vanished without a trace."

"So did the little sign I put up. '*Please wait until you have exited the premises before ordering the book from Amazon.*' When I first noticed it was gone, I figured some customer felt sufficiently offended to take it down. But I don't think that's what happened."

"You don't?"

"I think it was there yesterday when I closed for the night, and by the time I opened up this morning it was gone."

"It just disappeared."

"That'd be my guess."

"Like eBay and Amazon."

"But on a smaller scale."

"Like my Metrocard."

"And mine."

"What's going on, Bern? If this isn't a dream, what the hell is it?"

"I'm not a hundred percent sure."

"Well, what I am is a hundred percent baffled," she said, "so if you've got any kind of a clue, let's hear it. Because all I know right now is that the planet's gone crazy."

"Not the planet," I said.

"You mean it's just us?"

"No, I mean it's the entire universe," I said. "And what it's gone is mad."

"This'll sound nuts," I said. "I don't think it makes sense, but neither does anything else. You remember the book I was reading?"

"Vaguely. We talked about it, and then I went to the Cubby Hole and drank some more scotch, so my memory could stand refreshing."

"*What Mad Universe,*" I said, "by Fredric Brown."

"It's coming back to me," she said, and thought about it, and her eyes widened. "No! Bern, is that even possible?"

"You tell me."

"Alternate worlds," she said. "Or universes, whatever. An infinite number of them, like monkeys with typewriters."

"And we were in one of them for our whole lives."

"And then this morning—"

"*Tilt!*"

"And now we're in a different universe," she said, "the same as the original in most ways, but there's no Amazon in this universe, and no eBay either."

"And Bowl-Mor is back on University Place where it belongs."

"And our Metrocards changed color and turned into SubwayCards, and Mowgli brings books to you instead of raiding your shelves and turning into an online entrepreneur."

"And the city streets are the same, except for one important difference."

"What's that, Bern?"

"No CCTV. No security cameras. No need to smile, because you're not on *Candid Camera.*"

"And Two Guys—"

"Is right where it's always been, but the guys aren't from Luang Prabang anymore."

"They're from Whatsit in Whatchamacallit."

"Dushanbe."

"Right."

"In Tajikistan."

"Whatever you say, Bern. They know how to cook, I'll give them that. You know what? I think you must be right."

"About . . ."

"About what happened, or what's happening, whatever. Did you read the book through to the end?"

"In bed," I said. "propped up on a pillow, with a cup of chamomile tea on the night table. I was tired, but I was caught up in the book, and then I turned the last page and closed the book and turned off my light."

"And?"

"And nothing. Next thing I knew it was morning."

"And you were in a parallel universe."

I thought about it. "You think I did this," I said.

"What I think," she began, and then there was a knock on the door. We turned toward the sound, just in time to see the door open to admit a big man in an expensive suit that looked as though it had been expertly tailored for someone else.

It was Ray Kirschmann, the best cop money can buy, and it was oddly comforting to see that he'd made the cut in our brave new universe.

"Don't get up," he said, unnecessarily. "Somethin' smells good, but from the looks of it you both get to join the Clean Plate Club. Shame I didn't show up a few minutes earlier."

"Ray," Carolyn said, "there are those who'd say it's a shame you showed up at all."

"Just so you're not one of 'em, Shorty. Reason I'm here, Bernie, I noticed you closed up but left your book table out on the sidewalk. Aren't you worried about shoplifters?"

"It's only shoplifting," I said, "if it takes place inside the shop. But no, I'm not worried. You could argue that anybody who swipes a book off the bargain table is doing me a favor."

"Well, somebody did you three favors," he said, "by takin' three books. And then he wrote you a note." He drew out and unfolded a sheet of notebook paper. "'In a hurry. Am taking three books.' There's no signature."

"The note itself is miracle enough."

"It doesn't stop there, Bernie. When he folded it he tucked this in."

He held up a ten-dollar bill.

"Now you might not care if somebody walks off with a

book," he went on, "but I figured Mrs. Rhodenbarr's son Bernard would just as soon hang onto the cash, and ten bucks sittin' on an untended table doesn't last long in this town."

"So you brought it here."

He nodded, handed me the bill. "That's all I got," he said. "Bernie, Shorty. Next time I'll try to get here before you run out of food."

"In the universe I remember," she said, "that ten dollars would have wound up in Ray's pocket."

I shook my head. "He does like to supplement his income," I said, "but not by stealing petty cash. On balance, I'd say he's the same old Ray."

"I guess. I'd find him easier to take if he'd cool it with the height jokes. I've got a perfectly good name, the one my parents picked out just for me, and it's not Shorty."

"Well—"

"It's nothing important, Bern, just something for you to keep in mind next time you shuttle us into a new universe. Same Ray but no more short jokes."

"I'll keep it in mind. You really think all of this is my doing?"

"What else could it be? Look what's changed. Security cameras. You hate them, you can rant for hours about them—"

"For hours? Really?"

"Maybe it just seems like hours, but you do go on and on about them, how they put you out of business the way desktop publishing shut down all the little print shops on Hudson Street."

"Well, they did."

"And Bowl-Mor. It's really there?"

"You want to walk over there now? Rent a pair of shoes? Bowl a couple of frames?"

"Maybe later, Bern. But Bowl-Mor means this has to be your doing, Bern. It was nothing more than a neighborhood bowling alley, and if the neighborhood really needs a bowling alley I suppose somebody will open another one sooner or later. But for you it was a whole symbol of gentrification and the impending end of Greenwich Village as we know it."

"When I saw it this morning," I recalled, "I didn't really think anything of it, because it looked as though it had been there forever."

"And in this world, it has."

"And eBay and Amazon, and the way Mowgli changed from being a supplier to a customer—"

"It's as if you somehow absorbed the knack of world-building from Fredric Brown's book, and when you woke up you were in this brand-new world of your own devising."

"That sounds—"

"I know how it sounds. Do you have a better explanation, Bern?"

"No," I said. "On the one hand it sounds utterly crazy, and at the same time it's not only oddly plausible, it's the only possible explanation around."

"Uh-huh."

"But—"

"But what?"

"Metrocards and SubwayCards. I've used a Metrocard just about every day since they introduced them. It's so much better than having to buy tokens, and you could refill the thing with a credit card, and except for the cost, it's like having a master key that unlocks every bus and subway car in the city. What did I ever object to about my Metrocard?"

"The name," she said.

"Huh?"

"You don't remember?"

"Remember what?"

"'Metrocard? What kind of a boneheaded name is Metrocard? You know what the Metro is? The Metro's what people in Paris call their subway. The Paris Metro, you hear the word Metro and you think Paris, you don't think of hopping on the L Train and riding it all the way out to Canarsie.'"

"I said that?"

"More than once, Bern. 'In London it's the Underground, or maybe the Tube. In New York it's the subway. The word is New York City's gift to the world. When a couple of yuppies in a gentrified tenement give their bathroom a new look, do they finish the walls with Metro tiles? When someone jonesing for a hero sandwich makes the bad decision to pass up a proper Italian deli for a fast-food chain, does he pick a place called Metro?'"

"I wonder why I felt so strongly about it."

"I think it was around the time you were breaking up with a girlfriend. I can't remember which one."

"They sort of merge in memory," I said.

"If you're going to use it to get on the subway, you said, then they ought to call it a Subway Card. And you didn't like the colors, either."

I thought a moment. "Orange and blue. Oh, because they're New York Mets colors."

"'Why the Mets? When those clowns have three men on base, they're generally all on the same base. What about the

Yankees?' You thought a Subway Card ought to have pin-stripes."

"A full-fledged rant," I said. "Whoever she was, it must have been a bad break-up. You know, it's beginning to come back to me. I guess I felt strongly at the time. But all these years later?"

"I don't know how it works, Bern, but the thought must have lingered in a couple of your brain cells, and when your unconscious mind got around to ordering up a new universe—"

"That's what I did? Specify what I wanted in a new improved world?"

My right hand was resting on my knee, and she laid a hand of her own on top of it. "I can't think of any other explanation," she said. "The book you were reading handed you a key, and you—"

"Waved it aside," I said. "And picked the lock."

9

Lunch hour ran a little long that day, and we could have gone on talking clear through to sundown, but Carolyn had to put the finishing touches on a Dandie Dinmont whose owner had entered him in a show coming up in a few days in Trenton, New Jersey. "She thinks he's a shoo-in for Best of Breed, probably because there won't be all that many Dandie Dinmonts making the trip to Trenton. But what she's got her heart set on is for Naughty Prince Andrew to get first place in the Terrier group."

"Has he got a chance?"

"Well, he's a nice-looking dog," she said, "but what do I know? I just wash 'em."

"And buff their nails," I said, "and trim around their ears, and make them come out looking like they spent a week at Canyon Ranch."

"I do what I can. And, if Prince makes his mama's dream come true, I'll get a nice bonus."

So she had every reason to get back to work on the naughty prince, and for my part I wanted to be back in my bookshop. I'd never had a better morning there, surrounded by people who not only cared about books but were surprisingly eager to buy them, and who knew how long it would last? Maybe it was just a morning thing, maybe now that the sun had reached its zenith this new book boom would sink slowly in the west . . .

Not so. I walked out of the Poodle Factory, cast my eyes westward, and saw half a dozen people standing there, having conversations that I could only presume to be at once literate and literary, while they waited for me to open the store.

The Screaming Mimi was on the counter where I'd left it, but I barely got to look at it over the next several hours. Now and then I'd pick it up and read a paragraph or two, and then someone would come along and I'd mark my place and close the book.

But I did get to one of the elements I remembered from previous readings. There was a character named Godfrey, a thoughtful old drunk whom everybody called God, and a couple of pages in he let us in on a key principle of his personal philosophy. You could get anything, God contended, if you wanted it badly enough.

The whole novel, mystery and love story and all, stemmed from that notion.

I said as much to a woman who asked me what the book was about. "So the reason I can't lose those ten pounds," she said, "is because I don't really want to?"

"Well—"

"In other words, let's blame the victim? Is that what you're getting at?"

There are questions no one should ever be fool enough to answer, like *Do these jeans make my ass look fat?* So I kept my mouth shut, but she went on waiting for my reply.

I said, "First of all, I'm not getting at anything. Fredric

Brown came up with the line in a book he wrote in 1949, and who knows if he believed it himself? He put it in the mouth of one of his characters, but that doesn't mean it was part of his own personal credo."

She thought about this, nodded.

"And his point, or the character's point, wouldn't be that you don't want to lose the weight. It's that you don't want to badly enough."

"Like priorities."

"Exactly," I said. "You want to lose ten pounds, but you don't want to walk around weak with hunger, and you don't want to deplete your energy to the point where it affects your work and well-being."

"That makes a certain amount of sense."

"I'd say so. And you don't want to deprive yourself of perfectly legitimate pleasure, and that makes sense, too."

She was smiling now. "So I'm not a bad person," she said, "just because I get the occasional yen for something gooey from Krispy Kreme."

"Who doesn't? And there's another point, which I hesitate to bring up, but I think it's relevant."

"Oh?"

"It's also purely subjective, just my own personal reaction to the evidence before me. I don't know what makes you think you need to lose ten pounds, but you don't."

"Well," she said, and colored a little, and averted her eyes. And, not long after, she bought eight books, and not one of them had anything to do with diets or weight loss. She told me her name was Gretchen Kimmel, and she asked me mine and repeated it as if to fix it in her mind. She paid with a credit card—and, like Mallory Eckhart a few hours before her, she jotted down her phone number in case I, um, needed it.

And would I? Well, who knew what I would or wouldn't need or want in this unlikely world?

I added her to my phone's list of contacts. If I wanted to—badly enough, that is—I could give her a call.

Long before I had a bookstore, I was caught up in the fantasy of owning one. I pictured myself chatting with well-read men and women, hosting Sunday afternoon poetry readings while off to one side a Juilliard student would be playing a Schubert violin sonata. There'd be Chilean Riesling to sip and cubes of Jarlsberg to nibble, and I'd be the affable host, with a jacket and tie, or even an ascot if I thought I could carry it off.

And, by the time the wine and cheese ran out and the customers drifted away, wouldn't the host have bonded with some bright and charming young lady?

I always figured running a bookshop would be a good way to meet women. And once every third blue moon it actually was, but it was a rare day indeed when someone like Mallory Eckhart made a point of giving me her number, and I was flat-out gobsmacked when Gretchen Kimmel did the same.

Two in one day? Incredible. A third, obviously, would be out of the question.

I was thinking about this, even as I was having another go at *The Screaming Mimi,* when a hand appeared without so much as an *ahem* and held a pamphlet with a homemade look to it between my eyes and Fredric Brown's words.

I looked up. The woman holding the pamphlet was tall and slender. Her dark hair looked as though she'd cut it herself after an apprenticeship with Vidal Sassoon, and her dark eyes behind wire-rimmed eyeglasses took the Hot Librarian look to a new level. Think Linda Fiorentino in *The Last Seduction*. Think Katherine Moennig as Lena, Ray Donovan's assistant.

"I'm sorry to interrupt," she said.

I took the pamphlet from her and had a look at it. The title was there in two italic lines—*Dr. Newton's / Zoo*—above a vaguely oriental drawing of what was either a mythical creature or a lioness drawn by someone whose knowledge of the beast was limited to verbal descriptions. Across the bottom, in smaller and more self-contained type, it said *Bluett & Sons Ltd.* And there were three Chinese characters at the upper right.

I paged through it, noted the photographs, some in color, some in black and white. It was the privately printed exhibition catalog of an obscure exhibition, the kind of item that could sit for years on a shelf until the one right buyer walked in and swooned over it. I wanted to buy it, but would I ever sell it?

I asked her how much she was asking for it.

Her eyes widened, her lips parted. I thought I'd have to repeat the question, but she said, "I don't want to sell it."

"Then why—"

"I want to buy it," she said. "I found it in your Art & Antiques section, so I assumed it was for sale."

I turned pages, nodded thoughtfully, while being careful to keep my thoughts to myself.

I had never seen the thing before in my life.

Once, years ago, a householder walked in on me while I was going through the drawers of his desk. He was holding a baseball bat, and he looked ready to swing for the fences.

"Thank God you're here," I said. "I was afraid—well, never mind, but I'm really glad you're all right."

I don't remember where the conversation went from there, but I got out of there without being lined into center field or popped up behind third base, so I'd say that one belongs in the Wins column. The lesson here is that if you can't improvise on short notice you've got no business being a burglar, and while the skill's less essential in bookselling, it does come in handy.

"Dr. Isaac Newton," I said, "and who ever would have guessed that the man who figured out gravity from the falling of an apple would have a passion for small jade carvings of animals?"

"Oh, is it that Isaac Newton?"

"In a word," I said, "no." I read, "'*In the finest tradition of scholarship Dr. Newton allowed us a free hand in selecting or rejecting pieces from his collection as we wished. He further kindly allowed us to add a small number of carvings from other sources and a few important loans to help make the catalogue and exhibition more complete.*' Now the exhibition was staged in London in 1981, and while Bluett & Sons identify him as the *late* Dr. Newton, his death must have been fairly recent. The Isaac Newton everybody knows was *Sir* Isaac, not *Dr.* Newton, and gravity had its way with him in 1727, so—"

"So he couldn't have had that conversation with Mr. Bluett."

"Or his sons." I turned a page. "You know, this came in so long ago that it's almost like seeing it for the first time. I priced it at fifty dollars. That's lower than it should be."

"Does that mean you want to raise it?"

"That wouldn't be ethical. If you want it, I'm bound to honor the price I put on it."

"I see."

"But if you decide you don't want it," I said, "then I might adjust it upward."

Before I'd finished the sentence, she'd laid a fifty-dollar bill on the counter. "I like jade," she said. "Jade's important to me. Keep that in mind. If you get hold of anything you think might interest me, just let me know."

"How will I reach you?"

"I'm hard to get hold of. But I'll check in with you from time to time. Just set aside anything you think I might like."

She was gone, book in hand, before I could ask her name or her number.

It was getting on for four o'clock when I reached for the phone and called Carolyn. I told her I just wanted to make sure we were on for the Bum Rap.

"If it's still there," she said. "Yes, of course. I just told Naughty Prince Andrew's mommy her good boy's ready for his close-up, and she'll be picking him up sometime in the next half hour. Even if she's late, I'll be in the usual place at the usual time."

"As will I, but I might be a few minutes late. If you get there before I do—"

"You want your scotch on the table when you get there?"

"I don't want any scotch on the table," I said. "For either of us. We'll both have Perrier this evening."

Silence.

"Or, you know, order yourself a root beer or a Coke or a ginger ale. I don't want to tell you what to drink."

"You just want to tell me what not to drink. And I don't think it's because you've started worrying about the long-term possibility of liver damage. Bern, you're gonna do it, aren't you?"

"Well—"

"Correction: We're gonna do it. Right?"

"Unless you don't want to, but—"

"Are you kidding? I've always had to wheedle my way into keeping you company, and now that it's actually your idea for me to come along, you think I'm going to develop cold feet? I'll be there, and I'll be sober as a judge, and not the one on Fox News."

"Good," I said. "And speaking of cold feet, wear comfortable shoes."

A pause, and I could picture her rolling her eyes. "Bern," she said, "I'm a dyke, remember? That's the only kind I own."

10

I had hauled my table inside and cleared the store of warm-blooded creatures other than myself and Raffles, and I was trying to settle on one of the two neckties I keep in my back room, when the phone rang. It was an NYU classics professor who'd bought a book from me that morning, and who'd talked about downsizing his library. He was closing in on retirement and looking forward to life on the North Carolina Outer Banks, where he'd been spending vacations for years.

"I'll want to keep many of my books," he'd said earlier, "but one of the joys of changing my status to Professor Emeritus is knowing I'll never again feel the need to read anything by Livy or Tacitus or Herodotus or Thucydides or any of those household names. Oh, I'll keep this—" I'd sold him *Last Seen in Massilia,* one of the later volumes of Steven Saylor's *Roma Sub Rosa* series "—and my other Roman mysteries, and most of the alternate histories, like Harry Turtledove's *Gunpowder Empire,* and of course *Roma Eterna,* by that wonderful writer of speculative fiction—"

Et sic porro. We'd gone on to talk about the possibility of my buying those books that wouldn't make the trip south, and now he was calling to say he wanted to *carpe* what he could of the *diem* before *tempus* commenced to *fugit.*

He wasn't far away, in NYU-owned faculty housing on West

Third Street, and if I could come this evening he could promise a 50-year-old Armagnac to lighten the task of appraising his books.

"A pleasant alternative to the omnipresent Cognac," he said. "One grows jaded, if you know what I mean."

"A phrase that came to mind," I told Carolyn, "was *Strike while the iron is hot,* which would be *Ferrum dum calet* if the Romans ever said it, but I don't believe they did. But won't the iron still be on the warm side twenty-four hours from now?"

"Is that when you'll be seeing him?"

"Tomorrow evening at eight-thirty, at his presumably book-lined apartment."

"Tonight Perrier, tomorrow Armagnac. Will you wear that tie?"

When I got off the phone with the future Professor Emeritus, I'd decided on the tie with the scarlet and navy stripes.

"Why?" I fingered the knot. "Is there something wrong with it?"

"No, it looks fine."

"I generally put on a tie when I go somewhere to make an offer on a library. It makes me look like a more serious person, and you don't want to sell your books to someone who's not approaching the whole enterprise with a certain degree of gravity."

We were both glad to be at our usual table, not that there'd been anything wrong with the one we'd had the night before. Still, it was reassuring to find our table available, just as it was reassuring to note that Maxine was still Maxine.

"And I guess the same thing holds for burglary," she said.

"You wouldn't want your jewelry stolen by someone with his shirt open at the collar."

"I figure it's easier to get past the desk at the Innisfree if I look like someone who belongs in the building."

"I'm not sure that's the right tie for a Russian oligarch," she said, "but I get the point. And it gives me an opening, so I'll ask the burning question. How come?"

"How come?"

"How come I didn't even have to ask to get in on this?"

"Well," I said, "I think you're part of it."

"Part of knocking off the Kloppmann Diamond?"

"Part of the universe."

She frowned. "Bern, everything's part of the universe. That's what makes it universal."

"Part of this universe," I said. "The one we only arrived at this morning."

"Well, how could I not be part of it? I'm here, aren't I?"

I decided to back up and start over. "The first clue I got," I said, "was the Metrocard/SubwayCard business. Everybody else swiped a SubwayCard and thought nothing of it. But not me."

"Right."

"And not you, either."

"Bern, I walked to work. I can't remember the last time I used my . . ."

Her words trailed off.

"Your what? Finish the sentence."

"My Metrocard."

"That's what you still called it," I said, "and that's what you went looking for in your purse."

"And found a SubwayCard instead."

"So your awareness of things," I said, "was still planted in the world we both went to sleep in last night. It's like the two of us just got here this morning, and everybody else has been here all their lives."

"You're right," she said. "It's all new to me, the same as it is to you. You're the one who read the Fredric Brown novel, and you're the one who tilted God's own pinball machine and sent us reeling into another universe, and that's why Bowl-Mor's where it's supposed to be and the security cameras are all gone and Amazon's just a river in South America. All those things, they're all about you, Bern."

"I know."

"You're bringing me along tonight," she said, "and I'm excited about it and grateful for the opportunity, don't get me wrong."

"But?"

"But what you also did was bring me along into this different world. Bern, I was surprised to find a SubwayCard in my purse. But everybody else in the five boroughs said 'Oh, right, there's my SubwayCard, right where it's supposed to be.'"

"Except for the people who take cabs."

"Or Orrin Fucking Vandenbrinck, in his block-long limousine. How'd you manage it, Bern?"

I took a sip of French soda water. "I don't know," I said. "I don't have a clue how I made any of this happen."

"Your unconscious mind, working its magic while you slept?"

"And doing it all without leaving any footprints. Unless—"

"Unless what?"

"Well, maybe whatever part of me made this happen, maybe it realized something. Maybe it knew that for this to be the best of all possible worlds, I needed for my best friend to see it the same way I did."

"Because otherwise how could we really talk?"

"We couldn't, not like this."

"We're a team, aren't we, Bern?"

"I'd say we always have been."

She straightened up, took a deep breath. "Orrin Vandenbrinck," she said, "won't know what hit him."

I wasn't a hundred percent convinced of the hopelessness of Vandenbrinck's situation. But we did stand a chance, and that was all I asked. In a world of security cameras and pickproof locks, I hadn't even been able to get in the game. Now at least I got my turn at bat.

In my apartment, I'd had a hidey-hole built into a bedroom wall for almost as long as I'd occupied the apartment. It was the work of a skilled carpenter with a comforting disregard for law and order, and it was commodious enough to keep just about anything safe from prying eyes. Money, jewelry, burglar's tools—it had held them all, at one time or another, and if you didn't know your way in you'd have to tear down the building to find it.

After one too many times when I'd been forced to make an inconvenient trip uptown, I'd tracked down my carpenter friend and found he still had both his skills and his lamentable but convenient antisocietal attitudes. He worked his magic, and so I came to have a second hiding place, a little smaller than the first, in Barnegat Books' back room. I tricked it out with a second set of everything I needed to get safely in and out of your house, and visited it when the occasion arose.

It had done so that afternoon, and I'd moved a bookcase and hunkered down, poking here and pushing there, as if seeking to open one of those wooden puzzle boxes on offer in Chinatown novelty shops. I couldn't really see what I was doing, but my hands remembered the routine, and found what I was looking for. Not without effort; the secret compartment was more crowded than I remembered. Still, there'd be room enough for a diamond, wouldn't there? Even a large diamond?

I decided there would. And now I had a little ring of picks and probes in one rear pocket, while the other held two pairs of those blue rubber gloves every nurse in America puts on and takes off and throws out and replaces ten or twenty or thirty times a day. I'd call this a good policy, it's brought staph infections way down, but I can't help picturing a landfill somewhere that looks as though the local Smurfs have been molting.

"'I shall arise now,'" I said, "'and go to Innisfree, and a small cabin build there, of clay and wattles made.'"

"What's that, Bern?"

"*The Lake Isle of Innisfree.* William Butler Yeats, and I looked it up in the Untermeyer anthology a few hours ago to refresh my memory, but that's all that stayed with me. He's going to plant rows of beans, I forget how many, and have a hive for the honeybee."

"Is there such a place?"

"It's an uninhabited island," I said, "in the middle of a lake in Sligo, not far from where Yeats spent his childhood summers."

"Clay and wattles, huh?"

"So he said. I think it was reading Thoreau that steered him in that direction, although I can't remember coming across any wattles at Walden Pond. Are you ready? There's no rush if you want to finish your drink."

She looked at her glass, which was either half full or half empty, depending on how you see the world. "One good thing about drinking Perrier," she said, getting to her feet, "and it may be the only good thing, Bern, is you don't feel the need to finish it."

Ten minutes later we were standing across the street from Orrin Vandenbrinck's new home, doing our best to look unobtrusive.

"Apologies to Billy Yeats," she said, "but I don't see a whole lot of clay and wattles. Glass and steel, that's what I see."

What I didn't see was any of the security cameras that I'd spotted the night before, when spotting them had taken no great effort. They'd stuck out like a little row of sore thumbs, so much so that it could only be intentional. The security camera you're aware of doesn't provide evidence that you committed a crime; it dissuades you from so doing in the first place.

And I'd assumed there was another layer of security, a couple of cameras I couldn't see, in case I was too stupid or strong-willed to be dissuaded. If so, they could still be here, as invisible as ever.

But it certainly didn't seem very likely.

"The penthouse takes up the entire top floor," I reported. "It has its own express elevator, one that makes only two stops, the lobby and the penthouse. There are two other elevators in the building, but one of them's for One to Twenty, and the other makes its first stop at Twenty and tops out at Forty-one."

"How do you know all this, Bern?"

"Amazon and eBay may be gone," I said, "but the rest of the internet hasn't changed. A few minutes online and you can find out almost anything. You want to see a floor plan? Want to read specs?"

We had taken up our posts across the street so that we could watch people coming and going, but nobody was coming and nobody was going. A fellow who was either a doorman or an admiral in the Latvian navy was poised to open the door for people headed in or out, and had more time on his hands than the Maytag repairman.

"He won't be a problem," I told Carolyn. "He'll be so thrilled at the opportunity to open the door that he won't give us a second look. But there'll be a concierge behind the front desk, and his job's got to be every bit as boring as the doorman's."

""How do we get past him, Bern?"

"We act as though we belong. Try to look prosperous."

"In these clothes? I mean, I suppose I look all right—"

"You look terrific, Carolyn."

"—and these days a lesbian haircut is suddenly an acceptable fashion statement, but my outfit is kind of down-market."

"That's because you're rich enough not to care."

"Yeah, right."

"And if he stops us," I said, "all he's gonna do is deny us access. He's not about to call the cops."

"'Officer, these two have no business in the building.'"

"You could say that about most of the tenants."

"'They're just here for the clay and wattles.'"

"If we refuse to leave, then he might pick up the phone. But if we go quietly, we'll be out the door in thirty seconds, and five minutes later he'll have forgotten he ever saw us."

She took this in, thought about it. "Okay," she said. "Let's do it."

The fellow behind the desk, also in the Latvian Navy but years too young for the Admiralty, was reading a book. I suppose it's a professional thing, but I can't see someone so disposed without wondering what's got their attention. Under other circumstances I might have approached the desk for a look, or even asked him what he was reading.

Not tonight. I urged St. Dismas to keep him engrossed in whatever it was, and with Carolyn at my side I headed for the elevators. I wanted to look purposeful but unhurried, and I may or may not have made a good job of it, but my efforts weren't enough to keep the young man from saying "*Sir?*"

I kept going, because I had every right and reason to be where I was, and my name wasn't *Sir* anyway, and—

That might have worked, but when he repeated the word, just a little bit louder and with a little bit more conviction, I stopped in my tracks.

And turned toward the voice, and put a puzzled expression on my face even as I took a step or two in his direction. I counted to three, willed my expression to change from puzzlement to comprehension, and snapped my fingers to indicate that light had dawned.

"Ah then," I said, and the *TH* of then may have verged on Z. "I haff not seen you before," I said, aiming an index finger at him, "and zis means zat you haff not seen me before, eh? Eh?"

"Uh, I don't—"

"You do not know me," I said, "and how could you?" I smiled broadly as I continued to approach the desk. "I did not wish to take you away from your book. May I see what you are reading?"

Wish, what. My Ws could almost have been Vs.

He colored slightly, held up *Blue Moon*, the last Reacher novel before Lee Child brought his brother in as coauthor.

"Ah," I said. "Is good?"

"Well, I haven't gotten all that far, but—"

I stopped him with a hand, indicating that I was merely being polite and my question wasn't one he need feel he had to answer. "Istvan Horvath," I said. "Apartment 29-D. And you are?"

"Peter. Um, Peter—"

"Peter-Peter?"

"Peter Tompkins."

"Pumpkins, yes?"

"I beg your pardon?"

Big smile. "Peter. Eater of pumpkins, yes?"

"Uh—?"

"Is a poem, yes? For children. 'Peter Peter Pumpkin Eater.' No?"

"Oh, right," he said. "Peter pumpkin eater. I get that all the time."

Oh, I'll just bet you do, Pete. "Next time," I said, "I will remember you, Peter-Peter. And you will remember me."

"Of course," he said. "Have a good evening, Mr. Horvath."

11

The first elevator, with the numbers 1 through 20 arrayed above it, was maybe twenty yards beyond the front desk, with its more ambitious fellow right alongside it. Then there was a stretch of wall space, filled in part by a painting by the long-lost bastard son of Franz Kline and Jackson Pollock, and then, far enough from its fellows so you wouldn't choose it by mistake, was the discreetly unlabeled private elevator that went straight to the penthouse.

I pushed the button for Door #2. It opened without a sound, we entered just as silently, and it closed even as I pressed 29.

Carolyn, her lips moving no more than those of a promising ventriloquist-in-training, said, "Ishan Horbat?"

"Istvan Horvath," I said, "and I forget what he did and does, but he can look forward to a long and luxurious life, provided he doesn't try to go back to Croatia."

"Therezh really suzha person, Bern?"

"There is," I said, "and he owns Apartment 29-D, but he wouldn't have picked up the phone if the concierge had called, because I guess he prefers spring to fall."

"Huh?"

"He's spending October in Buenos Aires, where I understand it's lovely this time of year, but then so is Manhattan.

And there's no camera in the elevator, and even if there was I don't think Peter-Peter has lip-reading down pat, so you can talk normally."

"Oh," she said, normally enough, and the whisper-quiet elevator stopped as imperceptibly as it started, and the door opened, and we stepped out on the 29th floor.

The elevator, given the slightest encouragement, would have whisked us all the way to 41, just a single flight of stairs below the Kloppmann Diamond. But even without closed-circuit assistance, the front desk afforded a good view of the elevator, and the numbers above it that indicated where it was. I'd read *Blue Moon*, and found it admirably fast-paced and gripping, but that didn't mean young Peter might not want to reassure himself that Mr. Horvath and his lady friend had in fact gone where they were supposed to be.

I'd say the hallway was empty, but I'd be slighting the potted plants stationed here and there, and the generic abstract canvases on the walls. But there were no human beings, and of course no cameras, and I found the D apartment and rang the bell, just to make sure.

When no one answered it, I took out my set of tools. The lock was a Rabson, and about as pickproof as locks got before the current generation of electronic sentinels, but the inner workings of a Rabson lock are as familiar to me as my own apartment. I let us in almost as swiftly as I could have done with Mr. Horvath's key, flicked the light switch, and ushered Carolyn inside.

* * *

"You're glowing, Bern."

"Glowing?"

She nodded." Positively radiant. It really does it for you, doesn't it?"

"Even after all these years," I admitted, "and God knows how many locked doors. All I have to do is let myself in where I don't belong and I get the same thrill I got the very first time I did it."

"When you were just a boy."

"A good little boy," I said, "in all other respects. I wonder if Istvan Horvath has ever had the pleasure himself."

"Of breaking and entering?"

"Of seeing the inside of his apartment."

"It's all furnished, Bern. Pretty luxuriously, in fact."

"But pretty generically, wouldn't you say?"

"Like he picked a decorator out of a phone book and handed him an AmEx card. No, you know what it looks like?"

"What?"

"Like the building staged it," she said. "You know how they do on the *Flip or Flop* shows? On HGTV? Where you buy some pigsty of a house—"

"But one with good bones."

"Right, good bones. Because the last thing you'd want is a house with osteoporosis. And what you do, you rip out a few walls and spring for a new roof and build an enormous island in the kitchen, or maybe an archipelago. And then, before you have your open house, you hire a company to stage it, because a nicely furnished place has more eye appeal than empty rooms and bare walls."

"If I were selling condos to rich people," I said, "I might do that. If I'm asking upwards of a million dollars for an apartment, paying a couple of thousand to have it staged wouldn't be out of line."

"Not at all."

"And the buyer, if all he wants is an investment in New York real estate and a place where he'll spend maybe three weeks a year—"

"'This looks nice, Mr. Real Estate Agent. How much more for the furniture?'"

"There you go," I said. "Or maybe, 'You vhant two million six for this? Okay, but for zat you got to trow in ze furniture. So vhat do you say? Haff ve got a deal?'"

She gave me a look.

"What?"

"The accent. The same one you trotted out for Peter-Peter. Is that supposed to be Croatian?"

"I don't really know what a Croatian accent would sound like," I said. "I was just trying for all-purpose foreign."

"Well, in that case I have to say you nailed it. Now what, Bern?"

"Now we make ourselves at home," I said, and took out the two pairs of blue hospital gloves. "We'll give Peter some time to forget us, and let other people have a turn on the elevator. And I don't honestly think anybody's going to dust this apartment for fingerprints, but let's not leave any. Just in case."

We spent a long half hour in 29-D. It was a large one-bedroom apartment, with views south and west, and an abundance of empty drawers and closets and kitchen cabinets argued for Horvath's never having spent a night here.

In the bedroom, Carolyn kicked off her shoes and stretched

out on the queen-size bed. "If they staged the place," she said, "they didn't cut corners. They went with down pillows and sheets with a high thread count."

"You look like you're settling in for a nap."

"I'm tired enough. There's something exhausting about adjusting to a new universe."

"No kidding."

"But there's something invigorating about it, too. So I'm tired and wired at the same time." She put her arms over her head and stretched, in a manner that looked familiar.

"Oh," I said.

"Huh?"

"The way you were stretching just now. It reminded me of something, and it took me a minute to figure out what."

"Raffles, right? Or just about any cat, they all do it, but it's Raffles you'd have been reminded of."

Sure, that must be it, I could have said.

But what I said was, "Actually, it was a photograph I saw ages ago. It was probably around the time I first let myself into somebody else's residence."

"'*One Burglar's Beginnings.*'"

"Something like that."

"When you were at an impressionable age."

"Evidently."

"I don't suppose it was a picture of a cat."

"A woman," I said. "She was, you know, stretching."

"Stre-e-e-etching."

"And the expression on her face was a lot like the expression on yours just now."

"Oh?" Her expression was different now, and hard to read. "Uh, what was she wearing, Bern?"

Oh, God.

"As a matter of fact, she wasn't wearing anything."

"You don't say. Who was she, Bern?"

"Just a woman in a photograph."

"Just a woman in a photograph," she echoed. And, as with any echo worthy of the name, the words bounced off the walls.

"Oh, all right," I said. "It was Marilyn Monroe."

"In a lesbian bar," she said, "you wouldn't believe what somebody will tell you, especially as it gets close to closing time. The compliments come thick and fast, and if the woman uttering them has had enough to drink they can get pretty extravagant."

"I can imagine."

"And if the recipient of the compliments has had enough to drink, even the most extravagant of those compliments begins to seem reasonable. Now I've been on both ends of that particular spectrum, Bern. If I've had enough to drink and if I'm sufficiently eager to go home with some sweet young thing, who may not have struck me as that sweet or that young earlier in the evening, well, there's no limit to the outrageous things I might tell her."

"I can—"

"Imagine? Well, maybe you can and maybe you can't, but while you're at it you can try to imagine some of the verbal bouquets that have been tossed in my direction when it's my turn to be the sweet young thing. What's the line, '*Shall I compare thee to a summer day?*' Well, I've been compared to plenty of summer days in my time, and a few April evenings, and I've been drunk enough to believe that the particular hot number sitting next to me not only believed I was beautiful but that she was right."

Maddeningly, *I can imagine* was the only phrase that came to mind, but I was damned if I was going to trot it out again.

"But in all the dyke bars in all the boroughs in New York," she said, "nobody ever tried to tell me I looked like Marilyn Monroe."

"I never said you looked like her, Carolyn."

"You said—"

"I said something about the way you stretched reminded me of her pose in a particular photograph."

"Right. I'm short enough for Ray Kirschmann's smartass remarks to go over my head, and somebody who wasn't looking to go home with me once told me I was built like a fire hydrant, and my hair is dark and I keep it short, and half the time I walk around smelling like wet dog, so why wouldn't I remind you of the world's foremost blonde bombshell?"

"Look," I said, "I'm sorry."

"You're sorry?" There was a glint in her eye, the hint of a smile on her lips. "Bern, you paid me a more outrageous compliment than I ever got in Paula's or the Duchess. That's nothing to apologize for."

"Well, you're a very attractive woman."

I could tell she was about to deflect the compliment, but instead she let herself take it in, and glowed a little.

Then she straightened up and said, "That's very sweet of you. It's probably the nicest thing anybody ever said to me who wasn't a drunk lesbian looking to get laid. But tonight what I am first and foremost is your henchperson, remember? And don't we have work to do?"

12

The hallway of the 29th floor was as unpopulated as when we'd arrived. There were six apartments on the floor, and for all I knew all their owners were in Buenos Aires. I led Carolyn to the elevator, and watched the indicator while it made its way up to 37 and then descended to the lobby. When it had stayed there while I counted off thirty seconds, I summoned it with a blue-clad finger.

It responded. We entered, and the door closed, and that same finger took us to 41. The door opened, and a heavy-set man with his back to us was locking his door. He turned, looked at me, looked at Carolyn, and said, "Is nice out?"

"A beautiful evening," I assured him, and held the door until he had taken our place on the elevator.

I looked around. There was a staircase at either end of the hall. The elevator, unsurprisingly, was in the middle of the building, which put both staircases an equal distance away, and I stood there like Buridan's donkey, starving to death, unable to choose between two bales of hay.

But that wouldn't happen to us. I'd read a book of John Barth's, *The End of the Road*, and I'd absorbed its most important lesson. When you have to make a choice, and all else fails, take the one on the left.

* * *

I explained all this as we were walking soundlessly over the thick unpatterned carpet. "At least we're making a choice," I said, "but it may not be the right one. According to the blueprints online, only one of them has a flight of stairs leading to the penthouse. The other one never goes higher than Forty-one."

"And you don't remember which is which."

"If I did—"

"Right."

Wrong, as it turned out. The one on the left, which is to say the staircase at the front of the Innisfree, led only down—to the fortieth floor for starters, and then on to the lobby and, for all I knew, a basement and a subbasement and a dank and forbidding dungeon.

We turned around, retraced our steps, pressed on. We didn't see anybody, which was a comfort, and the rear staircase ran in both directions.

Before we climbed the up staircase, I put a finger to my lips, and Carolyn rolled her eyes to indicate I needn't have bothered. Her comfortable shoes had crepe soles, and I was wearing my Saucony running shoes, although I couldn't remember the last time I'd run anywhere. So our footfalls were silent, and concrete stairs don't squeak.

The door at the top was just a plain unornamented slab, painted the same muddy blue as the surrounding walls and the stairs themselves. There was no knob to turn, just a handle to pull. I wrapped a blue hand around it and tugged it just enough to assure myself that it wasn't going to budge, then checked out the lock immediately below it. It was, I was neither surprised nor dismayed to note, another Rabson.

A whisper. "Bern? Are you sure there's nobody home?"

We'd been over this before. If all was as it was supposed to be, Orrin Vandenbrinck was in a house seat at the DeLorean, one of a cluster of small off-Broadway theaters on Fifteenth Street just east of Union Square. *A Definite Maybe,* a new play by Efrem Seeger, was opening tonight, and Vandenbrinck had a substantial interest in the production. According to *Page Six* of the *New York Post*, he had a comparable interest in one Gillian Fremont, the ingénue cast in the leading role. "This represents a significant step up for the fetching Ms. Fremont," the anonymous reporter told us, "and we can only assume she has talents unreflected in her résumé."

So that meant he was at the theater now, and the final curtain wouldn't come down until after ten, and there was sure to be a party afterward. Even if they skipped it and came straight home, we'd be long gone.

But did that mean the penthouse was empty?

The bodyguards, those two blocks of granite, would most likely be in the theater, or waiting in the limousine, or downing shots of slivovitz at the bar across the street; one way or another, they wouldn't be far from the body they were guarding. But who was to say what other souls might be on the Vandenbrinck payroll?

I put my ear to the door, as if that was going to tell me something. If you're near a door, take a minute and put your ear to it. Hear anything?

I didn't think so.

There was no doorbell to ring, because this was an emergency exit, not how anyone came calling. It offered a way out for the residents should an electrical failure render all the building's elevators *hors de combat*. And yes, the lock could be opened from either side, because building staff and early responders might need emergency access, and it's good it was there, because how else could a burglar expect to get in?

It was, thank God and Mr. Rabson, essentially identical to the Rabson that had done such a good job of safeguarding Apartment 29-D. I'm sure the Innisfree's master key would open both of them; unless some paranoid international miscreant had installed an extra lock or two of his own, the master would get you through any door in the building.

But then so would my picks and probes.

I stood for a moment, my tools at the ready, and listened. The only sound I could hear was Carolyn's breathing, and then I couldn't even hear that, because she was holding her breath.

I went to work, and it seemed to me I could feel the Rabson putting up a show of resistance, then resigning itself to the inevitable and giving way with a soundless sigh. Ridiculous, of course, because all it was was a piece of machinery, and any apparent resistance could only be attributable to disuse.

For all I knew, I was the first person ever to turn its tumblers—with or without a key.

I pocketed my tools and took hold of the door handle. I waited, listening and hearing nothing, and then I gave just enough of a tug to move the door a half-inch or so.

Enough to rule out the presence of an additional lock on the inside, a chain lock or a sliding bolt or some similar annoyance.

I looked down at Carolyn, two steps below me on the staircase, and found her looking up at me. Her eyes asked if there was a problem, and mine sought to assure her there wasn't. Still, I listened for a long moment.

And heard nothing.

And opened the door.

13

We stepped into a kitchen that might have been a wet dream of Bobby Flay's. It had everything you'd find in the *Oh-My-God* kitchens on HGTV, the island and the quartz countertops and the ceramic tile backsplash, but it didn't stop there. A dozen gleaming copper frying pans in graduated sizes hung overhead. There was an enormous knife rack, there was an even larger spice rack, there was every kind of rack except the kind that had come in so handy during the Spanish Inquisition.

It was a hell of a kitchen, but it got less of my attention than it might have, because when I stood there and listened, I could hear something that hadn't reached me when we were on the other side of the fire door.

Carolyn clutched my arm. She heard it, too.

I closed my eyes, listened harder. Human voices. A conversation, and while I couldn't make out any of the words, the intensity got through. We were not alone in the Vandenbrinck penthouse, and whoever the other people were, they had more right to be here than we did.

I glanced over at the door we'd come through.

And then the conversation stopped, and I heard muted music, and then another voice, a voice that was trying to tell me something that it felt I needed to know.

"It's TV," I whispered to Carolyn. "It was some sort of dramatic scene, and now it's a commercial.'

"I guess it's not Netflix," she whispered back.

"Or HBO."

"Whatever it is, Bern, if there's a TV on there's somebody watching it."

"Unless it's a tree falling in the forest. He left the lights on in the kitchen, so why couldn't he leave the TV running in the living room?"

"I guess he doesn't worry much about the Con Edison bill. Is that where it's coming from? The living room?"

I didn't know. "It's toward the front of the building," I said, "which is a logical place to put a living room, but this place has got drop-dead views in all directions, so who knows? But if the TV's on over there—"

I pointed. She nodded, and we headed in the opposite direction.

A penthouse doesn't have to be large. All it has to be is on the top floor of an apartment building, and it can share that floor with other apartments. (In point of fact, there was a time when a top-floor location wasn't required; the word was once applicable to an outhouse or shelter built onto the side of a building, having a sloping roof.)

Never mind. This one was on the top floor of the Innisfree, and it had that floor all to itself. And, trust me, it was large.

I don't know about the sloping roof.

* * *

We walked toward the rear of the building, and away from the sound of the television set. There were lights on throughout, and doors were open, and as far as I could tell we had that part of the apartment all to ourselves.

But we kept quiet all the same.

Carolyn didn't ask where I was leading her, or why we were passing various rooms without giving them much of a first look, let alone a second one. I saved my explanation until I found the room I was looking for.

It was darker than most of the others, illuminated only by a bronze bedside lamp with a Handel shade. But it was very obviously the room I was looking for, and when we'd crossed its threshold I closed the door and turned on the overhead lights.

"The master bedroom," I said, not in a whisper, but not far from it.

"They don't call it that anymore, Bern."

"They don't?"

She shook her head.

"Why not?"

"Because it's a reference to plantation culture and the whole language of slavery. If you're going to tear down statues of Robert E. Lee and Stonewall Jackson, how can you in good conscience call this a master bedroom?"

I frowned. "So what are you supposed to call it?"

"The primary bedroom."

"Suppose it's the only bedroom in the place?"

"Then you wouldn't have to call it anything, would you? You'd just call it the bedroom."

"The primary bedroom," I said.

"That's the term I hear the most."

"On that *Flipflop* show? You know what I bet? I bet Vandenbrinck calls it the master bedroom."

And it looked the part. The bed, flanked by a pair of boxy black night tables, was king-sized at a minimum, and looked to me to be six inches to a foot longer and wider, suitable for an NBA point guard, if not a center. For people of ordinary size, it was big enough to sleep three or four of them; if they were there for a pursuit more active than sleep, I couldn't guess how many it might accommodate.

The walls held half a dozen oil paintings of various sizes, each housed in a carved and gilded frame. And each painting showed a woman, and none of the women could have been more attractive if she'd been painted by Titian. In four of the paintings, the subject was alone. A fifth showed two women, a pneumatic blonde and a not-quite-boyish brunette, and the redhead in the sixth painting was accompanied by two men who might have come straight from Gold's Gym.

Nobody was wearing any clothes.

Was one of the paintings there to hide a wall safe? No, as a quick check revealed. They were just there for the appreciative aesthetic response they might engender.

"He doesn't know much about art," Carolyn said, "but he knows what he likes, and now so do we."

She looked at each painting in turn, paying particular attention to the one that showed the two women. "Doesn't that look like it would hurt, Bern? I mean, not just her hand but halfway to her elbow."

"Um."

"But the blonde seems to like it, going by the expression on her face. And you have to admit it's hot."

I didn't argue the point.

"And these three. Doesn't that look complicated?"

"I suppose if you'd been doing yoga all your life—"

"Maybe, but that's the least of it. I mean from a mental standpoint. I just think it would be confusing. Bern?"

I'd been looking at the painting, which did in fact appear complicated from just about every standpoint, and now I looked at her and found her looking back at me.

"Bern, did you ever?"

"What? Oh. Well, once."

"Two boys and a girl, like the picture?"

"The other way around."

"You and two girls?" She cocked her head. "Anybody I know?"

"I don't think so. I'd seen this woman a couple of times, and we were never going to be Dante and Beatrice or Heloise and Abelard—"

"Or A-Rod and J-Lo."

"—but it would do to improve the idle hour. And one night we went out to dinner and when we came home her roommate was there, and the three of us sat around smoking."

"Smoking? You don't smoke."

"I don't smoke tobacco," I said. "Or anything else in years, but this was a long time ago. In fact it was before I had the store, so that meant it was before you and I knew each other."

"And you got stoned."

"I got a little high. We passed one joint around, and everybody got a slight buzz, and my girl and I started kissing, and I expected the other one to disappear into another room, but the one I was kissing pulled away and told her roomie, 'Oh, Bernie's a good kisser. You should kiss him and see for yourself.' And it sort of went from there."

"So it was your date's idea."

"It was. I mean, they were both attractive, so it's not as though the idea never entered my mind, but it never would have occurred to me to try to make it happen. And afterward I thought about it—"

"I'll bet you did."

"—and it dawned on me that they'd planned this and it was something they'd done before."

The whole conversation was part of a what you'd call a walk-and-talk if it turned up in an Aaron Sorkin script, because along with the paintings and the enormous bed, the room held a pair of glossy black dressers that were a match for the night tables. One of them taller than it was wide, the other wider than it was tall; a while back I'd have thought of them as a highboy and a lowboy, but in the spirit of desktop printing I thought of the tall one as Portrait and his brother as Landscape.

I started with Portait's top left-hand drawer and worked my way through one drawer after another. They all held clothing, and all were at least half-full, and I didn't need to look at labels to know that he didn't do his shopping at Kmart. There were two sock drawers, two underwear drawers—boxers and briefs—and three drawers that held nothing but dress shirts, most of them in their original wrapping.

A walk-and-talk, except that I let my blue-gloved hands do the walking.

"So your three-way turned out to be a one-and-done, Bern?"

"I'm trying to think if I ever saw either of them again," I said, closing one drawer only to open another. "I'm pretty sure I didn't."

"Didn't you enjoy it?"

"It was kind of confusing and unreal, and part of that may

have been the dope I smoked. It was exciting, but mostly in the sense of *Oh my God look what's going on here.*"

"Like fulfilling a longtime fantasy."

"Something like that, yeah."

"But you never went back for more?"

"No, and what stopped me?" I was at Landscape now, moving on from polo shirts to turtlenecks. Why on earth would anybody have so many clothes? "Oh, right."

"You met someone else," she said, "and fell in love."

"I had to leave town. I, uh, went to somebody's house in Larchmont, and nobody was home."

"But the door was open."

"Not at first," I said. "But soon enough. I made out okay, but one way or another I managed to arouse suspicion, and I didn't have a store to run, and the days were getting shorter and the thermometer was dropping, so why not spend a few weeks on the island of Tobago?"

"Why Tobago?"

"I have no idea, but while I was there the cops arrested some joker who'd been kicking in one door after another in Larchmont and Mamaroneck, and they took the burglary I'd committed and put it on his tab, and if he even realized it was one he hadn't done, why make a fuss? His lawyer pleaded him out and he went away for a while."

"And you came home."

"Uh-huh."

"And never saw the two girls again."

"Never."

Close a drawer, open a drawer. It had to be here. Hadn't Vandenbrinck told one TV reporter he didn't believe in bank vaults, because why spend a lot of money on something you couldn't lay your hands on whenever you got the urge?

The New York One interview had made YouTube, and I'd played it a few times and watched him smirk while he explained how the Kloppmann Diamond could be expected to improve his love life. "When you hang a stone like that around a woman's neck," he said, "it tends to get her in the mood. I mean, imagine how you yourself might feel, if that was the only thing you were wearing."

It was hard to read the interviewer's expression. Did she want to fuck him or kill him?

Maybe both.

"Bern?"

"It's got to be here," I said. "He told the whole world where the banks could stuff their vaults. By God, he was going to keep it in his apartment, and you know he's planning to bring his new girlfriend here tonight, when she's already flushed with excitement from her off-off-Broadway debut—"

"Bern."

"—and he'll lead her straight to the bedroom and show her the Kloppmann, and the next thing you know she'll be naked and he'll be hanging sixty million dollars around her neck."

"Bern," she said, "is this what I think it is?"

14

It could hardly have been anything else.

I've been to the Museum of Natural History a handful of times over the years. It's an easy walk from my apartment, and I could certainly go more frequently, but because it's always there it's easy to overlook.

Have I ever gone there on my own? It seems to me my visits were always with one lady friend or another, and the women in question were young mothers, and the child for whose benefit we'd gone to the museum wanted to see the dinosaurs. I have nothing against dinosaurs, but I don't care if I never see another.

It seemed to me that an early visit had included the Hall of Gems and Minerals, but it hadn't made that much of an impression on me, and anyway it would have been before the Kloppmann stone came into the museum's possession. All I could recall, and that but dimly, was scanning the exhibits with the eye not of a connoisseur but of a thief. *Was there a way to get in and out of the place, my pockets stuffed with gems? No? Well, then, the hell with it.*

So I hadn't ever been up close and personal with the diamond, but I'd certainly seen photographs of it—once when the museum announced the forthcoming deaccessioning, and again when the hammer came down at Sotheby's and the stone's new owner, a smug Orrin Vandenbrinck, picked it up and struck a pose.

It was egg-shaped, and it was the size of an egg, too, although of some bird significantly smaller than a chicken. The color was a definite blue, but a more complicated blue than came across in a photograph, and the phrase that came unbidden to my mind was *sky-blue pink.* I don't even know what that means, but it seemed to fit the stone.

It was, of course, a cut gem, and possessed forty-nine facets, although I wouldn't have welcomed the task of counting them. Fine gold wire was so arranged as to secure it so that it could be suspended from a gold chain, and I took each end of the chain in a gloved hand and let the stone dangle from it a few inches in front of my eyes.

Then I let the stone rest on the upturned palm of my right hand, and closed my hand around it, and quite of their own accord my eyes closed, and for a timeless moment there was nothing at all in the world but me and the stone.

"Bern? Where'd you go?"

I opened my eyes, took a breath, and opened my hand. The diamond sparkled in the low light of the bedside lamp. Carolyn was sitting on the bed, and it wasn't hard to tell where she'd made her discovery. The drawer of one bedside table was open, and nearby on the bed was a three-inch-square jewelry case, its hinged lid open.

"I just opened the drawer," she said, "and there it was."

"I never got it before."

"Got what, Bern?"

"Jewelry," I said. "Gems. I got the status symbol thing, and the *I'm giving you this because I love you so much* aspect, and the artistic merit of some pieces of jewelry, even costume jewelry with cut glass, if the design was pleasing. But this thing has its own energy, it's like a living thing."

"I know. I thought it was going to burn my hand, but it wasn't heat. It was something else."

"Which I'll call energy," I said, "maybe because I don't know what it means." I stepped closer, fastened the chain around her throat.

Her eyes widened.

"Your eyes are blue," I said.

"You never noticed before?"

Of course I had, but it was as if I was seeing them for the first time. I said, "When Richard Burton bought the Kloppmann for Elizabeth Taylor, he said it was because of the way it would complement her violet eyes. I thought it was just a good line, but now I can see what he meant."

"If Elizabeth Taylor wore this, I have to wonder what it's doing around my neck."

"It looks like it belongs there," I said.

I looked into her eyes, and she looked back into mine, and something happened. And I don't know what it was, any more than I know what happened when I closed my hand around the Kloppmann Diamond.

Each time, something happened. But don't ask me what it was.

"Bern? We should get out of here."

"You're right."

"I don't know what time he's coming back, but—"

But the longer we stayed there, the greater the risk. A wise burglar gets in and gets out, with as little time as possible between arrival and departure.

She got up from the bed, walked around its great circumference, leaned over to smooth its satin sheets. I opened and closed a few dresser drawers at random, reassuring myself that I'd left them as I'd found them.

Not that it mattered. The first thing Vandenbrinck would look for, the first thing anybody would look for, was the diamond.

The next few minutes verged on slapstick. Carolyn reached for the clasp of the necklace and couldn't manage to get it open. I took a turn, and my fingers couldn't begin to cope with the mechanism, and I didn't get anywhere. And then she brushed my hands aside and took hold of the necklace and lifted, and, its clasp still fastened, it cleared her head with room to spare.

She put it in the plush-lined case. I took the case from her, opened it, drew out the necklace, closed the empty case and returned it to the night table drawer.

Why? So that he might open the drawer, see the case where it belonged, and just take it for granted that the necklace was still in it?

No, that was ridiculous. I went back for the case, put the necklace in it once again, closed the case and found room for it in the inside breast pocket of my blazer.

Buttoned my blazer. Unbuttoned my blazer. Wondered why I was standing there like a ninny, buttoning and unbuttoning my blazer.

And so on.

* * *

I opened the bedroom door and motioned Carolyn through it. I followed her, and I started to close the door, and tried to remember whether it had been open or closed when we arrived.

Ridiculous. If I couldn't remember whether Vandenbrinck had left it open or shut, why should I think he would remember? And what difference could it make if he did or didn't?

We moved in silence, retracing our steps, and I was listening for the television set at the other end of the apartment, or whatever it was that we'd heard. And as we reached the kitchen, I was able to hear what we'd heard earlier, a conversation. As before, I couldn't make out what was being said, but as we crossed the room and reached the door through which we'd come in, I could tell they were having an argument.

Earlier, I'd locked the door once we were on the right side of it. That had just been a simple matter of turning a bolt, and that's all it took now to unlock it. I'd need my tools to lock up again from outside, and I got them out of my pocket, and closed the door on an argument that had gotten a whole lot louder in a matter of seconds.

And then—

"Bern? Were those gunshots?"

When we'd descended one flight of stairs, Carolyn put a hand on the door leading to the 41st floor, and I shook my head and pointed downward. Neither of us had said a word since Carolyn had asked about the three sharp noises we'd heard, loud enough to be clearly audible through the fire door, and we went down another flight before I explained that Mr. Horvath and his companion ought to take the precaution of boarding the elevator on 29.

"That means walking down another twelve flights," I said, "and it's probably not really necessary, but—"

"But better safe than sorry," she said, "especially if what we heard was gunfire. At least we're walking down and not up."

"Trust you to find the bright side."

"I know," she said. "It's my relentless optimism that makes me so adorable. That was a gun, wasn't it?"

"I don't see how it could have been anything else," I said. "The real question is whether the gun was being fired in the apartment or on television."

"And?"

"I think it was the real deal."

"Somebody shot somebody."

"Or shot *at* somebody and missed. Or got annoyed at a picture on the wall, or a television set, or maybe a computer."

"There have been times," she said, "when my iMac was lucky I don't own a gun. But that didn't sound like somebody shooting a computer, did it?"

"No. It sounded like somebody shooting a person."

"That's what I thought."

"After the first few flights," she said, "walking downstairs gets to be almost as bad as walking upstairs."

"In a way," I said, "it's worse. Walking upstairs, sooner or later you get out of breath and have to take a break. Walking downstairs, you just keep going until your legs fall off."

"Does that happen before or after we get to 29?"

"We'll know in a few minutes. And believe me, this is nothing compared to walking all the way down from the top of the Washington Monument."

"When did you—"

"Class trip," I said. "Senior year in high school. There was a local businessman who picked up the tab every year to give a little boost to the patriotism of every kid who made it through Thomas A. Hendricks High School."

"Who was Thomas A. Hendricks?"

"A local boy who served as vice-president during Grover Cleveland's first administration. But only for eight months."

"What happened after eight months?"

"He died, but at least by then he'd done enough to get a school named after him. It was a great trip, although I can't remember much of it. First time I ever stayed in a hotel. On the eleventh floor, which was farther from the pavement than I'd ever been in my life. The idiot I shared a room with kept filling paper bags with water and dropping them out the window."

"You sure that wasn't you, Bern?"

"No, I was the idiot who walked down from the top of the Washington Monument. We went up in the elevator—"

"I should hope so."

"—and the view was spectacular, you could see for miles, but what high school kid cares about that?"

"If there was a water faucet and a supply of paper bags—"

"That might have made a difference, at least to one of us. But once I'd spent a couple of minutes looking in every available direction, I was ready to get back on the elevator."

"So why didn't you?"

"Well, it had other things to do. Another group of tourists, mostly teenagers, had streamed in when our group got out, and once it emptied out at the bottom there'd be yet another batch on their way to the top." I shook my head at the memory. "I didn't give it any thought at the time," I said, "but if you ever start thinking you've got the worst job in America, think about the poor son of a bitch who spends eight hours a day piloting that elevator."

"There was an elevator operator?"

"There was," I said, "and I don't know how he could stand it, going up and down forever in a little box packed to capacity with obnoxious kids. I was as obnoxious as any of them, and even I couldn't stand it, all jammed together like anchovies, and the idea of having to spend precious minutes waiting for the damn thing to get there, well, the hell with that. 'You peasants can wait,' I announced. 'I'm taking the stairs. Who wants to join me?'"

"How many took you up on it?"

"Not a single one, which gives you an idea of my leadership abilities. But that was fine with me, because I'd be the only one who did it, and maybe that would impress some sweet young thing. So I set off on my own, and by the time I'd descended a small fraction of the 896 steps—"

"You counted them?"

"No, of course not. That's the number in the brochure they gave us. Or at least that's the number I remember, but if you want to go count them yourself—"

"I don't think so."

"Anyway, after I'd covered a few flights, I decided my idea might not have been as brilliant as I'd thought. Because there was nothing to look at but the blank walls, so the view never changed. And by then I'd gone too far to turn back, or at least I thought I had."

"Like Macbeth, Bern. So far stepped in blood, di dah di dah di dah."

"Something like that. And then my legs started to feel it."

"Mine have been feeling it for a while now."

"And it got worse," I remembered. "And it didn't really help to stop for a rest, and instead I tried to speed up, because I wanted the whole business to be over as quickly as possible, and that just made it worse."

"Hearing about it," she said, "isn't helping."

"Just one more flight. Here we go. See the number on the door?"

"Twenty-nine."

"So it is. Gloves?"

"Oh, right."

I summoned the elevator with an ungloved index finger, and it didn't take long to get there. Even if it had, neither of us was about to suggest taking the stairs. We rode to the lobby in silence, standing side by side, staring straight ahead, as if we didn't really believe we weren't sharing the space with a security camera or two.

When we got there, the only person in view was our old friend Peter, and his face brightened when he remembered my name. "Mr. Horvath," he said.

"Peter-Peter," I said. He managed a smile, and we sailed past him and out onto the street.

15

"His smile looked a wee bit forced, Bern. I get the feeling he doesn't like being called Peter-Peter."

"With any luck at all," I said, "we'll never set eyes on him again, or he on us. He'll have a chance to forget the whole thing. And if he doesn't, well, months from now he can take it up with the real Mr. Horvath."

"I'm gonna make some tea."

"Good idea."

"Or we could have a drink," she offered. She raised a hand, her thumb and forefinger about two inches apart. "I think there's this much left in the bottle, but maybe a drink's not such a good idea."

"It sounds like the answer to a prayer," I said, "but who was it who said the real sign of maturity is the ability to delay gratification?"

"Whoever it was," she said, "he can't be a whole lot of fun to hang out with."

We were at Carolyn's studio apartment on the ground floor of a four-story building in Arbor Court, one of those back streets in the West Village that your cabdriver never heard of. We usually get there on foot, but not after a downward trek of 221 steps.

And no, I didn't count them. But from the 42nd floor to the 29th was thirteen flights of stairs, at seventeen steps to a flight—well, I'd say do the math, but I've already done it for you, so why bother? While it's not quite a fourth of my descent of the Washington Monument, it was enough to put us in a taxi.

Carolyn told the driver we wanted the corner of Barrow and Hudson, and that was challenge enough for him. That left us just around the corner from Arbor Court—well, a couple of corners, but close enough. And before long we were settled in, I on the couch and she in the wing chair, with mugs of Earl Grey and a plate of Nutter Butter cookies.

"These almost have to be stale," she said, "but how are you supposed to tell?"

"They taste all right. I'm starving, and they've got to be better than cat food."

"Marginally, Bern." She took her bright blue gloves from her pocket. "We're done with these, right? Shouldn't we get rid of them?"

"Probably."

"Gimme." I gave her mine, and she let herself out, and was back by the time I'd knocked off another cookie. "Down the chute," she said. "Have we got anything else that might be hard to explain?"

I patted a pants pocket. "Burglar tools," I said, and patted my breast pocket. "And this."

"Right. Well, at least we don't have to worry about the gloves."

"That's a relief."

"Now that we've got it," she said, "what are we gonna do with it?"

"Good question." I took the case from my pocket, opened it, and let the necklace, stone and chain and all, drop into my open hand. The surge of energy, like a soundless hum, was palpable.

"It's like it's alive," I said.

"Well, maybe it is, Bern. If animals and vegetables can be alive, why leave out the mineral kingdom? It certainly felt alive when I was wearing it."

I got up and took a few steps, and a moment later she was wearing it once again. She'd taken off her blazer earlier, and now the diamond rested on her dove-gray sweater. She was looking at it, and so was I, and it all felt uncomfortably strange.

Because that meant I was looking at her chest, which is to say at her breasts, and this wasn't something I normally did. She was a woman, she had breasts, but she was my best friend and the friendship was an entirely platonic one, so much so that I neither looked at her chest nor took pains to avoid looking at her chest.

"Bern," she said, "what the hell are we going to do with this?"

"I've been wondering that myself."

"There's a pawnshop on Fourteenth Street, but somehow I don't think that would work."

"You're probably right."

"When you decided to steal it, what did you have in mind?"

"I didn't really think it through," I admitted. "I guess I figured just getting it away from Vandenbrinck would be triumph enough. As far as selling it—well, how do you unload something worth sixty million dollars?"

"Beats me. Isn't there a way to sell something like that back to the insurance company?"

"It's been known to happen. The companies hate it, but if

they can get out of paying the face amount of the policy by handing over a small fraction of that amount to whoever stole it, well, the larger the numbers, the easier it is to rationalize it."

"So we could do that?"

"We could try," I said, "if we could find a go-between, and if we could all trust each other, and there's already a whole lot of ifs in that sentence. But none of it matters, because the stone's uninsured."

"What???"

"I said—"

"I know what you said, Bern, but you're kidding, right? Who buys something for that kind of money and doesn't bother insuring it?"

"Orrin Vandenbrinck."

"Why, for God's sake?"

"Partly because he doesn't believe in it. 'A man buys life insurance, he's betting that he'll die. He's placing a bet he hopes he'll lose. He's betting against himself, and why would I do that?' It's not a difficult stance for him to take given that there's no wife or kids in the picture, no one who'll be ruined by his death."

"Or even disappointed, Bern. But if the Kloppmann Diamond disappears, he's out all those millions. Why?"

"That's the part he doesn't talk about," I said. "In one phase of his illustrious corporate career, our man played it fast and loose with an insurance company. Nobody's in a rush to do business with him."

"So he can't get a policy that'll cover the diamond?"

"He'd probably be able to, sooner or later—if he'd agree to keeping it in a safe-deposit box instead of a night table drawer. But that's no longer his problem."

"Because he doesn't have the diamond anymore."

"No."

"We've got it."

"And you're wearing it," I said, "and it looks great on you."

"It feels strange."

"It does?"

She nodded. "But it also feels kind of nice. It's like when Archie or Ubi lies on top of me. It almost feels like it's purring."

I thought about it. "Maybe you should keep it."

"Very funny."

"I wasn't trying to be funny."

"Well, you can't be serious. What could I do with it?"

"What you're doing now."

"Yeah, right. Can you picture me walking into Henrietta's with this thing around my neck?"

"I guess it'd fit in better at the Cubby Hole."

"Bern—"

"There's such a thing," I said, "as owning something for one's private enjoyment."

And I pointed, and her eyes followed my finger to the far wall, where a small canvas nestled within a gallery frame.

"My little Chagall," she said. "It's right there where anybody can see it, but they all assume it's a copy."

"I don't have many visitors," I said, "but anybody who shows up is apt to notice the Mondrian, and make the same assumption. The last woman I brought home asked me if I painted it myself."

"Well, you did, Bern. Not the one you've got in your apartment, it's the real deal, but you painted one that looks an awful lot like it."

We talked a little about her Chagall and my Mondrian,

and how they'd come to be where they were, and the particular pleasure that came from owning them. While we talked, both of her cats came out from wherever they'd been hiding. Archie, the sable Burmese, was the more adventuresome of the two, and he was comfortably nestled in her lap before Ubi, the Russian Blue, padded across the room, paused to consider a leap onto the couch, then found a spot he liked at his mistress's feet.

"He's stretching," she said. "Does he remind you of Marilyn Monroe?"

"Not particularly. Carolyn, I hope you know I didn't mean anything by that."

"I know."

"It just struck me, and—"

"I know."

Long pause. She petted the cat in her lap while the other one took an interest in her comfortable shoes. She cupped the Kloppmann in one hand, as if weighing it, then took it off and held it in both hands and gazed into it, as if into a crystal ball.

"Bern," she said, "I'm a lesbian."

"No kidding."

"I've been a lesbian all my life. And I've always known. I knew before I had any idea there even was such a thing."

"When your parents gave you dolls, you pushed them away and demanded a cap gun and an Erector set."

"No, I played with dolls. I loved my dollies, Bern. But instead of wanting to dress them up—well, you get the picture. The point is I'm a lesbian."

"I get the picture," I agreed, "and as far as the point is concerned, I got that the day I met you."

"Really? One look and you knew I was gay?"

She'd come into the bookstore within a week or so of my

assuming command. She bought a book by a Dorothy, I forget whether it was Dorothy B. Hughes or Dorothy Salisbury Davis, and we got to talking.

"You said you had a hangover," I reminded her.

"Straight women get hangovers, Bern."

"You said you had a hangover because you spent the whole night drinking Cutty Sark at the Mona Lisa and couldn't find anybody to go home with."

"Oh."

"So I jumped to a conclusion," I said, "and had a soft landing."

"It didn't put you off?"

"Not at all. And a day or two later I wandered into the Poodle Factory, and we talked some more, and then one afternoon we met on the street, having both locked up at the same time, and you asked me if I liked the Bum Rap, and I hadn't discovered the place yet. So we went over and had a couple of drinks."

"And never left," she said.

"We hit it off," I said, "as I've never hit it off with anybody—"

"Same here."

"—and very early on I thought thank God she's a lesbian—"

"'Because otherwise I'd have to sleep with her, and she's an ugly little troll.'"

"—because this way we can really be friends," I said. "I never had a close friendship with a woman before, because sex always got in the way."

"But with this troll—"

"Oh, stop it, will you? You must know you're an attractive woman."

"To some people," she allowed.

"To most people."

"Right. I'm just another pretty face." Her blue eyes bore into mine. "Bern, I can't seem to say what I want to say."

Then leave it unsaid, I thought. Because something funny was going on, and it was every bit as unfamiliar to me as my green-and-white SubwayCard.

And I was afraid of it, and where it would take us.

But I waited in silence, and she took her time, and then she told me one more time that she was a lesbian.

We already established that, I could have said. But I didn't, because I knew where this was going.

"But I'm having feelings tonight that I never had before."

"I know."

"You do?"

"I'm, uh—"

"Having similar feelings yourself?"

I nodded, because it had all at once become difficult to speak. It was, in fact, getting difficult to breathe.

"I don't know when it started," she said. "But it was already going on when we were cooling our heels in 29-D."

"Chez Horvath."

"When I stretched? I certainly didn't have Marilyn Monroe in mind, I don't even know if I ever saw the picture you were referring to, but I was trying to look sexy."

"Well, it worked."

"I didn't know that's what I was trying to do, but it was." She frowned. "'It was? I was?'"

"Whatever."

"Even earlier," she said. "When we were at the Bum Rap,

drinking our Perrier? I was looking across the table at you and I thought how nice you looked."

"I had the same thought about you."

"And in the elevator, after you flimflammed Peter-Peter with your all-purpose accent, I had this out-of-nowhere flash that you'd open the door and we'd rush into the bedroom and . . ."

"Right."

"But of course we didn't, and it's not as though I really expected us to. It was just this passing thought, but in all the years we've known each other it's a thought I've never once had, and there it was."

"Uh-huh."

"And what do I see when I look at you? I see my best friend in all the world, a man who knows me better than anybody else could ever know me. The one person in the world I've always been able to trust, the one person I've always felt safe with."

She opened her hands, looked at the diamond, closed her hands around the stone, and looked at me.

"And I'm a lesbian," she said, "and I've always been a lesbian, and I always will be a lesbian. I'm not bisexual, I've known plenty of bisexual women, and there are people who'll tell you bisexuality isn't a real thing, but they're wrong, it is a real thing. But it's not me."

She took a breath.

"So why do I want to go to bed with you, Bern? Why do I want to rip your clothes off and screw your brains out? Because I do, and I'll be damned if I can figure out why."

16

There was a pivotal moment after which anything might have happened. But it passed with no off-ripping of clothes or out-screwing of brains. Neither of us said anything, and then each of us said the other's name, and then the room went silent again.

"I think it's universal," I said.

"You mean everybody in the world feels this way?"

"God, could you imagine? No, I mean it's this universe as opposed to the one we were in yesterday."

"The old universe," she said. "The real world. Or is this the real world?"

"Whatever world we're in," I said, "is the real world."

"Because we're in it."

"Right."

"Did you do this, Bern?"

"I don't know what I did or didn't do. It happened while I was asleep, remember?"

"But you designed it. Bowl-Mor, SubwayCards, the internet still firmly in place—but no Amazon, no eBay."

"And no security cameras or pickproof locks. I have to admit it's got my fingerprints all over it."

"Good thing you were wearing your Smurf gloves. Bern, if you designed this world for us—"

I held up a hand. "I may have been the architect," I said. "I may have been the one who designed the building. But I had help furnishing the rooms."

"From me?"

"We're not only in this together," I said. "We got into it together. Look how astonished you were to find a SubwayCard in your purse."

"Bern, how could I have done anything? I never even read the book."

"*What Mad Universe*."

"Right. I never read a word of it."

"You asked me about it. I showed it to you and explained the premise."

"That's true," she said, and if we'd been in a cartoon I'd have seen a light bulb taking shape over her head.

"What?"

"When I got back here last night," she said, "I'd been to the only two remaining lesbian bars in Greenwich Village and struck out in both of them, and I blamed the world."

"The universe."

"Whatever. And I thought about some of the bars that have disappeared over the years, and what it's done to the dyke social scene. Two women can get married now, Bern, but how are they supposed to find each other in the first place?"

"That's hardly the first time you've had that conversation with yourself."

"I know, and I've also had it with you, haven't I? But it hit me last night, and I thought about Fredric Brown."

"And wished he would open a bar for lesbians?"

"I thought about alternate universes."

"Oh."

"I was in bed at the time, so it was probably the last thing I was thinking about when I fell asleep. Or passed out, whatever you want to call it, and the next thing I knew it was morning."

"And you had a SubwayCard in your purse."

"If I'd passed by Sheridan Square," she said, "I could have checked. Two Boots opened a pizza parlor where the Duchess used to be. They've even got a pie that they call The Duchess, as a sort of homage to what used to be."

"And you think—"

"I just wonder if the old joint's back in business. Is it possible?"

"I'm beginning to believe everything's possible."

"Maybe it is. And maybe Paula opened up again in the old location on Greenwich Avenue."

"Do you want to go take a look?"

She thought it over, shook her head. "What I want to do," she said, "is get rid of the albatross."

"The Kloppmann."

"I'm fine with having the Chagall on my wall. For one thing, it looks as though it belongs there."

"It does."

"And I stole it myself, years ago, and nobody's knocking on doors looking for it. It's beautiful, but it's not a painting. It's a lithograph."

"Pencil-signed," I said.

"And numbered, and it was worth a few hundred dollars when I got it, so what can it be worth now? A few thousand tops?"

"Could be low five figures."

"Really? That's more than I'd have guessed. But the Kloppmann is something else entirely. What are we gonna do with it, Bern?"

The first thing I did was turn on the television set. We'd had a look at New York One as soon as we'd arrived at her apartment, and there'd been no report of anything related to the Innisfree. This time a cheerful announcer told us about a devastating fire in the Bronx and a drive-by shooting in Brownsville that had killed a seven-year-old girl in another apartment.

"It may be a different universe," Carolyn said, "but in certain respects it's no better than the last one we were in."

But once again there was nothing about the Innisfree.

Maybe the shots we'd heard in Vandenbrinck's penthouse were on the TV. Maybe whoever was watching it had turned up the volume, or maybe the adrenaline in our veins had just made it seem louder.

Or maybe TV had nothing to do with it and two actual people were having an argument, and one of them shared Al Capone's opinion that you could get further with a kind word and a gun than with a kind word alone. Three shots fired, perhaps into the ceiling to make a dramatic point, perhaps into one's companion to make it even more dramatically.

We'd heard it, because we were only a couple of rooms away at the time. But Vandenbrinck's was the only apartment on his floor, with nothing over his head but the roof and the sky, and there was no reason to assume anyone was home on the floor below his, not in a building that by all reports was largely empty.

And if you were some shifty foreigner with an unlaundered

fortune, and you heard what might or might not have been gunshots in another apartment, would you reach for a phone and call 911?

"I think we're all right," I said. "At least until Vandenbrinck and the next Sarah Bernhardt get home from the after-party. And it would be nice if the diamond could pass into another pair of hands before that happens."

"Do you have any particular hands in mind, Bern?"

"I wish. I could name three or four men and one woman who could identify themselves on LinkedIn as receivers of stolen goods. But it's been a long time since I tried to deal with any of them, and I don't know if they're still in business, or still have the same phone numbers."

"Do you want to try?"

"No," I said, "because for one thing they're a bunch of crooks."

"In a business like that? Go figure."

"There's not one of them I'd trust. And they'd be miles out of their league anyway with something that last changed hands for an eight-figure sum."

"Isn't there anybody else?"

"In all my life," I said, "I've only known one man I could go to with something like this."

"Can't you call him?"

"Not unless they have phones in heaven."

"He died?"

"Years ago. He was murdered. You'd remember him."

"Oh my God," she said. "Abel Crowe."

* * *

Abel Crowe.

Good fences make good neighbors, as you've very likely heard, and Abel Crowe was unquestionably a good fence, and was held in high regard by his fellow tenants on Riverside Drive—until one of them killed him in a very unneighborly fashion. It happened the day after my own last meeting with Abel. Carolyn was with me, and so were some interesting if inanimate objects I'd brought along with me.

One was rare edition of Spinoza's *Ethics.* Baruch Spinoza was a special passion of Abel's, who was apt to quote the Dutch philosopher whenever the opportunity arose, and he'd have been an eager customer for the book, but I'd brought it as a gift.

I'd also brought a pair of emerald tear-drop earrings and a Piaget wristwatch. I'd acquired them earlier that evening, in the residence of a couple named Colcannon, even as Carolyn had been lifting their Chagall lithograph from its hook on the wall.

And hadn't there been something else as well? Oh, right. A 1913 Liberty Head Nickel, one of five in existence, with a likely value at the time of a quarter of a million dollars.

I'd left it with Abel. And, not twenty-four hours later, it got him killed.

"Abel Crowe, Bernie. He was such a sweet man."

"The operative word," I said. "I've never known anyone with so prominent a sweet tooth."

"I saw one of those T-shirts the other day. '*Life is Uncertain; Eat Dessert First.*' I thought of him right away."

"I miss him," I said. "He was a pleasure to do business with, but it was more than that. I always enjoyed his company."

"And it hit you hard when he was killed."

"Well, if I hadn't brought him the damn coin—"

"You can't blame yourself, Bern."

"I know that, but—"

"It wasn't your fault."

I shrugged.

"Bern? You said you miss him."

"I do. I mean, it's not as though I spend half my time thinking about him, but he does come to mind. Whenever I see a book by Spinoza, or when an enterprising waiter makes sure I get a good look at the pastry wagon, or—well, you get the idea."

"It's not the only idea I get."

"Huh?"

"Bern, is it safe to say that you missed Abel Crowe even more than you missed Bowl-Mor?"

I looked at her. I said, "I think I know what you're getting at."

"I'd be shocked if you didn't."

"Carolyn, the man spent the war years in Dachau, that's where he developed the craving for sweets."

"I know."

"And he wasn't a boy in knee pants when he went there. He was a grown man." I closed my eyes, ran numbers in my head. "Jesus," I said, "even if he was still alive, he'd be dead by now."

"Unless this is really the best of all possible worlds, Bern."

I picked up my phone, checked my contacts. "No listing for him, and how could there be? He was a few years gone before I finally broke down and bought a cell phone."

"It's hard to believe we ever got along without them."

"I know. Even if Abel somehow survived, what are the odds he's still in the same apartment?"

"You remember that apartment, Bern?"

"At Eighty-ninth and Riverside. I was there, oh, probably eight or ten times over the years."

"I was there two of those times," she said. "The night we brought him the V-Nickel, and before then, on the Fourth of July, when he invited us to watch the fireworks over the Hudson."

"I remember the evening."

"And I remember the apartment," she said, "and the only way anybody would leave an apartment like that is feet first. Trust me, Bern. If Abel's still got a pulse, he's still in that apartment. His number's not in your phone?"

I shook my head.

"You must have had it written down somewhere. An old notebook or something like that?"

"I wouldn't begin to know where to look," I said. "Oh."

"*Oh?* Oh what?"

"It was one of those numbers I didn't have to look up," I said, "and evidently I still don't." I picked up my phone. "But what are the odds he still has the same number?"

She rolled her eyes.

"It's ringing," I reported, "probably in a gentrified brownstone in Williamsburg, where someone with a Wall Street job *and* five or six tattoos will let it ring eight times before picking it up and saying something ironic. And then—"

And then it stopped ringing and I stopped talking, and a familiar voice, a voice I understandably never thought I'd hear again, said, "Yes? Hello?"

17

“Bernard,” he said. “And the beautiful Carolyn. Please, come in. *Mi casa es su casa,* as the Spaniards say, and who are we to question their sincerity? And perhaps it is enough that they say it. ‘The endeavor to understand is the first and only basis of virtue.’”

“Spinoza?”

He nodded, led us into the living room. The view over the Hudson was as magnificent as ever, even now that New Jersey was beginning to sport a skyline of its own.

“All goes well with you both? So my eyes assure me, Bernard. It seems to me a very long time since we’ve seen one another, but neither of you has aged a bit. You both look exactly as I remember you.”

As did he, remarkably enough. He didn’t look either young or slender, not by any stretch of the imagination, but he stood straight and moved gracefully and appeared quite elegant in a maroon velvet smoking jacket over pale gray trousers. His feet, which had always been a source of discomfort to him, looked happy enough in wine-colored carpet slippers.

“But please,” he said. “Sit down, make yourselves comfortable. I’ve put out a few things.” The marble-topped coffee table held half a dozen large china plates, and the selection on offer included éclairs and cupcakes and sacher torte and, piled high on one plate—

"Girl Scout Cookies," he announced. "There is a child in this building, just a little bit of a thing, and it is her ambition to outsell all the other members of her coven."

"I think they call it a troop," Carolyn said.

"You know, I believe you're correct. Young Madison is the sales leader at last reckoning, and this is a source of considerable pride to her. Rather than point out that pride is pleasure arising from one's thinking too highly of oneself, as Spinoza reminds us, I've entered into the spirit of the occasion and established myself as her number-one customer. The Girl Scouts have a dozen varieties this year, but these are my favorites." He pointed. "Adventurefuls. Caramel deLite Samoas. Carolyn, have one of these. Toffee-tastics. And, of course, the irresistible Thin Mints. Bernard, they call these Tagalongs, don't ask me why, but you must have one."

One of the chocolate éclairs was calling to me, but I did as I was told.

"And now please tell me what you would like to drink. Are you both still partial to scotch? I have a particularly nice single malt, not quite as assertive as Laphroaig but similarly a product of the isle of Islay. Or, if you'd prefer something less peaty, I can offer you Dewar's, which is always reliable."

I'd always found it so, and the single malt sounded worth investigating. But Carolyn and I glanced at each other, and I told Abel we were passing up alcohol for the evening.

"As am I," he said. "I had a brandy after my supper, but I don't think it needs any reinforcement." He pointed to a tall glass on the table. "I'm treating myself to an Einspänner, and if it weren't prideful of me to say it, I'd tell you it's every bit as fine as the beverage they serve at Café Frauenhuber." He beamed. "The oldest coffee house in Vienna," he said, "and both Mozart and Beethoven entertained there, playing dinner music for the customers. Of course that was before my time, but not much had changed, and I doubt much has changed since."

It depended, I thought, on what universe one was in.

An Einspänner, it turned out, was a couple of shots of *Espressokaffee mit Schlagsahne*, and you sipped the coffee through the whipped cream. I don't know that it would be worth a trip to Vienna, but it was ample compensation for a taxi ride from the Village.

So we sipped the espresso through the *schlag*, and we ate Girl Scout cookies and Mittel European pastries, and Abel said it was good we'd called when we did, and not a week before or a few days later.

"I am between ocean liners," he said, and explained that in recent years he'd taken to spending the greater portion of his time on cruise ships. "My health is good," he said, "but the years take a toll, you know. And my personal physician, who is by no means an alarmist, suggested I consider what I believe they call assisted living. You are acquainted with the term?"

"From a distance," I said.

"It's a distance you'd be well advised to keep, Bernard. It's a first step. You pay an exorbitant price and move into less inviting quarters than you presently occupy, and they have all manner of group activities available, shuffleboard and yoga classes and macramé workshops, all of which you do everything in your power to shun. And you dine one or two or three times a day in the dining hall, where you are presented with a wide choice of unpalatable dishes, all approved by some insufferable dietician, and when your mind decides it prefers dementia to a true awareness of its circumstances, they shift you to the Alzheimer's ward and join you in the fervent hope that the end's not too far off."

I didn't know what to say to that. Carolyn said, "You make it sound—"

"Better than it actually is," he said, finishing her sentence for her. "I decided perhaps dying was not so bad, when one considered the alternative, and then I sought refuge in the words of Baruch Spinoza, and before long I was in my stateroom on a Holland America ship. The *Oosterdam*, if I remember correctly."

"Your friend Spinoza opened a travel agency?"

"What he wrote, and what I read, is this: '*A free man thinks of nothing less than of death, and his wisdom is a meditation, not on death, but on life.*'"

I let the words wash over me, and Carolyn asked Abel to repeat it, and he was more than happy to comply.

"Okay," I said. "I kind of get it. But where does the Roosterdam come in?"

"The *Oosterdam*. Or I suppose it could have been the *Rotterdam*. It doesn't matter."

I had another cookie. I believe it was a Toffee-tastic, but it may have been one of the Adventurefuls. That's one more thing that doesn't matter.

"Do you know what a cruise ship is, Bernard? Carolyn?"

She shook her head. I said, "I know what Samuel Johnson said. '*Being on a ship is like being in jail, with the added hazard of drowning.*'"

"And perhaps that was so in the good Dr. Johnson's time, but my experience is a good deal different. A cruise ship is a luxurious version of assisted living. The food is excellent, and you can eat and drink whatever you want at any hour of the day or night. Your bed is made up shortly after you get out of it, and the linen is always clean, and at night they turn down your bed and place a mint on your pillow. If you don't want to leave your cabin, they bring you your meals. If you're not feeling well, there's a doctor a few decks below, and he doesn't tell you to take two aspirin and call him in the morning."

He went on. You had fifteen hundred or two thousand fellow passengers, and could spend as much or as little time with any of them as you wished, and when the cruise was over you never had to see any of them again; you stepped off one ship and onto another, with a whole different array of passengers, and different singers and musicians and comedians to entertain you of an evening. There was a library, there was a game room, there was a gymnasium, and there were restaurants and bars and cafés at every turn.

"And there's a conveniently located desk," he said, "occupied by an obliging woman with nothing she'd rather do than book your next cruise. You can go from one ship to another, and sooner or later I contrive to get on one that drops me in New York, where my apartment is just as I left it. And I'm here for as long as I want to be and then I get on another ship." He beamed. "This coming Wednesday I board the *MS Volendam*. Even as we speak it is cruising the St. Lawrence River from Quebec City, and it will stop in New York on its way to Fort Lauderdale. There I'll transfer to the *MS Zuiderdam* for a 66-day circumnavigation of South America."

Carolyn: "So it's just one Dam ship after another?"

"And one country after another," he said, "and one port after another, and sometimes I get off and sample what a new port of call has to offer, but at least as often I spare my feet and remain comfortably aboard. The ship's library almost invariably has something I can read with pleasure, and I always have Spinoza at my side." A sip of Einspänner, a Thin Mint. "'*Not to laugh, not to lament, not to detest, but to understand.*' The perfect companion, my cherished friend Baruch. He takes up so little space in one's luggage, even as he fills one's mind and replenishes one's spirit."

18

"But look at the hour! Surely you've both spent too much time already with a loquacious old man."

I didn't have to look at the hour, as the chiming clock on his mantle was busy announcing it. It must have chimed every fifteen minutes since our arrival, but I'd not once noticed it, nor had I ever thought to glance at my watch.

And how could I regret a single moment of the time we'd spent with this particular elderly gentleman?

"If this is purely a social call," he went on, "I assure you it could not be more welcome. But would I be wrong to suspect that there's an element of business to it, one you find yourselves too polite to mention?"

"Well, there is something," I said, and drew the jewel case from my jacket pocket. Abel took it in both hands and held it as if waiting for a word from the treasure it held, and maybe he got that word, because something showed in his eyes.

He lifted the lid, and said something in German that certainly sounded heartfelt. He lifted the stone from its case, held it between his thumb and forefinger.

"Bernard, is this—"

"It is."

"Of course it is," he said. "It could be nothing else on earth or in heaven. When Richard Burton gave it to Elizabeth Taylor, she had it set in a ring, then complained it was too heavy to wear."

Carolyn: "So she didn't wear it?"

"Of course she did. She loved having it on her finger, even as she delighted in complaining about it. Then, after he'd died, she sold it and a few other pieces and donated the proceeds to African children." He held the stone to the light. "To a good cause," he clarified, "that sought to keep them from dying of a lamentable disease, but I don't recall which one."

He drew a jeweler's loupe from the pocket of his smoking jacket, which suggested that he'd suspected I'd be bringing him something. While he studied the stone, he said, "The Kloppmann Diamond. Do you know its history?"

"Some of it."

"It is an alluvial diamond, which is to say that erosion over the centuries freed it from where it had formed, probably beneath the coastal waters of the South Atlantic Ocean. Those waters eventually washed it ashore, on the west coast of what we now call Namibia, named for the Namib Desert. At the time, of course, it was German Southwest Africa, and would so remain until Germany's colonies were redistributed after the First World War. The word *German* was dropped from its name, and as South West Africa it was a British mandate, administered by the Union of South Africa."

"Who was Kloppmann?" Carolyn wanted to know. "And is it true that he just picked it up off the beach?"

"Someone picked it off the beach," he said, "or found it by digging in the sand at the water's edge. But it wasn't Gerhardt Kloppmann. It would have been some native, very likely of the Herero people, who found the stone, and Kloppmann took it from him, probably paying him with a bullet, or sending him to a camp."

There was no rushing Abel, and we were happy to listen to every word of the history lesson, but you don't have to. The German colonial administration conducted a four-year campaign of genocide against the Herero, and it was a genuine dress rehearsal for the Holocaust, one that played out years before anybody ever heard of Adolf Hitler. For illustration, Abel quoted one General Lothar von Trotha: "'*I destroy the African tribes with streams of blood. Only following this cleansing can something new emerge.*'"

The Herero population was reduced, one way or another, from eighty thousand to around fifteen thousand. German combat losses ran to 696 soldiers, and Gerhardt Kloppmann was not among them. He returned to Europe, where he held onto the stone just long enough to get his name permanently attached to it. Then he sold it for an unrecorded sum and went on to die rather heroically in the early years of the World War.

And so on.

The stone changed hands a few times, always at a higher price, and often enough tainted by some sort of scandal or tragedy. A maharajah got his hands on it, and the press began calling it the Star of Uttar Pradesh, but the name never caught on; the maharajah and three of his wives died violently in a palace coup, and their royal jewels disappeared, and a while later the Kloppmann surfaced in the possession of the pretender to the throne of Ethiopia.

Italy invaded that country in 1935. Emperor Haile Selassie went into exile, but his older cousin, whose claim to the throne was no stronger than his grip on the Kloppmann, chose to remain in Addis Ababa.

"His name escapes me now," Abel said. "Although I do recall that a London journalist dubbed him Haile Unlikely. He stayed in Addis, where he lived just long enough to regret his decision. Someone must have taken the diamond to Rome, and from there it went to Zurich."

And so on.

"And now you are here," Abel said, "for which I am deeply grateful. And you have brought me this extraordinary object, this Kloppmann Diamond, and for that I am—"

"Not so grateful?"

"Still grateful," he said, "because who would wish to be spared the thrill of holding such an item in his hand? But what on earth am I to do with it? I assume you wish to sell it."

"Of course."

"Do you have a price in mind?"

"I was hoping you might."

"*Gruss Gott.* Carolyn, have you held the stone in your hand?"

I said, "She was the one who found it, Abel. She picked the right drawer to look in."

"And did it speak to you, my dear?"

"It hummed," she said, "but silently. I don't know how to explain it."

"No one could explain it better. Bernard, I think you should keep it. I think Carolyn should wear it. Not in public, obviously, but at home of an evening."

"I suggested as much," I told him, "but she doesn't like the idea, and on reflection I don't blame her."

"No," he said. "Neither do I. The most recent owner, the mean-spirited little man whose name escapes me—"

"Orrin Vandenbrinck."

"Dutch?"

"Once upon a time," I said. "An ancestor of his washed up in Nieuw Amsterdam around the same time as Peter Stuyvesant, but that wouldn't account for more than a narrow slice of his DNA. But he's proud of the name. He told one reporter he looks forward to the day when everybody calls it the Vandenbrinck Diamond."

"An ambition worthy of the fellow. Does he know the stone is gone?"

"He might. New York One didn't, as of a few hours ago. He was at the theater, and there would have been a party afterward, and he could still be out celebrating. But he might be home by now."

"I can't see that it matters," he said. "It's still the Kloppmann Diamond. It's still impossible to sell." He frowned. "Bernard, it begins to come back to me. The last time I had the pleasure of your company, yours and Carolyn's, you brought me something very nearly as impossible to sell. Not a precious gem but a comparably precious coin."

"The 1913 nickel."

"It was one of five," he recalled, "as opposed to one and only one Kloppmann Diamond. I had much the same feeling then that I am having now. I was honored that you brought it to me even as I wished you hadn't. Of course I want to participate in its sale, but how can I possibly do so? Where am I to find a buyer?"

I didn't have an answer, or anything to contribute, so I stayed silent. Carolyn started to reach for a cookie, then changed her mind and withdrew her hand.

"Not Rotterdam," he said forcefully, as if I'd dared to suggest that particular city. "It's a large enough stone that it might be cut into smaller stones, each still large enough to be of value but entirely unidentifiable as having been part of a greater whole. But that would be a crime, Bernard."

Oh?

"Against nature," he clarified, and took another look into the diamond's innards. "It would be like kidnapping Helen of Troy and selling off her organs for transplant." He frowned. "Forgive me, Bernard, Carolyn. That is an unfortunate image. But it makes a point."

"Vividly," I said.

"And the pittance one would net through such arrant vandalism would not provide much of a motive. The Kloppmann amounts to ever so much more than the sum of its carats. But to whom could one sell it?"

He was on his feet, still holding the stone, pacing to and fro as an aid to thought, talking as much to himself as to us. There were enthusiasts of one sort or another for whom the pleasure of ownership was sufficient in itself, and their egos were sufficiently inflated without being able to boast of their treasures. Not a few Van Goghs and Rembrandts—and, he'd been given to understand, at least one superb Vermeer—reposed in private galleries the world would never see, the unlawful property of owners who could neither show them nor sell them.

"If it were orientalia," he said, "there's a man I know in San Francisco with access to collectors in Hong Kong. If it were a painting, there are avenues I could explore. Or a singularly desirable coin or postage stamp. But with a diamond, do I know anyone? Do I know anyone who knows anyone?"

No one seemed to come to mind.

"Hold this for me," he said, and fitted the gold chain around Carolyn's neck. "I won't be a moment."

He left the room.

"And here I am," Carolyn said, "wearing the albatross."

I looked at the Kloppmann, and, God help me, at the breasts it was adorning.

Abel wasn't gone long. He returned to tell Carolyn that she really rocked the Kloppmann, although those weren't the words he used. "So I say once again," he said, "that you should keep it for your private enjoyment."

"And I say once again," she said, "that it's not my style. I'm for tailored clothes and sensible shoes, Abel, and maybe my class ring from Erasmus High if it's a special occasion. Here, you hold this."

"If you insist. Bernard, the details are lost wherever an old man's memories go, but when you brought me the 1913 V-nickel I seem to remember giving you two choices."

That's how I remembered it.

"A small sum, an almost insultingly small sum, on the spot. Or, as an alternative, a percentage of whatever sale price I might eventually realize. I have to admit I don't recall the numbers."

I could have refreshed his memory. He'd offered $15,000 cash or half of what he estimated might be a hundred thousand, and I'd had enough celebratory drinks to roll the dice.

"Nor do I recall the details of the aftermath," he admitted. "I did in fact find a buyer, and I trust I turned your share over to you, and you were happy with the outcome?"

"I had nothing to complain about," I said.

"Then perhaps it will please you to learn that the offer I'm prepared to make you tonight is similar in nature. You can go home with thirty-two thousand dollars, or you can wait for me to find a customer—in which case I'll pay you a fourth of whatever sum I receive."

"Thirty-two thousand," I echoed.

"For an item that recently changed hands for sixty million, and yes, I admit it's insulting."

"I'm not insulted, Abel."

"Shall I tell you how I arrived at the figure? I went to my safe and counted the cash in it. It came to thirty-seven thousand, and I make it a point never to have less than five thousand cash on hand."

"And that's what you'll have left if you give us thirty-two."

"But what I hope you'll do," he said, "is what you chose to do before. I'll be looking for a man with long eyes."

"A man with long eyes?"

He frowned. "It doesn't really work in English, does it? *Ein Mann mit langen Augen*, and I'm not sure it works any better in German, but it means a very patient investor willing to bide his time. He might have to hold Herr Kloppmann's namesake gem for years before the right opportunity presents itself."

"And it might take you years to find this Mr. Long Eyes."

"It might, but when I do I'll get a minimum of a million dollars from him, because I won't take a pfennig or a kopeck or a farthing less. And you would get a fourth."

I thought about it. He was offering me a significantly lower percentage of this particular bird in the bush, but it was a much bigger bird.

None of which mattered.

"I'll take the thirty-two thousand," I said.

"You're certain?"

I said I was, and he left the room again, but it didn't take him as long this time, perhaps because he'd already done the counting. The money he handed me was in hundreds, used and out of sequence, and when he invited me to count it I told him I didn't need to, and then counted it when he insisted. It was all there, of course, three hundred and twenty bills, which he then apportioned into three envelopes, which in turn found their way into various pockets of mine.

"I thought you might have long eyes yourself, Bernard."

I explained that I had a pressing need for cash. "That's why I went to work tonight. I didn't really expect to find the Kloppmann, but I figured there'd be something worth taking in his apartment, or somewhere else in the building."

"Thirty-two thousand for a sixty million dollar treasure. I feel as though I've insulted you."

"I'm never insulted when someone gives me money," I said. "Besides, there's another way to look at it. I didn't spend all that much time in the building, but if you add in research and prep, it might come to four hours max. So that means I just earned eight thousand bucks an hour for my labors, and it may surprise you to hear this, but that's a higher hourly return than I generally net running a secondhand bookstore."

19

"Cruise ships," she said, in the cab heading downtown. "I think I'd be all the time waiting to get somewhere."

"For a while. You'd be waiting to get home, and then after a few weeks your mind would hit the Reset button, and you'd realize that where you were was home."

"In the middle of the ocean."

"In a well-appointed stateroom on a high deck. You have to admit it sounds more inviting than Assisted Living."

"God's waiting room," she said. "Though given the demographics, you would probably get a similar vibe on a cruise ship. This next cruise he's taking, on the Somethingdam—"

"To Fort Lauderdale?"

"No, the long one, the one that takes two months to circle South America. Say you've got two thousand people on board, not counting the crew, and what do you suppose the median age is?"

"Somewhere between Medicare and Dead."

"That many old people on a long cruise, at least a few of them are sure to be in the frozen food locker by the time the Doubledam gets back to Lauderdale."

"Or buried at sea, the way Abel wants to go."

She frowned. "You know, I'm positive they quit doing that years ago. I read something, don't ask me where. For ages they had to deep six anybody who died at sea, for health reasons, but refrigeration made that unnecessary, and it's not really the frozen food locker, there's a specific space designed for the purpose."

"But the ocean floor is still an option, according to Abel. He's witnessed a couple of burials at sea, complete with bagpipes. And he always checks that box, because he likes the idea."

"Of spending eternity in What's-his-name's Locker?

"Davy Jones."

"Right. Of lying on the bottom of the ocean and getting eaten by crustaceans?"

"What's not to like?"

She made a face. "Anyway," she said, "according to what I read—"

"Uh-huh. I won't ask you where you read it. I'll ask you *when* you read it."

"Gee, I don't know. A couple of months ago."

"I bet you had a Metrocard in your wallet, didn't you?"

"Huh?" She looked puzzled, until she didn't. "In this universe—"

"In this universe," I said, "if Abel wants a watery grave, that's what he gets."

Back in Arbor Court, I took the bills from the three envelopes and dealt them out in two equal stacks, each of which just fit in an envelope. I gave one to Carolyn and kept the other.

Carolyn weighed her share in her hand. "Bern," she said, "this is too much."

"For a sixty-million dollar diamond? I think the word Abel used was pittance."

"That's not what I mean and you know it. My share's too much. You did all the work."

"I opened one lock."

"That's more than I did."

"It was a Rabson," I said. "With what I've taught you, and all the time you spent practicing, you could have opened it yourself."

"You think? I'm way out of practice."

"It's not something you forget. It's like falling off a bicycle."

"I don't know, Bern."

"I do, and it's beside the point. We're partners in this enterprise. We went into it together and we came out of it together, and if we'd walked into a roomful of cops, we'd have both faced the same charges. And if I'm the one who opened the lock, who picked the right drawer to open?"

"Fifty-fifty, huh?"

"Even Steven. The goose gets the same amount of sauce as the gander."

Years ago I'd had my crafty friend build a third hidey-hole, this one at the rear left corner of her closet. She headed for it with the envelope and returned moments later, still managing to look unconvinced. She couldn't take issue with my arguments, she said, but it still didn't seem right. Wasn't I the senior partner? Shouldn't I get more?

"You're absolutely right," I said. "As you may have noticed, we've got one envelope left over."

"This one? It's empty, Bern."

"And it's mine," I said. "I'm keeping it. Hand it over."

She watched as I made a show of brushing some imaginary lint from the empty envelope, then set about folding it and finding pocket space for it. Before I was finished, she rose from her chair and came over to where I was sitting and stood alongside me.

Our eyes met. If the diamond had brought out the blue of her eyes, well, the color was no less intense now that the stone was in a safe four miles uptown.

"Bern?"

I got to my feet. I knew what she was waiting for, but suppose I was wrong? Then what?

She gave the slightest nod, as if answering my unvoiced question.

I took her in my arms and kissed her.

We'd kissed before, far too many times to count. We'd kissed hello and we'd kissed goodbye, as friends do—not all the time, not even half the time, but often enough. Some of our kisses were air kisses, and some were blown across the room to the recipient, but most were on her cheek or mine, and now and then there was a brief meeting of our lips.

Once, after several lessons, she succeeded in opening a reasonably complicated lock. She beamed, I put a hand on either side of her face and planted a kiss on her forehead.

Funny what you remember.

There was friendship in our occasional kisses, and affection. Women, straight or gay, kiss their same-sex friends in that fashion, as do many gay men. In my experience, straight men limit themselves to hugs, and even those embraces are awkward as often as not.

So whenever I kissed Carolyn or she kissed me, there was something gender-related in the act. But there was never a sexual element, never anything flirtatious, never any conscious or unconscious implication that the kiss could be a prelude to . . . well, to anything.

This was different.

"I'm a lesbian."

"I know."

"I wasn't just telling you. I was telling both of us."

"Okay."

"Kiss me again. Oh, gee. It's not just the novelty of it, is it?"

"No."

"You're so much taller than I am. Even when you bend your knees and I get on my tiptoes."

"They say everybody's the same height lying down."

"And it's true," she said. "I told you about the skyscraper I pulled out of the Duchess, didn't I? Back before it turned into a pizza place. The basketball player?"

"A forward for the New York Liberty, wasn't she?"

"Just a point guard, but she was taller than you, Bern. You know what? I don't want to talk about her."

"Good."

"Let's lie down," she said. "Can we do that?"

20

* * *

21

What, you wanted more than three little asterisks?

Well, I'm afraid that's all you get. Whether you bought the ebook or the paperback or the hardcover trade edition, you would have received the same troika of typographical stars for Chapter Twenty. That's even true if you went whole hog and put the deluxe signed-and-numbered Limited Edition on your American Express card.

Three asterisks, like it or lump it.

See, if you wanted the details, the blow-by-blow account, so to speak, you would have had to spring for the signed and lettered Collector's Edition, limited to 26 copies (as in A to Z). Handsomely illustrated, sumptuously bound in glove leather, housed in a custom-made titanium case outfitted with a combination lock.

The price? Well, really , what difference does it make? All 26 copies were spoken for well in advance of publication. There's always the chance one will turn up in the aftermarket, but—

No, just a joke. There is no lettered edition, no spelled-out version of those asterisks.

There are, even in this confessional age, matters one keeps to oneself.

22

"Wow, Bern."

"Says it all, doesn't it?"

"There's a voice in my head telling me that this doesn't change a thing, and there's another voice saying it changes everything. And I have the feeling they're both right."

"I know what you mean."

"Really? Because I'm not sure I do. This is about as good as I've ever felt in my life, like I'm floating on a cloud, and I'm loving it, but at the same time I'm terrified of falling."

"What I'm feeling," I said, "isn't all that different."

"This isn't the first time I've been to bed with a man. You knew that, right?"

"It seems to me you mentioned it."

"Ages and ages ago, before I was completely out. I mean, I always knew I was gay, and that I didn't have the kind of feelings for boys that I had for girls. But when I was in high school, girls didn't take each other to the junior prom. I gather it's no longer unheard of."

"Very few things are."

"Well, I wasn't in the running for prom queen, but I wasn't a complete bowwow either, and I got asked on dates. And my date might kiss me goodnight, and if I dated somebody more than a couple of times we might make out a little. And I didn't find it disgusting. It didn't do anything for me, but it didn't make me vomit."

"Which might have been awkward," I said, "in the back seat of somebody's father's Plymouth."

"Anyway, everything got amped up in college. Orientation Week was barely over before a third-year Phys Ed major orientated the hell out of me. One glance and she knew what I was, and after one evening in her dorm room, so did I."

"And you never looked back."

"That's mostly true," she said, "but you start wondering if maybe this is a phase you're going through, and if you're comfortable with the whole idea of never getting married and never having children and never being able to let the world know who and what you really are, because back then—"

"Right."

"And you get the thought in your head, like how do you know for sure you wouldn't enjoy sex with a guy if you've never had it? And, you know, Bern, it's a fair question."

"Sure."

"And, you know, a couple of drinks makes it easier to go through with something like that. Maybe more than a couple, maybe enough rye and ginger to shut up the voices in your head, or at least turn down the volume."

"That's what you drank? Rye and ginger ale?"

"Or the occasional Seven and Seven. That was Seagram's Seven and Seven-Up."

"I remember. It tasted—"

"Like crap, but it got the job done. And so did I. I did my research, I performed my experiment, I analyzed the results and drew the only possible conclusion."

"You were a lesbian."

"I was," she said, "and I am. Even in a universe that decided to turn a somersault and put me in bed with my best friend. And it didn't take anything stronger than Perrier to get me there."

"Unless you count the *Einspänner*."

"What, coffee and Reddi-Wip?"

"I don't think Abel would use anything but real whipped cream."

"You're right. Bern, I've been meaning to ask. Have you been up against it?"

"Up against what?"

"Like financially. Strapped, in a bind, whatever. I know the store hasn't been doing all that well, even if you had a decent day today—"

"More than decent."

"—but you own the building, and you've got residential tenants who pay rent, and I thought that was keeping you above water."

"It is. Why?"

"You told Abel you had an urgent need for cash."

"Did I say urgent? I thought the word I used was *pressing*."

"Maybe you did. What was pressing you, Bern?"

"Nothing. It was a convenient way to explain a decision I'd already made. I could have quoted Omar Khayyam."

"A loaf of bread, a jug of wine, and thirty-two thousand dollars?"

"I was thinking of '*Take the cash and let the credit go.*'"

"Take the thirty-two," she said, "and let the quarter of a million go. Believe me, I'm fine with it, Bern. I don't know what I'm gonna do with my sixteen thousand, and its not as though

I was drooling at the thought of major money. But last time, with the V-nickel—"

"I decided to roll the dice."

"Right."

"And how did that turn out?"

"Badly for us," she said, "and a lot worse for Abel. But that was in a different world, Bern. In this world Abel's alive and well, and looking to sell the Kloppmann for a minimum of a million dollars. Don't you think he'll do it?"

"He may. He's prepared to sit on it for as long as it takes, and there's a good chance it'll hatch sooner or later."

"You always said that he was the one fence you could trust absolutely."

"*Absolutely* might be a stretch. You're the only person in the world I trust absolutely. But as far as sharing the proceeds from a transaction is concerned, yes, my trust in Abel is as complete now as it was when we left him the V-nickel."

She looked puzzled. Understandably so, I suppose.

"Nothing in this world," I said, choosing my words carefully, "would keep Abel from treating us honestly."

"But?"

"But suppose there's a reverse somersault, and we do a backflip into the previous universe? Where do you figure that leaves us?"

23

"Oh," she said. "My. God." Her eyes, not that far from mine, were bluer than ever. "Could that happen?"

"How do I know?"

"You're the one who read the book. Fredric Brown, remember? *What Mad Universe?*"

"I read the book," I agreed, "and between the time I closed it and the time I opened my eyes in the morning, which I'll point out was something like twenty-one hours ago—"

"Really? Shit on toast, is it really four-thirty in the morning? Where did the time go?"

"Wherever it went," I said. "I'd say it was well spent. And sometime a wee bit more than twenty-one hours ago, while I was sleeping, I must have done something to launch us out of one world and into another. I don't know what I did, and God knows I don't know how I did it, but I can't argue that it wasn't my doing, even if I didn't know I was doing it."

"Bern, I'm just glad you took me with you. But to get back to the book—"

I held up a hand. "It's just a book," I said. "A novel, and you know Randall Jarrell's definition of a novel, don't you? He said it's a book-length work of fiction with something wrong with it."

"What's wrong with *What Mad Universe?*"

"What's wrong with it is that it's not an instruction manual. It's fiction, it's a work of the imagination. Now Brown's imagination was second to none, and he took the longstanding notion of parallel worlds and made a rich and satisfying story out of it, but that doesn't mean a person can read his book and learn how to go world-hopping."

"But isn't that exactly what you did, Bern?"

"Um."

"And I know the book is a novel, and that all he was trying to do was write a story. But how can you be sure it's pure and simple fiction?"

"Fiction is never pure," I pronounced, "and rarely simple, and if that has a familiar ring to it, it's because that's what Oscar Wilde said about the truth. You think Brown was drawing on more than his imagination?"

"It's possible, isn't it? Isn't that what writers do?"

"I don't know what they do," I said, "or how they do it, but if they didn't do it I'd have a store full of empty shelves."

"And nothing to read."

I thought about Fredric Brown. As productive as he was, it was hard to believe he ever did much of anything that took him away from his typewriter. But how could I know where he went in his dreams, and what world he was in when he opened his eyes? "*Where do you get your ideas, Mr. Brown?*" "*Oh, they just come to me. Or, in special cases, I go to them . . .*"

"Bern," she was saying, "I really like the universe we're in right now."

"So do I."

"I haven't used my SubwayCard yet, but I figure I'll like it just as much as my old Metrocard. Just so it gets me through a turnstile, or onto a bus. And I have to say Amazon was handy,

I could order anything from a T-shirt to a trilobite and they'd deliver it in no time at all. But I've got more T-shirts than anybody needs, and what do I want with a trilobite?"

"I was wondering."

"And I like a world without security cameras, and not just because it makes it possible for my best friend to go on doing what he does best. And I even like having Bowl-Mor back where it used to be, and who knows? Maybe one of these days Two Guys will find itself between owners again, and we'll skip lunch and bowl a few frames."

"It might be fun."

"If this lasts," she said. "But you're not sure it will?"

"What I think," I said, "is that anything's possible. We could spend the rest of our lives in this tailor-made world. Or we could drift off to sleep and wake up in yesterday's universe."

"And if you had to guess?"

"If I had to guess, that's all it would be. A guess."

"And?"

"I think this is going to turn out to be temporary," I said. "And I think the time frame is more a matter of days than years."

"Days."

"It's just a feeling. I'm not basing it on anything. I could be completely wrong, and we could remain here forever."

"But if your gut feeling is right—"

"There's a backward somersault in our future."

"While we're asleep."

"I don't know that being asleep is an ironclad requirement. I suppose it could happen while we were awake. But I think it's more likely while we're unconscious, and presumably dreaming."

"If we fell asleep now, Bern, and it happened now—"

"I hope it doesn't."

"Me too, but if it does. Would you wake up back home on West End Avenue?"

"Would I do a backflip of my own?" I thought about it. "I don't see why unintentional teleportation should be part of the picture. I'd probably wake up in the same place I went to sleep."

"In bed with me, and both of us naked."

"Oh."

"Which at the moment feels perfectly wonderful, but how would it feel in another universe?"

"Oh."

"Bern, wherever we wind up, we'll still be best friends, won't we?"

"Forever," I said.

"But will our friendship still have this, um, new dimension?"

"I don't know."

"Neither do I."

She reached out a hand, touched me. We were best friends, and it was not unusual for us to touch one another, on the arm, on the shoulder, even a light pat on the behind.

But she was touching a part of me it would never have occurred to her to touch a day earlier.

"Bern," she said, "could we do it one more time? Just in case we never get to do it again?"

24

There's a dream I've had, with slight variations, for I don't know how many years. I'm behind the counter at Barnegat Books, having some sort of conversation with some sort of customer, when I realize that I'm not wearing anything between my shoes and my shirt. No one can tell, only my upper body is visible, but how can I avoid exposing myself while fetching the appropriate book, or freshening my cat's water dish, or doing whatever else I'm called upon to do in this particular version of the dream?

The answer, of course, is that I can't, and what generally happens right around this stage is that I become aware on some level that I'm having that damned dream again. At which point the details of the dream begin to grow wispy and slip away, and I may try to get back into the dream to find out how the conversation will turn out, but that almost always turns out to be impossible, and what generally happens next is I open my eyes and let my day begin.

Not this time. I lay there, eyes securely shut, while the dream concluded its disappearing act, and I kept them shut while I let myself recall where I was and how I'd come to be there.

The dream was over. My night's sleep was over. But what else had run its course?

Was I waking up in the same new universe in which I'd gone to sleep?

I was, I realized, afraid of what the answer might be. And, as long as I avoided opening my eyes, I wouldn't have to know what it was.

It's a stance one can only maintain for so long, and once I was out of the dream I don't suppose it could have been more than a minute or two of eyes-wide-shut before I gave up and opened them.

The first thing I saw was one of the cats—Archie, the Burmese—sitting on Carolyn's side of the bed and looking at me. God knows what he was thinking. "Don't ask," I told him, and looked around for his mistress, but what I found was the note she'd left on the coffee table:

I didn't have the heart to wake you. Running late myself because I've got an early appointment with a Labradoodle who needs a wash-and-set. So I'll use my green-and-white SubwayCard (!) and take the bus across Tenth Street. Take your time, I'll feed Raffles.

She'd underlined "green-and-white SubwayCard" three times, lest I miss its significance, and signed the note with a little heart.

I checked my own wallet, just to make sure, and found my own SubwayCard.

Whew.

I had a bath, then put on New York One, which told me nothing I needed to know, and yesterday's clothes, which passed the sniff test, albeit with not much room to spare. Tie? No tie?

I put it on, knotted it, then loosened the knot and unfastened the collar button.

Casual Friday.

It was 10:30 when I got out the door. I could have used my SubwayCard but it was comfort enough to know it was there. I walked to work, pausing at a Sheridan Square food truck for a bagel and coffee. There was no hurry, not on such a beautiful autumn morning, and so it was getting on for eleven when I set about opening my store.

There were customers waiting. Just two of them, a man and a woman, and I got the feeling that they had met for the first time that morning, waiting for me to open up.

Raffles greeted me as he always did, rubbing himself against my ankles. "Nice try," I told him, "but I happen to know you've been fed, and there's fresh water in your water dish." My customers contrived to deepen their new bond by joining in admiration of my cat, asking its name and, when it proved to be nongender-specific, whether it was a boy or a girl. They didn't seek to know if he was a Manx, so I didn't have to have that conversation again, but the woman did ask if she could pet him, and I told her it was okay with me if it was okay with Raffles. And apparently it was.

Twenty minutes later they left, each with a bag of books. He asked if there was a good place nearby for lunch, and I told him Two Guys From Dushanbe was great if you liked Tajik food.

"As in Tajikistan? I don't believe I've ever had it." To the woman: "Have you?"

She said she hadn't. Would she like to join him? Why yes, yes she would.

* * *

Shortly before noon I called Carolyn. "I've got a store full of people," I said, "and I suppose I could chase them out, but I walked to work and stopped along the way at a food truck, so I had a late breakfast, and—"

"You want to skip lunch."

"If that's not a problem."

"I love our lunches," she said, "but I'm not all that hungry myself. Maybe I'll go bowling."

"Seriously?"

"No, but it's nice to know I could if I wanted to. I'll see you in a few hours. Usual time? Usual place? Usual table?"

"You bet," I said.

Intermittently I'd become aware of the envelope in my jacket pocket. At one point I felt warm enough to take off the jacket and hang it over the back of my stool, and when I returned from showing a young woman where the Anne Rice novels were shelved, I saw the envelope showing. Anyone could reach behind the counter and walk out of my shop sixteen thousand dollars to the good.

That's more serious than having someone lift a book or two from my bargain table, and it's even worse if you think of the sum as half the price of the Kloppmann Diamond.

I took the envelope into the back room. As I found a spot for it in a desk drawer, I remembered my handy set of picks and probes, still in my back pocket. The New York criminal code is quite specific, labeling possession of burglar's tools a Class A misdemeanor, and you can do a year for it. I put my tools in the drawer with the envelope, and closed the drawer halfway, and changed my mind and returned the tools to my pocket.

Because you never know.

* * *

The high point of the afternoon was the reappearance of the winner of the Linda Fiorentino/Katherine Moennig look-alike contest, the woman who'd contrived to buy a book I hadn't known I owned. Once again she'd managed to slip into the store unnoticed, and once again she presented herself at the counter, but this time she set down not a single pamphlet but a stack of six books.

I told her it was good to see her again, and she reminded me that she'd said she would be back.

I took the top book from the stack. "Ah, Donald Westlake," I said.

"No, it says—"

"It says 'Tucker Coe,'" I said, because this is the first edition, published under that pen name fifty years ago. You didn't know Westlake was the author?"

She shook her head. Then why, I could but wonder, would she want the book? I'd priced it at $37.50, which seemed reasonable enough considering its very decent condition and the freshness of its dust wrapper, but if she didn't have a collector's interest in the author, didn't in fact have much of a clue who the author was, what would make it worth her attention?

Oh.

"Westlake wrote five books as Tucker Coe," I said. "They were all published by Random House between 1966 and 1972, during which time he published two dozen other titles as well, some under his own name, the others as Richard Stark."

"He must have been a busy man."

"A productive one, certainly." I opened the book to the page that listed Tucker Coe's other books. "Five books, of which this is the fourth, all of them chronicling the fictional career of one

Mitchell Tobin, who left the NYPD under a cloud and wound up operating as a sort of *de facto* private detective, all the while spending his free time building a wall around his house, and you can make of that what you will. The first book was *Kinds of Love, Kinds of Death,* followed in due course by *Murder Among Children* and *Wax Apple.* Then this book, and a couple of years later he published the final volume, but it's not listed here, because when this book came out he hadn't written it yet. Still, I ought to be able to remember the name."

"It's all very interesting . . ."

"*Don't Lie to Me.*"

She recoiled as if slapped, and the dark eyes looked as though they might burn a hole through her eyeglasses. "It *is* interesting," she said, "and even if I were just saying so to be polite, I don't think it would amount to an actual lie, and even if you're an absolute stickler for the literal truth—"

"That's the title."

"The title?"

"Of the fifth and last book by Tucker Coe. *Don't Lie to Me.*"

"Oh."

"I didn't mean to suggest you were telling an untruth."

"It's all right. I understand."

I reached for the rest of the books, sifted through them, jotted down their prices. *Jade Dragon Mountain* by Elsa Hart. *The Song of the Jade Lily* by Kirsty Manning. *Gods of Jade and Shadow* by Silvia Moreno-Garcia. *Jade City* by Fonda Lee. *Jade: 5000 B.C. to 1912 A.D., A Guide for Collectors* by Mircea Veleanu.

Fitting companions, to be sure, for Tucker Coe's penultimate book, *A Jade in Aries.*

"A subtle pattern begins to emerge," I said. "You do know

that not all of these books are about jade? The Tucker Coe's the only one I've read, and I don't think the word *jade* appears anywhere but the cover and the title page."

"That's all right."

I jotted down prices and added them up, and I showed her the total, which was just under $140, and suggested we round it down to $125. I took three fifties from her and counted out change.

"I have a special fondness for jade," she said.

"I, um, figured as much."

"If you find more books—"

"I'll set them aside for you."

She took the receipt I'd given her, picked up my pencil, and jotted down a number.

"Or if you were to come into possession of actual jade objects," she said. "I know that's unlikely, you traffic in books, not in art and antiquities. But one never knows."

"Never," I agreed, and fingered the slip of paper. "You should put down a name. As an *aide-mémoire*."

She wrote something, folded the slip, passed it to me. "If your *mémoire* needs an assist, this should serve better than a name you've never heard."

She headed for the door, and I saw Raffles look up from his spot at the window to note her passing. She had that sort of presence.

I unfolded the slip of paper. Along with the ten-digit number, she'd printed *JADE* in block capitals.

It was a few minutes after the usual time when I got to the Bum Rap, and Carolyn was already at our usual table. Her rocks glass held a couple of ice cubes bobbing in a familiar amber liquid.

"I figured it'd be okay to get back to scotch," she said, "and I'm certainly in the mood for it, so I ordered this the minute I sat down. But I haven't had any yet, in case you don't think it's a good idea."

"I think it's a splendid idea," I told her, and caught Maxine's eye immediately, and said I'd have the same as Carolyn was having, except with soda. She went off to fetch it, and Carolyn reached for her glass, then left it where it was.

"So we can toast something," she explained. "We've got between now and when she gets back to figure out what to drink to."

I was ready. When my drink came I raised my glass and said, "Here's looking at you, kid."

We touched glasses, sipped. Her sip was more substantial than mine.

"This is just what I needed," I said, "but I'd better go easy. You remember I told you about the guy who wants to pour me some Armagnac and sell me some books?"

"Vaguely. Wasn't he a professor?"

"With leather elbow patches on his Norfolk jacket," I said, "he could hardly be anything else. He called to make sure I hadn't forgotten our engagement. And a good thing he did, because what with one thing and another, it had slipped my mind."

"One thing and another," she said. "This time yesterday—"

"We were sitting right here."

"Drinking Perrier. That seems so long ago, Bern."

"I know."

"Like ages."

"I know." I laid my hand on top of hers. "Anyway, it all came back as soon as he started talking. I'm supposed to show up at his apartment on West Third at 8:30."

"I can tell how much you're looking forward to it."

"I almost canceled," I said. "But with the kind of business I did today, morning and afternoon, I don't want to pass up a good chance to fill some of the empty spaces on my shelves."

"Because everybody knows you can't do business from an empty wagon. What? I just said—"

"I know what you said. It reminded me of my breakfast."

"Huh?"

"Didn't I tell you? On my way to work I grabbed coffee and a bagel from a food truck."

"So?"

"It was at Sheridan Square."

"Everybody has to be somewhere. So?"

"While I was standing there—"

"Eating your bagel, drinking your coffee—"

"—I looked across the square, and you know Two Boots? The pizza place?"

"What about it?"

"It's gone."

"Oh, yeah? Gee, I wonder when that happened. It's too bad, they had great pizza, although finding good pizza in New York has never been all that hard to do." She paused for breath, frowned. "Bern? Am I missing something?"

"Guess what's where Two Boots used to be."

"You're kidding. No, you're not kidding. The Duchess is back?"

"Like it never left," I said.

"Were there people in it? Probably not at that hour."

"I didn't get close enough to tell. I saw it in the storefront where Two Boots used to be, and it registered, but just barely."

"And you finished your breakfast and started walking. I don't suppose your steps happened to take you to Greenwich Avenue."

"I wound up on Tenth Street," I said, "so I had to cross Greenwich Avenue. Why?"

"That's where Paula's used to be, but from Tenth and Greenwich you'd almost need binoculars to see it."

"It didn't even occur to me to look for it. I wasn't thinking about the Duchess, I couldn't tell you what was running through my mind, but then just before I got to the store I did make a point of looking for Bowl-Mor, and of course it was there, right where it was supposed to be, and that made me think of the Duchess, and that was the first time I realized the implications."

"The implications?"

I nodded.

"Except for a period of a month or so," she said, "when I steered clear of the place because there was somebody I didn't want to run into, I was a regular at the Duchess. How many times do you figure I walked through those doors?"

"Probably quite a few."

"And I can't remember seeing a single implication, Bern."

I picked up my glass, found it empty.

I said, "The Duchess was a regular part of your life."

"Isn't that what I just got through telling you?"

"But it was never a part of mine," I said. "I'm pretty sure I never had a drink at the Duchess. In fact I don't believe I ever set foot in the place."

"Probably wise, Bern. There was a sign for a while, but not

for long. They took it down because too many people didn't get it."

She paused to thank Maxine for delivering a second scotch on the rocks, one she'd ordered without my noticing. Maxine cocked an eye at my empty glass, then looked a question at me. I nodded, even as the thought crossed my mind that this was probably Not A Good Idea.

"The sign," I prompted.

"Oh, right. '*Y Don't You Go Home?*' Except instead of spelling out the first word, W-H-Y, it was just the capital letter Y."

"I don't get it."

"Hardly anybody did, which was why it wasn't up there for more than a few days. What it meant was if you had a Y chromosome you weren't welcome."

"Subtle."

"Way too subtle. But you get the point. No men."

"I get the point," I said. "And you still don't get the implication?"

"I wouldn't call that an implication, Bern. It was pretty much out there. If a man walked in, any man, gay or straight, drunk or sober, he got the opposite of a warm welcome."

"The cold shoulder."

"Or worse, if he put up a fuss."

"So why would *I* want to make sure the Duchess was part of the best of all possible worlds? What would prompt me to blink it back into existence, along with Bowl-Mor and SubwayCards?"

"Oh."

"That was the implication, and it strikes me as pretty clear-cut. I didn't just bring you along for the ride, and I didn't dream us into this universe all by myself."

"I never read the book. I've read plenty of Fredric Brown, but not the book that got us here."

"But you asked about it, remember? And I told you the premise, and you thought it was interesting."

I let her think about it, and watched her thoughts register on her face on her face. "I got that we were in this together," she said, "but it's more than that. We did this together."

"That's how it looks to me."

"Me too." She put her hand on mine, and beamed across the table at me. "I'm proud of us, Bern."

My second drink was about halfway gone when Carolyn reminded me what I'd had for breakfast. "A bagel and coffee, Bern. Just one bagel?"

"Just one," I said. "But, you know, it was an everything bagel."

"So it was all tricked out with poppy seeds and sesame seeds and onion and garlic."

"And salt."

"But it was still just a bagel. What have you had since then?"

"A very busy day," I said.

"But no lunch. You didn't grab a snack at the store?"

"I'm not that crazy about cat food."

"So you're drinking on an empty stomach."

"I'm not sure of that. How long does it take to digest a bagel?"

She rolled her eyes. "At eight-thirty," she pointed out, "you're going to be seeing this professor, and you don't want to wind up being the absent-minded one. And what is it he promised you? Some kind of brandy."

"Armagnac. I think he said it was fifty years old."

"So's Martina Navratilova, but she's still got it. I think we should get something to eat."

"Where?"

"They've got food right here, don't they?"

I looked at her. "You don't remember," I said.

"What don't I remember?"

"The burrito," I said.

"Oh," she said, and her nose wrinkled, confirming that now she did indeed remember.

"They don't have a kitchen at the Bum Rap," I said. "What they have is a microwave oven, and the only thing I remember them having was burritos, and I ordered one."

"I remember."

"And I ate it, so that it could sober me up. But all it did—"

"I remember."

"—was make me fart."

"I remember."

"A Bum Wrap," I said, "with a W. That's what they called their burrito, and maybe they still do. I don't think it would be a good idea to have another one."

"Not now."

"Not ever, in any world we happen to find ourselves." I took a breath. "But you're right."

"I am?"

"I should get something to eat. I don't think I want Tajik food just now. It's delicious, but right about now my stomach might think it was a burrito."

"We could go to Paula's, Bern."

"Last time I checked," I said, "I had a Y chromosome."

"Guys have always been welcome at Paula's," she said, "Unless they make trouble."

"I'm rarely troublesome. Unless I've had a burrito."

"There were guys who came there on a regular basis, and not to hit on lesbians. I guess they liked the atmosphere. And the food, because Paula always had a good kitchen. Nothing fancy, but the woman's hamburger was world-class. Could you handle a hamburger?"

"Probably, if we tell them to hold the onion. And if the place even exists."

"If I brought back the Duchess," she said, "I wouldn't forget Paula's. I liked it better and spent lots more time there."

I thought about it. "My appointment's on West Third," I said, "and what I think I'd like to do is eat at one of the Italian restaurants on Thompson Street. A nice simple pasta dish, say, and espresso or cappuccino until it's time to walk around the corner and look at his books."

She didn't look enthusiastic.

"But there's no reason why you can't go to Paula's."

"You sure, Bern? I'd like to know if it's there, and if it's the way it used to be."

And who knows, I thought but didn't say. *Maybe you'll get lucky.*

25

They had tables set up outside at Rocco's, but by the time I got there it had cooled off enough to lead me to choose a table inside. I'd picked up a newspaper along the way, and I read it while I worked my way through a fritto misto antipasto and a generous order of spaghetti puttanesca. It was, I suppose, every bit as ethnic a meal as anything they could have served me at Two Guys, but Italian food never tastes ethnic to me. It just tastes like New York.

While that second scotch at the Bum Rap hadn't had me staggering, there's no question that I'd been feeling it. But I'd walked it off on the way downtown, and by the time I sat down and took the menu from the sad-eyed waiter, I felt clearheaded. I might not have been sufficiently so for an evening of illegal entry, but I'd say I was as sober as your average judge.

Un vino, signore? No, I don't think so.

There was nothing in the paper about the diamond, or about Orrin Vandenbrinck, or the Innisfree. I hadn't really expected there would be, but I was beginning to wonder. It was getting on for twenty-four hours since I'd passed us off as Istvan Horvath *et sa petite amie*, and the most enduring after-party in the history of off-off-Broadway couldn't have tied up Vandenbrinck for more than a few hours.

I ordered an espresso and said no to a suggested glass of

Anisette. But when I'd finished the espresso and asked for a second, I decided I'd like a cordial after all.

"But not Anisette," I said, and remembered the Andrew Vachss books Mowgli had sold me. "Perhaps a Strega."

That made the waiter happy, and the golden liquid he brought me did nothing to dampen my own spirits. It's name means *witch* in Italian, and I won't say it cast a spell, but it did a good job of balancing out the caffeine.

On my way to the West Third Street address, I realized I couldn't remember the professor's name. Had I somehow contrived to forget it? Had he even told it to me in the first place?

He would have had to introduce himself when he called, wouldn't he? But there'd been a lot of metaphorical water since then, under the bridge and over the dam, and it was evidently enough to wash away any name I might have heard.

So what was I going to tell the uniformed man on the desk? "*My name's Rhodenbarr, and good old What's-his-name in 4-G is expecting me.*"

What's-his-name's building turned out to be an apartment house six stories tall. It could have had a front desk, which in turn could have had an attendant, but it had neither. Instead there was a locked front door with a double row of names alongside it, each equipped with a button one could press.

I scanned the names. The one for 4-G said RUBISHAM and I studied it and pondered its pronunciation. The first syllable, I decided, might rhyme with either *tub* or *tube*, and if I'd ever in my life heard either version, it had slipped away to spend eternity with Judge Crater and Ambrose Bierce.

I pressed the bell. Or the buzzer, I couldn't say which, because whatever sound it made was behind closed doors and four floors over my head.

No answer.

I checked my watch. It was 8:32, so I was officially two minutes late, but I couldn't think that had led him to give up on me.

I rang again, longer and more forcefully this time, for whatever good that might do. And it did none, as far as I could see, because my summons went unanswered.

Curiouser and curiouser.

He'd phoned me twice, once yesterday and once this afternoon, but if he'd told me his phone number I'd promptly forgotten it along with his name. I checked my cell phone, clearly a fool's errand because I knew well enough that both of his calls had been to the Barnegat Books landline. But I went through the motions anyway, on the chance that there was a call to my cell phone I'd forgotten, along with apparently everything else, and while I was doing this a woman with Jay Leno's chin appeared at the front door.

I stepped aside and she stepped through it, looked at me, and showed what she thought of what she saw by very deliberately closing the door behind her. Not until it had clicked shut did she give me an icy smile and walk off to the left.

Fine. Be that way.

I rang the bell one more time, waited once more for a response that never came.

Then I let myself in.

A bright ten-year-old with a jackknife could have snicked back the bolt and opened the door to the lobby. That same kid wouldn't have had much trouble getting into the Rubisham apartment, but only if I'd lent him my tools and given him a few lessons.

I hadn't planned on unlocking the door to 4-G. I'd gone upstairs on the admittedly slim chance that the buzzer downstairs was out of order. I found the right apartment, poked the button, and heard the result, clear as a bell, from behind the door. When it went unanswered, I knocked, and knocked again.

It occurred to me that, if Professor Rubisham was old enough to retire, he might not be too young to have a heart attack, or join the I've-fallen-and-I-can't-get-up brigade. Like Jimmy Valentine in the O. Henry story, I could break a law and save a life.

Yeah, right. It was more likely that the guy was old enough to have a shaky memory, and that he'd simply forgotten our appointment. If he was home and in distress, I could help him; if not I could check out his library.

I opened the lock.

Inside, I found a three-room apartment, and it took me a few minutes to figure out what was odd about it. There was nothing hanging on the walls, no prints or paintings. The furniture was mostly from Crate & Barrel. No potted plants on the window sill, or anywhere else.

No coats in the closet, no clothing in the dresser drawers. Pots and pans and silverware in the kitchen, but no food in the cupboards and nothing in the fridge but a box of baking soda.

No toothbrush in the bathroom. No towels, either.

And not a single book, hardcover or paperback, anywhere in the apartment.

26

Paula's windows were dark, but not because the place was closed. The glass was deeply tinted, like a gangster's Cadillac.

Inside, the lighting was still on the dim side, but I could see the bartender and the patrons, even as they could see me. When they did the conversation died down, and on the jukebox Anne Murray went on letting us know she was "Just Another Woman in Love."

Carolyn saw me before I spotted her. "Hey, Bern! Glad you could make it. C'mere, let me buy you a drink."

Her voice carried, letting the world know that I was All Right, and the tension went out of the room. I joined her at the bar, where she greeted me with an air kiss, introduced me to three women whose names I promptly forgot, and ordered a drink for me and a refill for herself.

Minutes later the two of us and our drinks were at a candle-lit table against the far wall. A few minutes more and I'd brought her up to date.

"That's really weird," she said. "You're sure you had the right address?"

"I wrote it down." I showed her the slip of paper, with the time and the address and apartment number. "And the building was definitely faculty housing. Most of the buzzers just had last names on their nameplates, but a fair number of the names were preceded by D-R or P-R-O-F."

"But not 4-G."

"No, all it said was Rubisham. I checked, and it was the same way on the mailbox in the hall."

"Roobisham."

"I'm guessing at the pronunciation. I suppose the first syllable could just as easily be Rub, but what difference does it make? There's no such person."

"Then who called you, Bern? He wasn't just a voice on the phone, was he?"

"No, we were face to face yesterday morning. He bought a mystery set in Ancient Rome." I frowned. "We had a whole conversation. If he wasn't a classics professor, he went to a lot of trouble to sound like one."

"And the library you went over to appraise—"

"Was gone. There were built-in bookcases in the living room and what I suppose was the den, but they were as empty as the closets and dresser drawers."

"Empty bookshelves?"

"Except for a slight coating of dust. An empty dresser looks perfectly normal until you open a drawer, and it's the same with a closet. But an empty bookcase is empty in a whole nother way."

"I always look at a person's bookshelves to get an idea of who they are."

"I know. 'Do I really want to go to bed with a woman who owns every book Danielle Steele ever wrote?'"

"Self-help books," she said, "are the big Red Alert for me. But empty bookcases—what do they tell us about this bird?"

"About Professor Rubisham?" I'd had time to think about

this on my way to Paula's. "My guess is he retired and moved away, possibly to the Outer Banks, but most likely that was Mr. Armagnac's invention."

"Mr. Armagnac?"

"We might as well call him something. The actual Rubisham retired, or got the boot for sleeping with students, which used to be a perk back in the day. Or for all I know he upgraded his Ph.D. to an R.I.P. and left his apartment in a body bag. Whatever happened to him, it happened long enough ago for the dust to settle."

"On his empty shelves."

"Once he was out of there," I said, "a cleaning crew erased any lingering traces of his presence and got the apartment ready for the next tenant, whoever he may be, and whenever he may be scheduled to move in."

"Where does Mr. Armagnac come in?"

"That's a good question."

"When I say that, Bern, it generally means I haven't got a clue."

"There you go. I never laid eyes on him before yesterday morning, when he was just one more component of an antiquarian bookseller's perfect day."

"So he was never a part of the Metrocard universe."

"No."

I picked up my glass and looked into it, as if it had the psychic properties of a crystal ball. I do that a lot, with not much to show for it, but only when there's something authoritative to gaze into. When I'm drinking Perrier I might allow myself a glimpse of the bubbles, but I wouldn't be looking for the secrets of the universe.

I said, "Why lure me to an empty apartment? Whatever he

had in mind, he must have hatched his plan between his time in the store yesterday morning and his phone call later in the day. Was he looking to rob me?"

"Why would he do that?"

"For money, I suppose. I show up, he pulls a gun—"

"Really, Bern?"

"Who knows? Or he pours me an Armagnac with an added ingredient and I drink it and pass out, and then he goes through my pockets."

"And what does he find? Your SubwayCard?"

"For a while," I said, "I was walking around with sixteen grand in an envelope. But when I saw Mr. A., the closest I'd come to the Kloppmann Diamond was looking at pictures of it online. Even if he knew about my secondary career, he couldn't have guessed I was going to take a shot at the Kloppmann, or that I'd be successful. In fact—"

"What?"

"His first call was yesterday afternoon," I said, "and his initial suggestion was that I come over that night. But I pushed it a day because I was planning to go to the Innisfree."

"So he couldn't have known anything about the Kloppmann Diamond. Maybe he just thought you were the type to carry a lot of cash on your person. If you were looking to buy a library—"

"I was," I said. "That's why I showed up, not because I was jonesing for a pretentious glass of brandy. I didn't bring a lot of cash with me. I never do. And here's the thing, Carolyn. Even if he was sufficiently out of touch to think I might be worth robbing, he never showed up."

"That's a point."

"He invited me to the apartment, and called again this afternoon to make sure we were still on. And then, a couple of hours later, I showed up and he didn't."

"Why?"

"That's my question. Why?"

She looked at me, and her face showed an expression I'd only seen on it when she was reading Stephen King. I asked her what was the matter.

"Just a thought," she said. "Maybe he was luring you."

"Luring me to what?"

"An empty apartment," she said. "An apartment where nobody was likely to set foot until the next semester starts, which would be sometime after the first of the year. Bern, if he wanted to kill a person, and leave the person where he wouldn't be found for months—"

"Why would he want to kill me?"

"Maybe he's one of those paths."

"Huh?"

"A psychopath, a sociopath. A serial killer."

"Who goes from one used bookstore to another, hunting for victims."

"I guess it doesn't make a lot of sense."

"Nothing does, so don't apologize. But what I keep coming back to is he did what he could to make sure I was coming, and then he didn't show up."

"Maybe he chickened out."

"Or he grew a conscience and decided not to kill me after all. No, none of it adds up. He baits the trap, takes this empty apartment and furnishes it with an imaginary library, puts out an imaginary bottle and a couple of imaginary glasses, and leaves me stranded out on the sidewalk, ringing a bell that nobody's around to answer."

"He must have figured you'd let yourself in."

"Why would he assume that? Even if he suspects I'm not averse to a little illegal entry, why think I'd try to get into this particular apartment? What I'd think, in his position, is that I'd ring the bell long enough to know it wasn't going to get me anywhere, and then I'd utter a few colorful curses and go home." I picked up my drink, finished it. "Which, incidentally, is what I almost did. If I hadn't had my tools with me, I'd have called it a night."

"You'd have never known it was an empty apartment."

"I would have thought I'd been stood up, and I'd decide to give him a piece of my mind next time he walked into the shop. But he never would, and I'd forget about it."

"So what was in it for him?"

"That's my question," I said, "and if you can come up with an answer, I'd love to hear it."

She thought about it. Then she said, "Oh."

"Oh?"

"Shit on toast."

"Well, that clears things up. On the other hand—"

"Bern," she said. "If you were on West Third Street, ringing a doorbell, that's where you would be."

"Huh?"

"You wouldn't be anywhere else."

"No, because I haven't yet mastered the esoteric art of bilocation. What are you talking about?"

On the jukebox, Patsy Cline was singing "I Fall to Pieces."

"If you were on West Third," she said, "then he'd know for sure that you weren't on East Eleventh Street."

*　　*　　*

We reached the curb just as a cab pulled up to disgorge two women, one of whom gave my companion a big hello while the other pouted. "No time, Mags," Carolyn said, and steered me with a little push and hopped into the cab after me.

"Maggie Birnbaum," she told me. "Don't ask."

"I won't."

She leaned forward. "Eleventh and University," she told the driver, and sat back. To me she said, "It's quicker to walk half a block than deal with the one-way streets. And if something's going on—"

"We might not want to pull up right in front of it. You know, you don't have to come with me."

"Didn't we already have this argument?"

We had, while she settled her bar tab. I'd made my point, stressing that the world's most absentminded professor would have no reason to break into a secondhand bookstore, that a couple of hours ago I'd locked both the door and the window gates, and that you didn't need more than one person to have a wild goose chase. And she'd made hers, by telling me to shut up and get real.

The cab dropped us on the corner. Across the street, some sporty folk were leaving Bowl-Mor even as others were arriving. When the store turned out to be exactly as I'd left it, I told Carolyn, we'd catch another cab right back to Paula's. Or she could go on her own. Whatever she preferred.

What she preferred, she said, was for me to give it a rest. Paula's would still be there tomorrow. Or it wouldn't, if the universe did that backflip. She was good either way.

* * *

"False alarm," I said a few minutes and half a block later. "Lights out, door closed, window gates locked. Just the way I left it, and—"

I don't know how I intended to finish that sentence. Because I could see that the first part of the sentence was inaccurate, and that Barnegat Books was not exactly the way I'd left it.

The window gates were in the right position, but someone had made some surgical cuts in all the right places, as if with a laser that ate case-hardened steel for breakfast. The lock was still sound, but it was no longer securing anything, and with one hand and very little effort I drew the gates open.

The door itself has a window, so there's never been any reason to beef up its security; upgrading the lock or reinforcing the door itself wouldn't stop a brute armed with a brick.

But the door was locked, and its window was unbroken.

"I don't get it," I said. "Did they have a key? Because I don't see any scratches on the metal, and you could tell if they forced the door. My lock's the one Litzauer left me, and I can't believe it stopped somebody who had already severed the steel gates in three places. If you already swallowed the camel, why would you strain at the gnat?"

"Bern."

She was pointing to the section of the window closest to the doorknob. Someone with a glass cutter had inscribed a near-perfect circle five inches in diameter. The glass disc was still there, with an addition that was almost invisible in the half-light.

"Scotch tape," she said. "They cut the glass, they took it out without dropping it and breaking it. How'd they do that?"

"Suction cups."

"And then they put it back," she said, "and taped it in place. Did you ever do anything like that, Bern?"

I shook my head. I took my set of tools from my pocket, and knelt down, and Carolyn reminded me that I had a key. "Oh, for God's sake," I said, and put the tools away and found my key ring and opened the door.

27

My first thought, before we even got in that cab on Greenwich Avenue, was that we'd walk in on a scene reminiscent of Dresden after the bombing. Bookcases tipped over, books all over the floor, Raffles' water dish in pieces. But by the time I opened the door and switched on the light, my expectations had changed. My visitor, uninvited and certainly unwanted, may have been inconsiderate enough to vandalize a set of window gates, but he'd also taken the trouble to mend my window after he'd had his way with it. I didn't know who he was or what he wanted, but I was fairly confident he wouldn't make a mess.

Nor had he. I walked around, looking at bookshelves, glancing here and there. I have one set of glassed-in shelves where I keep the more valuable collector's items under lock and key, and it was undisturbed. He could have helped himself to whatever he wanted from the rest of my stock and I wouldn't know it until I chanced to look for a particular book and found it missing. But everything looked untouched.

As did both of the cat's dishes. The water dish still had water in it, and—

"Bern, where's Raffles?"

I looked over to the front window, where he's apt to be more often than not, dozing in a patch of sunlight. The sunlight wasn't there, of course, not in the middle of the night, and neither was the cat. Carolyn walked around, calling his name, and that had about as much effect as it generally does. I'm pretty sure Raffles knows his name, but he's never felt obliged to respond to it.

"He's probably in back," I said.

"When you lock up," she said, "you always leave the door to the back room ajar. So he can get to the bathroom."

Before he was rather cunningly foisted upon me, Raffles spent enough time in residence on Arbor Court to learn what Carolyn had long since taught Archie and Ubi—i.e., to use the toilet instead of a litter box. (She employed a training method popularized by Charles Mingus, the late jazz musician and self-acknowledged genius, who so trained his own cats. And no, I am not making this up, and if you don't believe me, maybe you'll believe Google.)

"I'm sure I left it open," I said, "and I'm also sure I left the window gates and the front door intact. Whoever broke in here closed the door when he left, probably with Raffles on the other side of it."

She hurried to the door, reached for the knob, then hesitated. "You don't think—"

"That somebody's lurking there? No, because the gates were drawn shut, disabled or not, and you'd have to be on the other side of them to manage that. You can open the door. If there's anybody lurking behind it, it'll be Raffles."

She opened it a few inches, and that was all that was required. Raffles put a paw through the opening, followed with the rest of his estimable self, and would have brought a tail along if he'd had one. He glanced briefly at each of us in turn, seeing nothing worth further attention, went straight to his water dish, sampled its contents, then strode the rest of the way to the spot he favored and made himself comfortable.

"If it's a clear day tomorrow," I told Carolyn, "sometime in the late morning the sun will show up, and he'll be ready."

"It's a good thing we don't have to understand cats in order to enjoy having them around." She wrinkled her nose, as if at an odor she was trying to pin down. "But I guess you could say the same thing for people."

"That's a point."

She started to draw the door shut, then remembered to leave it ajar. She asked me if I'd checked the cash register. I hadn't, but did so now, and nothing seemed to be missing.

I started to say as much, but stopped when I heard my name called. I looked at the front door, and there was a man on the other side of it, telling me to open up.

I couldn't make out his features in the darkness, and it took a moment for his voice to register. When it did I said, "Ray," but I said it to Carolyn, in a normal tone of voice, and it couldn't have carried to the door and beyond it.

He tried to turn the doorknob, but when I'd closed the door I'd automatically pushed the button to engage the snap lock, so that didn't get him anywhere.

"God *damn* it, Bernie!"

I heard that, of course, clear as a bell if less euphonious. Before I could respond, Ray Kirschmann gave the doorknob a good shake. It stayed locked, but the shaking was enough to dislodge the circle of window glass that had been (a) neatly removed and (b) just as neatly Scotch-taped back in place.

The sound of a glass disc smashing on a sidewalk after a fall of a few feet couldn't have been all that loud.

But it did get one's attention.

It also apparently froze one in place. *I have to open the door*, I thought, but I stayed right where I was, behind my counter. Carolyn was on the other side of the counter, looking hard at the door, but not taking so much as a step toward it.

The man at the door seemed the only one of us capable of action. I watched as he extended a careful hand through the circular opening and turned the doorknob on the inside, opened the door and stepped through it.

"Bernie," he said. "Carolyn. One of you want to tell me what the hell is goin' on?"

"Um."

He stalked across the room, extended a finger, poked me gently perhaps four inches north of my belly button, then hooked my tie and drew it toward him so that he could have a good look at it.

"Like I figured," he said.

I'd loosened the tie before tucking into Rocco's spaghetti, and tightened it again en route to what I thought was my appointment on West Third Street, only to loosen it once more on my way to Paula's. It was loose now, and my shirt collar unbuttoned, but it wasn't the state of the half-Windsor knot that was commanding Ray's attention, it was the tie itself, and I found myself looking down at it, wondering if it bore a telltale spot or stain.

"Red and blue," he said. "That's navy blue. Diagonal stripes maybe a quarter of an inch wide."

"I'd have to say that's a good description, Ray. You could phrase it in those very words in your report, if there was any earthly reason for you to write one."

"Bernie, Bernie, Bernie," he said, sounding deeply disappointed. "Why don't we speed things up, and whichever of you's got the Kloppmann Diamond cough it up and hand it over. What do you say?"

28

He dragged it out and gave it up a handful of words at a time, but here's the gist of it. Four or five hours ago, around the time Carolyn and I were drinking scotch at the Bum Rap, a pair of uniformed officers from the Ninth Precinct, responding to a 911 call, presented themselves at the front desk of the Innisfree Apartments and enlisted the aid of the concierge. That young man ushered them onto the private penthouse elevator, which whisked them up to the building's 42nd floor.

"You need a key for the elevator," Ray marveled, "but when you get upstairs there's no door and no key required, you step off right into the penthouse apartment."

"Damn," I said. "What'll they think of next?"

The two cops did a room-by-room search of the place, each of them holding a gun with both hands, making those herky-jerky movements when turning a corner, shouting out "Clear!" whenever a room proved to be empty. As every room in the apartment proved to be, unless you insisted on counting the dead man in the den.

"In the den," Ray said. "That's what I'd call it, with the big TV and the leather recliners. But there was a bookcase, so maybe Vandy called it a library."

"Vandy?"

"Like I need to say his name, Bernie? Like you don't know

who I'm talkin' about? You stole his diamond, the least you can do is remember his name."

I said I didn't know what he was talking about, let alone who.

That earned me an eye roll. "Orrin Vandenbrinck," he said, getting the name right, which surprised me; some years back, in an episode that involved Piet Mondrian, Ray had spoken the late Dutch painter's name innumerable times, and never once called him anything but Moon-Drain. "Now tell me you don't know who he is."

"Everybody knows who he is," I said. "He's the creep who got rich by hiking drug prices way past what anybody could afford." I didn't quite snap my fingers, but I did what I could to suggest that I was suddenly getting the picture. "The Klop-pmann Diamond, isn't Vandenbrinck the one who paid a for-tune for it? I forget how much, but it was a lot."

"You forget how much. Right. I'll tell you, it was a hell of a loss to the stage and the screen when Mrs. Rhodenbarr's son Bernard decided burglary was his ticket to fame and fortune."

I said, "The body in the den. Was it him?"

"Vandy? That would have made a lot of people happy, but no, it wasn't him. It wasn't anywhere close to bein' him. From his pictures, Vandy's a kind of a dopey-lookin' guy built like a dumpling. The guy in the den was somebody who got up every morning to shave his head and then spent half the day in the gym and the other half feedin' his face."

When the uniforms phoned it in, it was Ray who got the call. He'd confirmed what the responding officers had already determined, that the man in the den was indeed dead, and that the apartment was otherwise unoccupied. The dead man was dressed for comfort in royal blue sweatpants and a rugby-style shirt striped in yellow and green.

"Colorful," Carolyn said.

There was a wallet in a pants pocket, holding some two hundred dollars in cash and a New York State driver's license in the name of Jason Philbert.

"Except he didn't look like a Jason," Ray said, "any more than he looked like a Philbert. You saw him, Bernie. Did he look like his name ought to be Jason Philbert?"

Nice try. When I didn't respond, he said the dead man, in the flesh and in his driver's license photo, had a definite Eastern European cast to his features, and a couple of stainless steel teeth in his mouth that no Western dentist would have given him.

"If I had to make up a name for him," he said, "it'd be some collection of letters that don't belong together, hard to remember and tricky to pronounce." He made a show of concentrating. "Istvan Horvath," he said. "Ain't that a mouthful, Bernie?"

"Is that his name, Ray?"

He gave me a look. "You're good," he said. "I got to give you that. You didn't even flinch."

"Why would I flinch?"

"If Istvan Horvath and Jason Philbert turn out to be one pea in a pod, it's a hell of a coincidence. Because there's already a guy by that name livin' on the twenty-ninth floor, only he's not there at the moment on account of he flew from JFK to Buenos Aires around the end of August and nobody's seen him since."

"Until tonight," Carolyn suggested, "when he came home, took the penthouse elevator by mistake, tried to bench-press the refrigerator, and had a heart attack."

He gave her a look. "Not bad, Shorty. No, the Horvath from the twenty-ninth floor is still in B.A. Nobody wants to say how he made his money, but he made a lot of it, and now he's spendin' some of it while he looks for a way to make some more. And the one with the driver's license that swears his name is Jason Philbert coulda bench-pressed a Lexus, never mind a refrigerator, and it wasn't a heart attack that killed him. Somebody shot him three times, once in the chest and twice in the forehead."

Three shots.

"But would you believe there's a third Istvan Horvath?"

"Why not?" She gave her thumbs a rest and looked up from her phone. "I just looked it up, and guess what? Horvath's a pretty common name in Hungary, Ray, especially for ethnic Croatians. And Istvan is the local equivalent of Stephen."

That last was welcome news to him. "In that case, from here on in I'll give my tongue a rest and just call him Steve. Except for the third Horvath, because why should I change? I've known him for years, and I'll go on calling him Bernie Rhodenbarr."

I just looked at him.

"The guy on the desk," he said. "Nice enough fellow, name of Pete. He gave a pretty good description of the guy who passed himself off as Horvath and rode up to Twenty-nine. Average-lookin' guy, had a European accent."

"Well, that's me," I said. "I mean, he nailed it, didn't he? Of course any accent I have is New York, plus whatever trace of my Midwestern upbringing is still there. And I don't want to come off as vain, but I think we can safely say I'm a little better-looking than average."

"What you are," he said, "is a piece of work. You're also an inch or two taller than average, which Pete also said, and you maybe looked taller than you were because you had company, and it must have been you who got the elevator headed for the twenty-ninth floor, because your lady friend would need to stand on a box to reach the right button."

"A short joke," Carolyn said, and looked at her watch. "What took you so long, Ray?"

"Two people," I said, "and one has a European accent. And what exactly is a European accent, anyway?"

"Whatever it was, it got you on the elevator. And your outfit helped."

"My outfit? He saw by my outfit that I was a cowboy?"

"A navy blue blazer," he said. "With brass buttons."

"How many thousands of New Yorkers—"

"And a necktie, Bernie. Diagonal stripes of red and blue, narrow stripes. Jesus, he couldn't have given a better description of your tie if he'd strangled you with it."

I looked at him and he looked at me, and after a long moment I asked him if he honestly expected me to admit to anything, and he allowed that he didn't.

"So if there's no likelihood of a gotcha moment," I said, "maybe we could skip all that crap. Did you find any trace of my presence on the twenty-ninth floor?"

"No."

"Was anything missing from Mr. Horvath's apartment?"

"We'd have to ask Steve," he said, "and first we'd have to find him. But if you wanted to toss Steve's apartment, you'd have pretended to be some other guy on some other floor. You were just using Steve to get into the penthouse."

"How would I manage that?"

"Don't play dumb. You've got skills, we both know that."

"Any skills I may have had are rusty now. Ray, I've been out of that business for years now."

"Yeah, right."

"Technology forced me out of it," I said, and started the old rant about security cameras and electronic locks, and how for a burglar it was the examined life that was not worth living. I didn't get very far, though, because it dawned on me that he didn't know what I was talking about. Electronic locks? Security cameras? The whole of Manhattan on *Candid Camera*?

Not in his universe.

I stopped in the middle of a sentence, and he waved away the ensuing silence. "While we're skippin' crap," he said, "suppose we skip the usual crap that all you are is a bookseller. You don't have to cop to bein' a burglar, but how about you quit denyin' it?"

"I'm not denying the past, Ray. But do you have any idea how long it's been since I did any breaking and entering?"

He pointed to my front door. "From the looks of it," he said, "no more'n an hour or so."

"You can't possibly believe—"

"No, of course not, because you've got keys, and if you lost them you'd pick the lock, not vandalize your own damn store. So leaving out whatever you did or didn't do at the Innisfree Apartments, the question is when's the last time you let yourself in where you had no right to be, and walked out with what you had no right to take."

"And?"

"And we both of us know the answer, Bernie, and it probably won't come as news to your little buddy there, either." The smile he flashed at Carolyn went unreturned. "Sunday," he said.

"Sunday?"

"This past Sunday, sometime after nine at night. Or I suppose it could have been pretty much anytime Monday, because that's when they're closed. Like, you know, a Broadway theater."

"I broke into a theater?"

"A gallery."

"I stole a painting?"

"You couldn't, because they don't have any. It's the Ginseng Gallery on Lispenard, down below Canal Street, and what they specialize in is Chinese stuff."

"Chinese stuff."

"Old Chinese stuff," he said, "like from the Ying Yang Dynasty. And what they had on display when they locked up Sunday night, and what was gone when they opened up at ten Tuesday morning, was the Edgar W. Margate collection." He showed me a hand with the thumb and forefinger a little over an inch apart. "Twenty-one figurines about this big. You see one of 'em on your aunt's shelf, a little squirrel holdin' a nut, say, you'd say it was cute. A knick-knack, you'd say it was, and I'd agree with you, but Margate would tell you it was a priceless jade carving from the Ping Pong Dynasty."

I heard all the words, even Ying Yang and Ping Pong, but there was only one that stood out.

Jade.

"And you can swear up and down you don't know what I'm talking about, Bernie, but I know it was you."

"If you had evidence—"

"What I've got," he said, "is grounds for suspicion. Which means I'm dead certain of something I can't prove."

"And where does that leave us?"

"That's something for you to think about," he said, "while I use your bathroom. You okay with that?"

"*Mi baño es su baño.*"

"I'll take that for a yes," he said, and pushed open the door Carolyn had left ajar. I thought about twenty-one jade carvings, one of which was probably a squirrel holding a nut, and I thought about the fact that Ray Kirschmann was not the only person in the world—in this world, that is to say—who seemed unequivocally certain I'd stolen them, and I thought of another thing or two as well, and tried to make sense of it all, but I only got to do this thinking in the matter of seconds it took Ray to find his way to the light switch and flick it on.

"Jesus Ducking Christ!" he cried out, or would have if he'd been fitted with Auto-Correct. "Bernie, get in here!"

29

"He was dead," Ray said. "I swear to God he was dead."

I walked over to the gentleman in question. He was seated at my desk, his head thrown back, his arms hanging over the sides of the chair. His silk shirt was bunched up in front, so if there was a bullet hole in his chest I couldn't see it, but the two in his forehead would have been hard to miss.

"From the looks of him," I said, "he still is."

"Don't touch him, for Christ's sake."

"I just wanted to—"

"Check his body temperature? I already touched him, Bernie, and he's headed toward room temperature but he hasn't got there yet." He picked up one of the hands, as if to check for a pulse, then let it fall back. "I seen my share of corpses. If I had to come up with a number, what with the body temp and the beginnings of rigor mortis, I'd say two hours, maybe two and a half."

He looked at his watch and I looked at mine. "Ten fifty-four," I said.

"Close enough."

"So between eight-thirty and nine for time of death?"

"For a guess," he said. "The Medical Examiner might see it differently, so I can't say for certain. What I know for sure is he was a whole lot colder and stiffer a couple of hours earlier in a penthouse apartment on East Ninth Street."

"It can't be the same guy," Ray was saying. "The guy I saw was dead as a lox, and a woman from the M.E.'s office confirmed as much, and I saw him go out of there in a body bag. And this bird's a dead ringer for him, and they both bought their clothes from Izzy's Big and Tall Shop, but this one's wearing a different shirt entirely."

"Maybe he changed it."

He gave me a look. He'd been rattled at first, but I couldn't fault him for that. He'd seen what appeared to be the same corpse twice, and if anything I had to give him credit. He'd worked it out a lot quicker than I'd come to terms with my green-and-white SubwayCard.

In my defense, parallel worlds are more of a stretch than parallel people.

"Hell of a resemblance," he said, "and if they're not twins they've got to be brothers, or cousins at the very least."

"Or from the same little village in the Balkans," I suggested, "where they've spent the past thousand years humping each other's sisters."

"Or their own." He'd been checking pockets and turned up a wallet. "'Mason Dilbert.' That's Jason Philbert and Mason Dilbert, just in case you figured nobody in the fake ID business has a sense of humor."

He returned the wallet to the dead man's pocket. "I better call this in," he said. "But first I might as well ask. Neither of you's ever seen this guy before, am I right?"

"Not exactly," I said.

Not in person, I said, and not all by himself, which was why I hadn't put it together until I learned that there were two of them. Whereupon it had dawned on me that I'd seen the –ilbert Twins before, on TV, flanking their client.

"They were Vandenbrinck's bodyguards," I said, "and he may have referred to them as Heckle and Jeckle, which isn't that much of a stretch from Mason and Jason. He was showing them off, and his point was that the Kloppmann Diamond was safer with them guarding it than it would be in a bank vault."

"Bodyguards," he said. "I guess they look the part, except for bein' dead. So where's the body they were supposed to be guardin'?"

"No idea."

"And the diamond? Same answer?" He gave us each a long look, then treated himself to a sigh and a shrug. "The funny thing is I believe you. You never shot anybody, Bernie. You're three times as crooked as a corkscrew, but for all these years you've never been violent. But I've got to take you downtown, and I'm afraid you're in for a long night."

No surprise there.

But then he did surprise me. "Shorty," he said, "I'm cuttin' you a break. Go home."

She stared at him.

"Quick," he said, "before I change my mind. It's all a lot simpler this way. You were never here."

He didn't have to tell her twice.

He called it in, and while we waited for someone to show up he told me it'd be a while before I'd be allowed back in the store.

"So if there's anything you need," he said, "you better take it with you."

The only thing I could think of was the paperback on the counter.

"*The Screamin' Mimi*," he read. "I guess this here is Mimi, and she must be screamin', what with her mouth wide open like that. This is all you're takin', Bernie? A book?"

"This is a bookstore, Ray. What else is there to take?"

The question didn't call for an answer, nor did he offer one. But I could have answered it. There was an envelope in a desk drawer containing $16,000 in used hundreds—unless a visitor had come across it and decided to make it his own.

So the money might be there and it might not, and you could say the same for twenty-one artfully carved jade figurines, formerly (and still legally) the property of one Edgar W. Margate.

At one point I'd wondered if I'd get out of the interrogation room at One Police Plaza before the sun came up, but it wasn't even close. At that time of year, New Yorkers don't get their first glimpse of the sun until right around seven o'clock, and I was out the door and on the street a few minutes after four.

One thing I seemed to have in the new universe was good taxi karma. All I had to do was step to a curb and lift a hand. Not too many minutes later I was in Carolyn's apartment, waiting for my tea to be cool enough to sip. She had a cup of her own, and looked surprisingly fresh.

"I saw it was past four," I said, "and the first thing I thought was that's when Paula would close up, so either I'd find you here or I wouldn't have long to wait."

"Sometimes she'll lock the door and dim the lights and break the law by staying open a few extra hours."

"I never thought of that."

"And sometimes a person might spend some time there, knocking back the scotch, and when she leaves she might decide not to go back to her own apartment."

I hadn't thought of that, either.

"But what *I* did," she said, "is I never went anywhere near Paula's. I walked all the way here from the bookstore, and I passed within a block of the Duchess, but I didn't even stop to see who was there. I came straight home and got in bed right away, and my head was going a mile a minute, and I thought *This is crazy, I'll never be able to sleep.* And the next thing I knew I woke up coming out of a dream."

"I don't suppose you dreamed you were behind the counter at the bookstore, did you? With no pants on?"

"I don't think so, but I couldn't swear to it, because the whole dream was gone the instant I opened my eyes, and so was any chance I had of getting more sleep. I was out for two hours, and that's way less than eight, but I have to say it's a lot better than nothing. I feel pretty good." She cocked her head. "You, on the other hand, must be exhausted. Especially considering the kind of night you had."

"No, I'm okay," I said. "And it was a long night but it wasn't horrible."

"He didn't use a rubber hose on you?"

"No, and I wasn't booked or printed. He put me in a little room with a cup of coffee."

"To get your DNA, Bern. From the cup."

"Why would he do that? He already knows who I am."

"Oh, right."

"It's good I brought *The Screaming Mimi*. He left me there long enough to get through a couple of chapters, then came back and sat across the table from me and asked me a ton of questions."

"About Vandenbrinck and the diamond?"

"We barely touched on it. What he did was take me through Friday evening, from when I closed the store to when he turned up and walked in on us."

"What did you tell him?"

"The truth," I said. "Not necessarily the whole truth, and certainly not nothing but the truth, but if I'd been hooked up to a polygraph I'd have had a good chance of passing. I said I met you at the Bum Rap, I said we had a couple of drinks, and then I had an appointment so we went our separate ways. I told him where I ate and what I had for dinner."

"Oh? You didn't tell *me* what you had for dinner."

"Spaghetti puttanesca. I told him when I got to Rocco's and when I left, and I gave him the address on West Third Street, where I was supposed to meet some professor named Rubisham with an eye toward buying his books."

"You really did tell him the truth."

"Except I left out a few things. I didn't say that the joker who'd made the appointment wasn't Rubisham, that the real Rubisham moved out months ago and left nothing behind but his name on the mailbox. I left out the Norfolk jacket with the leather elbow patches, because in the telling the guy was just a voice on the phone. I agreed to look at his books because that's what I do."

"You left out the part about the Armagnac."

"Uh-huh. I also left out the way he'd gone out of his way to drop a word into our conversation."

She looked puzzled.

"Jaded," I said. "'*One grows jaded, if you know what I mean.*' Well, I hadn't known what he meant, but at least it was in English and not in Latin, and I let it go. Looking back, I'd say he was just looking for a way to get the word into the conversation."

"Jaded? Oh."

"As in jade. Professor Armagnac wanted to let me know he was interested in jade, but something kept him from coming right out and saying as much. And he's not the only one. Remember the customer I told you about, the one who bought a Tucker Coe first edition without knowing who actually wrote it?"

"You told me she bought it for the title, but I don't think you mentioned which one it was, and the only one I can think of is *Wax Apple.*"

I could have said *Don't Lie to Me* and launched another Abbott-and-Costello routine. Instead I supplied the title in question.

She echoed it. "*A Jade in Aries.* And she bought other books, didn't she?"

"All with *jade* somewhere in the title. 'I have a special fondness for jade,' is how she put it."

"You didn't tell me that."

"It didn't seem worth mentioning. Remember, this was all before Ray accused me of stealing twenty-one jade carvings from a gallery on Lispenard Street."

"He was really convinced you did it, Bern."

"I know."

"And so was Professor Armagnac, and Tucker Coe's girlfriend. Does she have a name?"

"She has a phone number," I said. "She jotted it down, and when I suggested she add her name, what she wrote was the word *jade* in block capitals."

"There are women named Jade, and some of them probably have sisters named Ruby and Pearl and Esmeralda, but somehow I don't think she's one of them. Bern? What do you figure happened to Mr. Margate's collection? Who really broke in and stole it, and why does everybody think it was you?"

I finished my tea, got to my feet. Carolyn's questions hung in the air while I walked over to the stove, filled the kettle, and set it on the burner. If I just kept watching it, I thought, it would never boil, and I would never have to explain the unexplainable.

I said, "This whole business with parallel universes is complicated."

"No kidding."

"More complicated than I thought. Look, a SubwayCard is just a Metrocard of another color, and it's nice to have the neighborhood bowling alley back where it belongs, and my life's easier all around without a security camera on every building."

"And?"

I looked at her, and felt an unfamiliar stirring, one with which I was becoming increasingly familiar. I guess the thought showed in my face, because she colored and lowered her eyes.

"And that," I said, "which is wonderful, even if it scares the crap out of me."

"You're not the only one."

"But what I guess I assumed is that the present would have all these changes, like the ones I've just mentioned. And the future would be however it turned out. But I thought we could count on the past to behave itself."

"Huh?"

"To mind its own business," I said, "and stay in its own lane."

"I'm a little confused here, Bern."

"So am I," I said, "which may be my point. Never mind. You asked three questions and I haven't answered them, have I?"

"That's okay. If you don't know the answers—"

"I think I do."

"Really?"

"I think everybody's right," I said. "I think it was me. I'm the one who broke into the gallery and walked off with the Margate Collection. I just wish I could remember it."

30

"Wednesday night we went to sleep in one world," I said, "and Thursday morning we woke up in another one."

"This one."

"Right. And certain things were different and others were exactly the same, but the lives we found ourselves leading were the same lives we'd led all along. Barnegat Books was doing better for the lack of online competition, but it was still the same humble establishment, and it still had the same affable fellow on a stool behind the counter."

"And the Poodle Factory had the same altitudinally-challenged lesbian washing dogs. So?"

"So Thursday morning I showed up, fed my cat, and sat behind the counter."

"The way you always do."

"Right," I said. "What about Wednesday?"

"Huh?"

"I know what you and I did Wednesday, back in our former universe. But what was going on in *this* universe, before you and I somersaulted into it? The bookstore didn't just spring into existence when the world went *Tilt.* It was already here, with books on its shelves and a cat snoozing in front of its window. Who fed Raffles Wednesday morning? And the day before that, and so on?"

"He didn't look as though he'd missed many meals."

"But who fed him?"

I let her think about it. She took her time, and I watched thoughts and emotions play across her face.

Then she was looking at me. "Paula's," she said.

"Paula's?"

"Remember how I couldn't wait to get there? Then I got there, and there it was, right where it used to be, and I felt this sense of relief." She frowned. "And then I stood there with one hand on the door and I was afraid to go in. '*Carolyn! We thought you were dead! Where've you been the past couple of years?*' And that was my best-case scenario, Bern. Maybe I'd be walking into a room where nobody knew me from Eve."

"But you steeled yourself and opened the door."

"I bit the bullet," she said, "and it turned out to be a gumdrop. I knew most of the women in the room, and they knew me, and they didn't have trouble recognizing me. They waved or nodded or said hello, but nobody made a fuss over me, because they'd seen me last week or the week before."

I thought about it. "Right," I said. "That makes sense."

"It does?"

"The only way Paula's could be where it is," I said, "is if it never went out of business, not in this universe. And if it was there all along, why would you stop dropping in for a couple of pops and a quick look around?"

"So Paula's never disappeared, is that what you're saying?" I watched her try to get her mind around it. "It was the same old place," she said, "and the same old crowd, but with enough differences to get your attention. There were two women I hadn't seen in ages, ever since they moved to Magdalena, New

Mexico. Except they didn't, they were still living in the same two rooms on Commerce Street."

"That must have been a fun conversation to have."

"It was a little awkward, but it would have been worse in a coffee shop. In a bar where everybody's drinking, a fuzzy memory's not such a big deal. And it was a good thing I ran into the Magdalena girls early on, because it prepared me for seeing Angie Berkowitz."

"An old flame? A bad break-up?"

"No, just a friend from the bars. But the last time I saw her was a year and a half ago at Redden's."

"What, on Fourteenth Street? The funeral parlor?"

"She was the guest of honor, Bern. Toxic shock syndrome, and it happened so suddenly that nobody could believe she was dead, but the open casket removed all doubts."

"And this evening—"

"She'd put on a couple of pounds," she said, "but all in all she looked fine. It was a shock to see her."

"I can imagine."

"But not a toxic one, and I caught myself in time to keep from telling her she looked natural, which is what everybody kept saying that afternoon at Redden's."

What they say about beer—that you can't own it, you can only rent it—is no less true of tea. When I got back from the bathroom, Carolyn was sitting on the edge of the bed, untying a shoe.

"I felt right at home in Paula's," she said. "There were things I had to adjust to, like Angie being alive, but isn't attitude adjustment what keeps all those distilleries in business? I may have remembered the world a little differently than Paula's other patrons, but aside from that I fit right in."

"Looking back," I said, "you always did."

She put the shoe down, uncrossed her legs, crossed them the other way, and dealt with the second shoe.

"Because I'm a Villager," she said, "who gets nosebleeds north of Fourteenth Street and the bends south of Houston. And I'm a lesbian. I'm a Greenwich Village lesbian, Bern, and that's what I've been since the first time I got off the D Train at West Fourth Street and walked into a bar on Minetta Lane."

She had the shoe off. She went on holding it in both hands while she told me how she'd felt walking into a lesbian bar for the very first time, all the fear and all the excitement.

Listening, I felt something myself. Not quite fear and not quite excitement. I decided it was anticipation. I was waiting for something, but what was it?

"I remembered that feeling tonight," she said, still holding the shoe. "Bern, it's late. Next thing you know it'll be time to open your store."

"You think they'll let me? It's a crime scene."

"You'll have show up, if only to feed Raffles. I think we should go to bed."

"God knows I'm tired," I said, "but I'm also wired. I don't think I could sleep."

"Good," she said, as she let go of the shoe. "Neither could I. Who said anything about sleeping?"

* * *

What I'd been waiting for, of course, was for the other shoe to drop. And it did, and after the asterisks had twinkled like stars in every available universe, we both slipped off to sleep.

By ten o'clock we were up and dressed and eating French toast and bacon at the diner on Hudson.

"I'm still a lesbian," she said, over a second cup of coffee.

I told her I was beginning to think I might be one myself.

"Last night in Paula's," she said, "there was this dark-roots blonde who really made the cheap look work for her, and I thought she was cute and I guess she thought I was, too, and we flirted a little."

"I'm shocked."

"I'll bet. Anyway, things were moving right along, and while it was a long way from a sure thing, there was a good chance I might go home with her. And I didn't think we'd get out of bed in the morning and race off to Bloomingdale's to pick out drapes, because there were already a few things about her I found irritating—"

"But she was cute enough to brighten an hour or two."

"Right. But what I kept wishing was that my buddy Bernie would show up."

"Really?"

"Really. And then you did. And a couple of women stopped their conversations and shifted into Wary Glance mode, and I looked, and it was you. And just like that I relaxed, and I hadn't even known I wasn't relaxed to begin with."

"The most confusing of all possible worlds," I said.

"It's a puzzle, all right. Last week I was bouncing back and forth between Henrietta's and the Cubby, while some other Carolyn Kaiser was hanging out in Paula's."

"I know how I spent this past Sunday night," I said. "I sat

home and watched *Billions*, and by ten Monday morning I was at the bookstore. But that was in another universe, and this world's Bernie Rhodenbarr was stealing little jade animals a block below Canal Street."

"Where'd he go? Now that you're here, what happened to him?"

"Beats me."

"And what happened to the other Carolyn? Did she disappear in a puff of smoke the minute I turned up?" She sighed. "I'm out of my depth here, Bern. The only thing I know is there's at least one cat in a bookstore on Eleventh Street. He hasn't got a tail, but he's got an appetite, so let's save a few minutes and take the bus."

"The bus?"

"I already checked," she said. "I've still got a SubwayCard."

31

The Crime Scene crew must have finished their business while I was downtown at One Police Plaza, answering Ray's questions in between chapters of *The Screaming Mimi.* They were long gone by the time I got there, but as far as the NYPD was concerned, Barnegat Books was still a crime scene, and they'd strung enough yellow tape to make their position clear.

They'd also swept up the broken glass and nailed a plywood board over the formerly glassed-in upper portion of the front door. And they'd even locked the door.

I used my key, shunted aside a few strands of CRIME SCENE DO NOT ENTER tape, and fed my cat. Carolyn lingered in the doorway long enough to determine that Raffles hadn't been hauled off to be booked and paw-printed, then headed off to open her own place of business.

I'd turned on the lights, and now I turned them off and relocked the door. The plywood hid the SORRY—WE'RE CLOSED! sign from public view, but the yellow tape and the darkened room behind it ought to get the point across. While none of it would keep out a sufficiently determined visitor, it was enough to discourage anybody who was just looking for something to read.

And, while it was too dark to read, there was more than enough ambient light to keeping me from bumping into things on my way to the rear of the store, where I found more yellow tape strung across the door to the back room. I dealt with the tape, then closed the door behind me.

I've been in rooms after the cops have conducted a thorough search, and they'll remind you of your attic after a family of squirrels has moved in. All they care about is finding whatever they're looking for, and they'll dump drawers and empty bookshelves in the process, and leave the resulting mess for you to sort through on your own time. I wasn't really expecting that kind of treatment, as the public portion of the store was as I'd left it, but all the same I braced myself as I reached for the light switch.

And relaxed. Everything was just as it should be. My guests had acted like the precise and scientific lab technicians they were, not like a couple of bulls from Manhattan Robbery on a treasure hunt. There was nothing to show that CSI had paid me a visit—aside from the yellow tape on the door, and the comforting absence of a dead body.

The first thing I did was check the drawers of my desk. I wouldn't have been astonished if my $16,000 had gone missing. I didn't think somebody with CSI would have pocketed my envelope, or even turned it up in the first place, but I couldn't absolutely rule it out. Ray Kirschmann, it has been said, would steal a hot stove—but only if he had to. If he'd found the money, he'd look for a way to maneuver me into bribing him with it.

More to the point, Ray never had the chance to open a drawer. He turned on the light, saw all that was left of Mason Dilbert, and seconds later had me and Carolyn for company.

But there were at least two people ahead of him. Mason

Dilbert, obviously—and whoever had put the three bullets in him.

And who would that be? My tweedy professor, whose name was neither Rubisham nor Armagnac, had contrived to make sure I wouldn't be at the bookstore at 8:30. Why do that unless he wanted to drop in himself? And what better reason to visit an unoccupied store than to steal something?

Not the cash in the envelope, and not the Kloppmann Diamond, either; he'd made the appointment Thursday afternoon, before I'd even launched Operation Innisfree. He undoubtedly knew about the diamond, everybody on the planet seemed to know about the diamond and the wretch who'd owned it, but why think any of that had anything to do with me?

He'd have come for the jade. Somebody had made off with the Margate collection, and everybody seemed to think it was me, and who was I to contend otherwise?

I thought about him, pictured him. He was older than I, though on reflection he'd looked a little young for retirement. He was slender and appeared fit, and while I hadn't seen him drop down and rattle off twenty pushups, I was willing to believe he was capable of it. His manner was professorial enough, and he'd peppered our conversation with Latin phrases and classical names, but all that meant was he'd done his homework.

I'll be damned, I thought. The sonofabitch was a burglar.

It wasn't that much of a stretch to put myself in his position. Say he'd scouted the Margate collection, either because he had a passion for jade or, more likely, he knew someone who'd be eager to buy it from him. Then, before he could act, some moonlighting bookseller beat him to it.

So why not burgle the burglar? A phone call or two to guarantee my absence, a little tradecraft to make short work of a couple of locks, and he'd be in and out before I gave up waiting for Godot on West Third Street.

He'd been in the store before, so he'd know his way around. At the very least he'd have had a quick look at the back room, and now the first thing he'd do was check out the desk.

If he'd done so, he'd have found the envelope. And, having found it, he'd have taken it in a hot second.

But he hadn't. Nobody had, because the envelope was right where I'd stowed it, its flap still sealed, and as far as I could tell no one had touched the thing, or even opened the drawer.

Could he have skipped the desk and gone straight for my hiding place? I turned and looked at the bookcase that stands in front of it. I'd moved it Thursday when I fetched my tools and rubber gloves, and I'd put it back in position, and it appeared to be just as I'd left it.

I returned to the desk, sat in my chair. Like the wooden desk, it had come with the store, and I'd never quite gotten around to switching it out for one of those ergonomic Herman Miller numbers. It had served me well enough, as it had served Mr. Litzauer before me, and I hadn't heard any complaints from Mason Dilbert.

Who couldn't have known about the jade, or had any reason to come looking for it.

I closed my eyes and moved pieces on an imaginary chessboard. Three of them, because I'd had a minimum of three visitors. It took me a while, but I came up with a scenario.

Mason Dilbert, determined to avenge his brother/cousin

(or to recover his employer's diamond, or both) was first on the scene. His past was shady enough to have equipped him with some basic skills, enough to force a simple lock with a strip of celluloid, but he'd need to cut his way around the more formidable mechanism that secured my window gates. Once he'd done so, he'd loided the door, closed it, engaged the snaplock, and—

And close behind him was a second man, one who found his way there by tailing Mason. He lurked, presumably in the shadows, while Mason performed his crude business of breaking and entering, then followed him inside. The gates were disabled, but the door was locked, and our second uninvited guest didn't have a strip of celluloid.

You can't buy a such an article in your neighborhood hardware store, but for a couple of dollars they'll be happy to sell you a glass cutter, and at some point some clerk had sold one to Guest Number Two. He'd probably owned it for a while and had a certain amount of practice with it, because he'd inscribed a near-perfect circle and removed the glass disc without shattering it or cutting himself.

He turned the knob, let himself in, found a flat surface and set the piece of glass on it, and made his way to the back room. And then what?

Oh, to have been a fly on the wall, you might be thinking right about now. I've had that thought myself, now and again, and I've concluded that there's no point whatsoever in being such a creature. It's not unlikely that Mason Dilbert was fluent in two or three languages and nearly so in a couple more, but it's safe to say that House Fly wasn't one of them. You wouldn't be able to understand a word, and there was always the chance you'd get swatted.

Which is what happened to Mason Dilbert.

One in the chest and two in the forehead. On our way out of Orrin Vandenbrinck's apartment, we'd heard the three shots that put an end to Jason Philbert, and not quite twenty-four hours later Mason got the same treatment. Ballistics analysis would determine whether the same gun had fired all six rounds, but you didn't need to run a test to assume a single shooter had accounted for both of the -ilberts.

And that was what the man who shot Mason wanted you to think.

Look, say you're him. For one reason or another, you want Jason Philbert dead. So you fire once into Jason's chest, and if that doesn't kill him outright it has him circling the drain, and to make assurance doubly sure you give him a double tap, two in the forehead.

But a day later, when you mete out the same treatment to his look-alike colleague, it's something else. It's an intentional pattern, an echo.

What it is, in fact, is a signature. An illegible one, because it doesn't spell out whose finger pulled the trigger, but it lets the world know that it was the same finger both times.

This whole line of thought raised as many questions as it answered, but they could wait.

Back to my scenario, on my imaginary chessboard. Mason's dead, shot three times. The man who shot him has done what he came to do, so why stick around? I couldn't be sure what had steered Mason to Barnegat Books, but it almost had to be connected to my own expedition to the Innisfree and its penthouse. Peter-Peter's description of the counterfeit Istvan Horvath and his much shorter companion had rung a bell for Ray Kirschmann, and maybe the desk attendant had come up with something else to suggest that Jason's killer could be found in a bookshop on Eleventh Street.

Did Number Two, the man with the glass cutter and the gun, have the same information? Or was he just tagging along in Mason's Size Thirteen footsteps?

What did it matter? He left his victim behind the desk, the books on their shelves, and the fly on the proverbial wall. He also left the glass disc on whatever flat surface he'd placed it, and he took the gun and the glass cutter with him and went out the door and off into the night.

And that left Number Three, Professor Rubisham or Monsieur Armagnac, call him what you will. If he was the pro I thought him to be, he'd have left the Norfolk jacket home and chosen something dark and unmemorable. His hands would be gloved and his feet sneakered, and in one of his pockets he'd have a set of tools not unlike mine.

Whenever he showed up, he'd know right away what he was looking at. He'd see the vandalized gates, the hole in the glass. If he got there soon enough, he might catch sight of the departing shooter. Sooner still and he might have heard the three gunshots, and waited out of sight until their source had made his exit.

Most likely, though, the *fait* had already been thoroughly *accompli* by the time he got there. In his position, what would I have done? Turned around and gone home, I'd prefer to think—but circumstances alter cases. What could he expect to net from Mr. Margate's jade? How dire was his financial situation? And what effect did the element of risk have on him? Was the fear paralyzing or perversely energizing?

He'd have waited a moment, and listened, and looked around to see who might be watching. And then he'd have turned the knob and walked on in. Maybe he'd have brought a mini flashlight, or maybe he'd have found that the dark was light enough, but either way he'd pad quietly to the rear of the store.

Would the door to the back room be open or shut? Would the light be on or off? Would he be aware of the smell of gunpowder, or would it be the corpse in the desk chair that first got his attention?

At that point he'd have abandoned all thoughts of little green animals. Knowing nothing of Heckle and Jeckle and tense times at the Innisfree, Number Three could only assume that both the man in the chair and the man who had made him incapable of getting out of it had been there with nothing on their minds but the Edgar Margate collection. The one he could see, his arms hanging over the arms of the chair, would be forever disappointed; the other had found the jade and fled with it—if in fact it had been there for the finding.

The one certainty was that there was nothing still there waiting to be found, and every reason for him to get the hell out. So he'd turned off the light and closed the door, and on his way out he did something that made it impossible for me to avoid feeling a kind of kinship with him.

I keep a Scotch tape dispenser on the counter, next to my cash register. When someone buys a single book, I generally slip it along with the receipt into a flat paper bag, and if I remember I seal it with an inch or so of tape. Number Three, God bless him, had picked up the tape dispenser and carried it to the front of the store, where he'd taken precious time to replace the glass disc and tape it in place.

And then he'd put the dispenser back where he found it.

32

"And then he let himself out, drew the door shut with the snaplock engaged, and fixed the window gates so they looked as though they were still doing their job. I can't help it, I have to admire a guy like that."

She rolled her eyes. "Of course you do, Bern. He remind you of anybody?"

"Not really. You see a lot of tweedy guys in the neighborhood. Academic types."

"That's it, eh?"

"I guess. I almost bought a Norfolk jacket once. I was looking at books at Housing Works and there it was."

"On the shelf," she said, "alphabetically positioned between *The Naked and the Dead* and *Nostromo.*"

"On a hanger, and in great shape."

"Only worn once, Bern. It went back in the closet when he didn't get tenure."

"It was a little tight in the shoulders," I remembered. "But even if it had fit like a glove I would have passed."

"Because who needs a belted tweed glove?"

"I looked in the mirror, and what I saw was a guy looking ill at ease in somebody else's jacket."

"So you hung it back on the rack for Mr. Armagnac to find it?"

"I don't think—"

"Neither do I. Bern, I'm with you, I have to admire the guy myself, and can't you think who he reminds me of? Cleaning up after himself, even taking the trouble to put the tape dispenser where he found it? Bern, name a burglar who picks a lock to get in and picks it again after he's out."

"Oh."

"His initials are B.R., if that helps."

"Oh," I said.

By the time we had this conversation, three days had gone wherever days go, and Barnegat Books, its gates and window glass restored and its yellow Crime Scene tape retired, was once again open for business.

And doing business, I'm pleased to report. The first customer, whose guilty pleasures ran to books that enumerated the many shades of gray, crossed the threshold just minutes after I'd finished feeding Raffles, and she didn't leave empty-handed. A Stephen King fan came in even as the Gray Lady was on her way out, and all morning long I had my share of customer traffic. It stopped well short of gridlock, but that was fine with me, and a few minutes after noon I brought lunch to the Poodle Factory.

"Pad Thai," Carolyn said.

"From Two Guys."

She frowned. "They're big on Thai food in Dushanbe?"

"Probably not."

"But Two Guys—"

"From Chiang Mai, and don't ask me what happened to the

two guys from Tajikistan. The Big Chef in the sky swung his cleaver, and they were suddenly gone."

"And another restaurant had taken their place."

"In no time at all."

"I don't understand it, Bern."

"There's a lot I don't understand," I said. "And it's beginning to dawn on me that all the things I don't understand have a single common denominator."

"What's that?"

"It's, you know, a mathematical term, and math was never my long suit, but it more or less means that there's a unifying element . . ."

"Bern, I know what a common denominator is."

"Oh."

"What I don't know is what this particular common denominator is."

"Oh."

"And what all the things are," she said, "that you don't understand."

"Oh," I said, for a third time. "Well, there's the way Two Guys morphs from Tajik to Thai in an eye blink. There's the way that young woman without a name bought up every book in the store with *jade* in the title, as a cute way of letting me know she wanted to get her hands on the Margate collection. And there's the way Mason Dilbert, who never met me and probably never heard of me, contrived to wind up sitting at my desk with the same three bullets in him as that carbon copy of him with the same name."

"Not quite the same name, Bern."

"Mason Dilbert, Jason Philbert. Close enough."

"And not the same bullets."

"They might as well have been. They had the same effect on Mason as they'd had on Jason, and allowed the two of them to go on being a matched pair. It gets your attention, it's so cute a development they could show it on Panda Cam, but—"

"But?"

"But it doesn't make sense."

"It doesn't, does it?" She lowered her eyes. "Bern," she said, "I get it, and what I get is that I don't get it. There's plenty of things I don't understand, starting with the fact that I'm a lesbian sleeping with my best friend."

"Um."

"Don't get me wrong, Bern. I had a good time last night. But that doesn't mean it wasn't strange. It felt perfectly natural, and it also felt perfectly strange, and if there's a common denominator for all of this strangeness, I'd love to know what it is."

"It's this universe," I said. "This best of all possible worlds. It doesn't make sense."

I wasn't improvising. I'd been thinking along these lines all morning, and I was prepared to make a strong case.

But I stopped when the door opened and two men entered the Poodle Factory. One was very tall, and would have had to stoop to get in the door even if he hadn't been wearing a turban. The other was short and slender and bareheaded, with generically Asian facial features. I'd never laid eyes on either of them before, and yet they both looked curiously familiar.

The tall one beamed and bowed. The short one moved busily around the room, his oval eyes seeking assurance that we were alone. Satisfied, he nodded to his companion.

Both men left.

"Bern—"

I held up a hand, and she didn't say anything after having said my name. And neither did I, and the door opened once again, and I recognized the man who crossed the threshold.

He glanced at Carolyn, then fixed his eyes on me. "You're Rhodenbarr," he said.

I didn't deny it.

"You know who I am," he said.

I nodded.

"Then you probably know why I'm here. I paid a lot of money for that stone. Do you know why?"

I shook my head.

"Because I wanted it," he said. "I still want it."

"I don't have it," I said truthfully.

"I know that."

"I never had it," I said, rather less truthfully. "I never laid eyes on it, let alone a hand."

""No, of course you didn't." Orrin Vandenbrinck may have been many things, but Human Lie Detector was evidently not among them. "You're a thief, but an admirably professional one. Why would you steal something you couldn't possibly turn into money?"

Why indeed?

"Someone else stole it," he said, "and killed one of my bodyguards in the process. Then he or someone else killed the other one. I've since replaced them."

With two men, I thought, whom we'd just met. One tall and wearing a turban. The other short, and, um, not wearing a turban.

"But how can I replace the Kloppmann Diamond? The thing's unique. It can't be replaced." His eyes held mine. "It can only be retrieved."

"Retrieved," I said.

"And that's where you come in, Rhodenbarr. I want to hire you. I want you to find out who has the diamond, and I want you to steal it, and I want you to return it to me."

"Just like that," I said.

"Just like that. Believe me, you'll be well paid."

Well, that was a load off my mind.

33

It was a good five hours later when I heard a familiar voice.

"Here he comes now," Maxine said.

She pointed at me—unnecessarily, I'd say, as the two people she was addressing had already turned to look at me. They were filling two chairs at what had become a table for three, and they looked glad to see me. Relieved, even.

"Carolyn," I said. "Ray." I took the available chair and told Maxine I'd have a beer. She named three brands, and I told her to surprise me.

"A beer," Carolyn said. "When did you ever order a beer?"

"Just now."

"No kidding. And when's the last time before that?"

"Oh, I don't know. An hour ago, maybe an hour and a half, and it was one of two that I had this afternoon, so the one I just ordered will be my third. But I think that'll be all right, as I don't plan on driving or operating machinery. Ray, what are you doing here, and what's that you're drinking?"

He said it was a Cosmopolitan, and it looked the part, filling a stemmed glass, garnished with a lime wheel, and blushing like a martini with an embarrassing secret.

"In a sensible universe," I said, "you'd be the one having the beer, but never mind. Oh, thanks, Maxine."

She'd brought me a bottle of Amstel and a glass, and I poured and sipped. Ray asked me if I was okay.

"Last I checked," I said, "I was fine. Why?"

"I was a little worried about you," he said. "I went over to your store. Middle of the afternoon, and the lights were out and the door was locked."

"I opened up when I got back from lunch," I said, "and I got two or three phone calls and sold about that many books, and then I said the hell with it and closed for the day. That's something you get to do when you own the joint."

"You left the bargain table out on the sidewalk."

"So?"

"And the sign that used to say five bucks a book, three for ten dollars? All that was crossed out, and somebody had changed it to 'All Books Free, Help Yourself!'"

"I probably should have made that 'Help Yourselves,'" I said. "Or maybe not. I'm addressing each reader individually, not collectively, so—"

"You own the store," he said, "and all the books in it, so nobody's questionin' your right to run the business any way you want. But you got to admit it's unusual."

"So?"

"So where'd you go, Bernie?"

I took a moment, and a sip of beer. "Well, it's no big deal," I said. "I've been feeling a little confused lately, you know? There's so much going on, and such a tremendous amount of sense that nothing makes."

"Including that last sentence," Carolyn put in.

"So what I wanted to do," I said, "was clear my head. I enjoy running a bookstore, I really do, but it's all mental, all things to think about and people with questions. And the phone ringing, and more questions. I wanted something physical."

Ray nodded. "You went for a long walk," he said.

"A short walk."

"Oh."

"Just half a block, really. I went bowling."

"Bowling," Ray said.

"Right."

"Around the corner at Bowl-Mor?"

"Where else?"

"Some years back," he said, "I used to bowl once a week. I was on a team, and the league was all cops and firemen."

"Did you enjoy it?"

"The bowling part," he said, "was somethin' I could take or leave. The fellowship, that was okay. How often do you get the chance to see cops and firemen and they aren't wishin' they could kill each other? And that explains the two beers you had, because what else do you do at a bowlin' alley?"

"It's no place for a Cosmopolitan."

"But you went there all by yourself, Bernie. Or were you meetin' somebody there?"

"No, I was alone."

"A grown man," he said, "all by his lonesome in the middle of the afternoon, tryin' to keep the ball out of the gutter, and maybe even knock down some pins. Did you keep score?"

"Of course I kept score."

"Did you cheat?"

"Did I cheat? Why on earth—"

"Just yankin' your chain, Bernie. Why'd you make the books free?"

"The books? Oh, on the bargain table." I shrugged. "I didn't want to haul it inside."

"You had to save your strength for Bowl-Mor."

"And if some of the books disappeared, well, I was okay with that. And if I changed the sign and made the books free—"

"Nobody would feel guilty," Carolyn said.

"Exactly."

"Well, if there was ever anything you'd know about," Ray said, "it's takin' other people's goods without feelin' guilty. You're a master at it."

I gave him a look.

"So maybe this is your way of givin' back, Bernie, and with a gift that keeps on givin'. How's it go, anyway? 'Give a man a fish and you feed him for a day. Teach him to steal a fish—'"

I sipped my beer. It was okay, but would never be my first choice for a drink to signal the welcome end of the workday. Still, it could have been worse. I could have been holding a stemmed cocktail glass and sipping a Cosmopolitan.

Ray had shifted conversational gears, but only slightly. He was going on about his early days in the NYPD, and the efforts of an old-time Hell's Kitchen gang to unload a van's worth of stolen carp and whitefish. "You can say a television set fell off a truck," he said, "but it's harder to make that case for a flounder. And if it takes you a month to move those hot TVs, well, you're in no rush, are you? But with the fish—"

I told him I got the picture.

"It's not so much a picture," he said, "as it is an aroma. Speakin' of things that don't smell right, I can't help thinking' about the Kloppmann Diamond, which I know you didn't steal, and those little green guys, which I know you did."

My first thought was of extraterrestrials, but of course he meant Mr. Margate's jade figurines. I'd have denied responsibility, but why bother?

"And it's not just a couple of burglaries," he went on. "There's two dead muscleheads, Stumblebum and Stumblebee, one in a penthouse and the other in a bookstore and each with three bullets in him. If we could clear up those homicides, it'd take a lot of the heat off."

"And I suppose that's a consummation devoutly to be wished."

"We'd be doin' our parts in the fight against global warming, Bernie. Be a feather in both our caps."

"That's what I was thinking earlier," I said, "though I can't recall that climate change entered into the equation. One thing about bowling, it frees the mind to wander off in other directions."

"Like a bowling ball," Carolyn said. "Before it winds up in the gutter."

I said, "What day is it? Wednesday?"

"Try Tuesday, Bern."

"Tuesday," I said. It seemed to me that we'd already had one Tuesday that week, but I couldn't swear to it. "Okay, give me a minute."

I found a pen, and started scribbling on the paper placemat. When I was done, Ray had a look.

"Names," he said. "Some I know and some I don't. Who the hell is Peter-Peter?"

"A notorious consumer of pumpkins," I said. "I'll explain

who everybody is, and I have some phone numbers, along with a few ideas on how you can round them up."

"Round 'em up? Why would I do that?" He thought for a moment and his eyes widened. "Well, I'll be damned," he said. "You're gonna do it, aren't you? You're actually gonna do it."

"Well—"

"Same old Bernie. Life hands you a lemon and you pull a rabbit out of it."

"No guarantees this time, Ray."

"That's what you always say, and you never fail to come up with that rabbit. I suppose you want to do this at your store, right?"

"That's what I was thinking."

"Might as well stay with the tried and true. When do you want to do this?"

"Today's Tuesday," I said.

Carolyn: "We established that, Bern."

"I was just making sure. I'd say Thursday, the day after tomorrow, because you want to strike while the iron is hot." I tapped the sheet of paper. "But some of these people may be hard to find, plus there are things I have to do before showtime."

"And most of them," Ray said, "are probably things I don't want to know about."

"Monday would give us both plenty of time," I went on, "to look before we leap. But a lot can happen in five days."

The table buzzed with clichés. *Haste makes waste. There's no time like the present. Time takes time. He who hesitates is lost.*

"One if by land," I said, "and hook if by crook. We'll do it Saturday. Early evening, say half past six. At Barnegat Books."

"You're gonna do it," Ray said. "I don't know how I'm gonna

get my hands on all these people, but that's nothin' compared to what you're gonna do. You're gonna make heads and tails out of all of this, and when all is said and done—"

"There'll be nothing left to say or do," Carolyn said.

"You said it, Shorty. When all is said and done, Bernie here's gonna be standin' in front of everybody with a squeezed-up lemon in one hand and a rabbit in the other. You'll pull it off, Bernie, and I got no idea how the hell you're gonna do it."

"What he's got," Carolyn said, "is faith."

"I guess."

"In you, Bern. And it's not hard to understand why. How many times has Ray rounded up the unusual suspects and lined them all up at Barnegat Books?"

"I guess it's been a few times over the years."

"More than a few times, and more than a few years. It's been a whole pattern in your life."

"If you say so."

"In your life and mine, Bern. You know, if you look at it a certain way—"

"If you look at what?"

"Our lives," she said. "Yours and mine. If you step back and take the long view and look at our lives."

We'd been stepping forward, not back, walking west along certain half-deserted streets on our way to Arbor Court. And now we weren't stepping at all, because we'd stopped for slices of pizza at a hole in the wall on Carmine Street.

"The long view," I said.

"Right."

"Of our lives."

"Uh-huh. On the one hand you're a burglar, you've got mixed feelings about it but it's something you've been doing pretty much all your adult life. And at the same time you're a literate guy and you like to read and have people around, so you've got this bookstore."

"And?"

"And that's your life, stealing things and running a bookshop. And I wash dogs for a living, and when I'm not doing that I'm bouncing around the dyke bars. The bouncing's been limited now that lesbian bars are on the endangered species list, and I'm not as bouncy as when I was younger, but I can still get back and forth between Henrietta's and the Cubby, and I probably drink too much, but doesn't everybody?"

"Just about. And that's your life?"

A nod. "And we both of us have our relationships, falling in lust with unsuitable partners and breaking up and starting over. And we're best friends, and we spend a lot of time together, and I'd be lost without you, Bern, and I like to think you'd be lost without me."

"Utterly."

"Those are our lives," she said, "and I'd say that makes us pretty lucky, both of us. But there's another way of looking at it."

"There is?"

"Uh-huh." She looked at her empty plate. "You know, this pizza's not bad. I don't know if it's as good as Two Boots, but it's got one great advantage. It exists, and Two Boots—"

"Is out of this world."

"Literally, now that the Duchess is back in business. Bern, part of me wants another slice, and part of me thinks I'm full."

"We could split one."

"Perfect," she said. "Brilliant."

And, after the slice of pizza arrived: "So what's the other way?"

"What other way, Bern?"

"Of looking at our lives. You were saying—"

"Oh, right. Well, looking at it a certain way, you're sort of a real-life fictional character."

"I am?"

"I guess we both are, but especially you. Like if you were in a book, you'd be a series character."

"Wouldn't I have to be in a whole series of books?"

She nodded. "Mysteries. Because you have this whole life, like I was saying, but if you just focus on certain episodes in your life, you're a detective."

"A detective? What, like Sam Spade?"

"No, not like him."

"Good, because he was only in one book, and if you're putting me in a whole series—"

"You'd be more of an amateur sleuth, Bern. You sell a few books, you break into a couple of houses. You live your life, you meet a girl and go to the movies, you drink scotch except when you drink Perrier—"

"Or beer, if I happen to be wearing bowling shoes."

"Whatever. You live your life and mind your own business, and every now and then you get in a jam and there's a dead body and it's up to you to do something about it."

"We're back to Sam Spade," I said. "'When your partner gets killed, you're supposed to do something about it.'"

"Sometimes the police think you did it, and you find the real killer in order to get out from under suspicion. Or you'll have some other reason to get involved. But there's a reason

Ray expects you to pick a murderer out of a hat, and that's because he's watched you do it so many times before."

I frowned. "It's not really something I do," I said. "It's something that happens."

"Repeatedly, Bern."

"But sometimes years go by," I said. "Yes, there have been incidents, a handful of them over the years—"

"It's gotta be ten or a dozen times, Bern."

"That many?"

"I could tick them off."

"You'd be ticking me off in the process. Ten times?"

"I bet it's more like a dozen."

"So this series could be ten or twelve books long."

"With each book centered on a time when you were playing detective."

"And the rest of my life, the great majority of my time, when I'm just out there doing what I do—"

"Nobody'd know about it, Bern. Because there'd be no reason to write about what you were doing between books."

The subject changed, and not a moment too soon. We headed for Arbor Court, and don't ask me what we were talking about, because my head was still in the earlier conversation. Something was troubling me, and I couldn't pin it down.

While we waited for a light to change, I said, "An amateur sleuth."

"Huh?"

"It's that word," I said. "As an antiquarian bookseller, I'm a professional. I haven't been hugely successful at it, but it's a field where keeping the doors open and the lights on is success enough."

"And?"

"I take a certain amount of pride in that. And I'm a professional burglar, too, and if I'm not completely proud of that, I give myself credit for being a cut above the clowns who kick doors in."

"So the idea of being an amateur sleuth—"

"Rankles," I said. "Makes me sound like a dabbler, a dilettante, an idler."

"I get it, Bern. But I don't know what else you would call it."

"There ought to be something."

"Maybe an extra word would take the sting out. 'A master amateur sleuth.' How's that?"

"Better, but—"

"'A virtuoso performer in the world of amateur sleuthery.'"

"I guess," I said. "I may be overthinking this."

34

At Arbor Court, with the cats fed and tea made, she said, "Bowling."

"I had to get away from the bookstore," I said, "and there were things I needed to do, but I wasn't ready to do them yet. And every once in a while for the past few years I've told myself that I really ought to go over to Bowl-Mor, and I never did, and then the building came down and all I had left was a resentment."

"'It was my bowling alley, and those heartless bastards knocked it down.'"

"Something like that, along with some guilt at having missed my chance. And now the universe was handing me a second chance."

"The new universe."

"Right, and how would I feel if I let it slip out of my grasp?"

"It might wind up in the gutter. So how'd it go?"

"It was okay," I said. "Once I got past the fact that I was wearing shoes that had been worn by hundreds of people before me, I managed to get into it."

"Were you any good?"

"No, but that wasn't the point. I kept score, but only because that's what you do. I think my worst game was around 120 and my best was something like thirty points higher."

"Three hundred is perfect, right? So half of that would be—"

"Mediocre at best," I said, "but I didn't care about the score. It was more of a meditation."

"I've heard of a walking meditation, Bern. I don't suppose a bowling meditation is too much of a stretch."

"The bowling was what my body was doing," I said, "while my mind was doing something else."

"And it worked, didn't it?"

"Well—"

"It must have worked, because as soon as you got your own shoes on again you hurried over to the Bum Rap and told Ray it was game on. So I guess that means you've got everything figured out."

I gave her a look.

"You don't?"

"What I figured out, or maybe I should say what dawned on me, is that there's nothing to figure out."

"Huh?"

"There are enigmas," I said. "There are elements that need to be figured out, but they're not going to be figure-outable."

"Is that a word?"

"Not in the real world."

"The real world."

Her words, an echo to mine, seemed to hang in the air, and we both sat up and listened to them.

"Bern, you're saying this world we're in right now isn't real."

"It is and it isn't."

"It feels real," she said, "and it doesn't, both at the same time, so I sort of know what you mean. We're right here now, aren't we? We're not holograms of ourselves and this isn't going to turn out to be some horseshit dream."

"We're here," I said, "and we're not dreaming."

"That's good," she said, "because that was the one thing that pissed me off royally about *Alice in Wonderland.* At the end, where she wakes up and her sister tells her it was all a dream. I was five or six years old when my father read me the Alice books, and even at that age I knew Lewis Carroll was copping out."

"You're still mad at him, aren't you?"

"You're damn right I am. Wonderland was real. What's the matter? Did I say something?"

"The Alice books. That's where they came from."

"It's where who came from?"

"I didn't pick up on it at the time, but Ray already rang that bell for me."

"What bell?"

"And I heard it, but I wasn't paying attention." I was on my feet, pacing. "What was it he called them? 'Stumblebum and Stumblebee?'"

"Oh, the bodyguards."

"First they were the bodyguards," I said, "and then they were the bodies. And who were the two brothers Alice ran into in Wonderland?"

"Tweedledum and Tweedledee," she said, "but that wasn't in Wonderland, Bern. She met them in the second book, *Through the Looking Glass,* so that would have been in Looking Glass Land."

"Spawned in the fertile mind of Charles Lutwidge Dodgson—"

"Alias Lewis Carroll."

"—and right at home in our brave new world, except they didn't get to enjoy it for very long. Look at their names, will you? They were straight out of Central Europe by way of Central Casting, and they should have had names appropriate to their origins—"

"Horvath," she suggested.

"—but instead they were Jason Dilbert and Mason Philbert."

"I think it was the other way around, Bern."

"What difference does it make? I went to sleep reading *What Mad Universe*, and I woke up a bench press away from Tweedledum and Tweedledee. Now they're both dead and I'm supposed to figure out who killed them, but I'm not sure anybody cares. You saw what an impression their deaths made on the man whose body they were guarding."

"He said he'd replaced them."

"Like a couple of burnt-out light bulbs, as opposed to the irreplaceable Kloppmann Diamond. And did you get a load of the pair he found to fill the shoes of Dum and Dee?"

"They were quite a pair."

"A Sikh who was tall enough for the NBA, even without the turban. And his silent partner, wrapped in a cloak of ninja invisibility."

"They looked familiar, Bern."

"I had the same thought. But did you ever see either of them before?"

"I don't think so."

"Mr. Tall and Mr. Small, together again for the first time."

"They looked as though they belonged together," she said. "Like if you saw one you'd expect to see the other."

I told her we could expect to see them both on Saturday.

* * *

That got us back to Tweedledum and Tweedledee, and Carolyn decided she wanted to refresh her memory of the boys—not Vandenbrinck's twosome, but Lewis Carroll's. Some years back a small library I'd purchased had included a Cadwallader Club limited edition of the two Alice books, bound in red leather with gold stamping. John Tenniel's illustrations are the ones everybody knows, but the Cadwallader edition featured two dozen dazzling color plates by Michael Trossman.

I never did get around to shelving the books, because I couldn't figure out a price, and then Carolyn had a birthday coming up and that settled that. And now she curled up on the couch with *Through the Looking Glass* while I had another go at *The Screaming Mimi.*

If you want something badly enough, you'll get it.

Right.

35

When I got to the bookshop Wednesday morning, my bargain table was still right where I'd left it. Only a single book remained, and I wish I could tell you it was Abbie Hoffman's *Steal This Book,* but would you believe me if I did?

I didn't think so.

I fed Raffles, then left the door locked and the lights off and spent the rest of the morning in the back room. I shifted a bookcase and accessed my designated hiding place, making deposits and withdrawals and generally taking inventory.

It was odd. All my life, I've never felt more at home than when I'm all by myself in somebody else's house or apartment, wholly caught up in the commission of a felony. And now I was in my own store and felt for all the world like a trespasser.

I told myself to get over it, and while the sensation lingered, it didn't keep me from doing what I was there to do. I spent most of my time at my desk, on the phone or the computer or both. Amazon and eBay were nowhere to be found. (Yes, I checked, even as I'd greeted the dawn by looking for my orange and blue Metrocard and finding instead—with a mix of relief and disappointment—my green and white SubwayCard.) But Google and Wikipedia were both alive and well, thank God, and I'd never been more grateful for their existence.

Online, I walked up one virtual street and down another

in the comforting anonymity the medium affords. You may recall the cartoon of a hound at a computer: "On the Internet, nobody knows you're a dog." I'm sure I left cyber-paw prints all over the place, one always does, but that prospect was way down on my list of Things to Worry About.

I spent the whole day in my office. I'd told Carolyn we'd be on our own for lunch, and I wound up missing that meal altogether. I never did open for business, so all I had to do when I left was put out dry food and fresh water for Raffles and lock up after myself.

By then it would have been time to meet Carolyn at the Bum Rap. My body found the idea of a drink very appealing, but my plans for the evening limited me to Perrier, and I didn't want to spend the next hour or so in conversation, not even with my best friend. I had things to do.

"'*Let us then be up and doing,*'" I said. I spoke the words aloud, because I'd had only myself for company all day, and sooner or later a stretch of solitude will have me talking to myself.

I walked along, trying to pull the rest of Longfellow's quatrain out of my memory. I got the next line, *With a heart for any fate,* but then I came up empty. I kept trying, saying the first two lines over and over, and there was a time when an otherwise unexceptional fellow declaiming to himself in trochaic tetrameter might have had people glancing at him, or pointedly *not* glancing at him, but times had changed, and no one took any apparent notice of me.

Because what do you think when you see a man in animated conversation with an invisible friend? That the city's really becoming overrun with ambulatory psychotics? That the last thing you want to do is make eye contact with this joker, and might it not be a good idea to, um, cross the street?

Not at all. You assume he's on a hands-free cell phone.

I took the subway here and there, and a cab or two as well, and sometime a couple of hours after midnight I put an actual key in a lock and opened a door without committing a felony. It was my own apartment on West End Avenue, and I had to remind myself that I had every right to be there.

I needed a shower, and had one. I needed a sandwich, and made myself one. I got in bed and stretched out and closed my eyes, and after a few minutes I sat up and opened them.

And got out of bed, and got dressed, and caught a cab downtown.

That was Wednesday, and the next few days weren't all that different. I got around a lot, sometimes on foot, more often by cab or subway. I had to remind myself to eat and sleep, but I managed to do enough of both to get through the days and nights.

And then it got to be Saturday.

I was in the Zone, that magical Eden of effortless concentration, wherein all one's attention is precisely focused and productively directed. A sunbeam thus mobilized through a magnifying glass will start a fire, and I felt just that sort of warmth building within me, and the gaze I fixed on a spot sixty feet away was just that perfectly aimed, and—

And my phone rang.

"Hell," I said aloud, and put down what I was holding, and dug my phone from my pocket, and saw who it was. "I'd better take this call," I announced, and while there were people around, I don't know that anyone was actually within earshot.

"You're talking to yourself again," I told myself, and pressed the button and took the call.

Ray Kirschmann said, "There you are, Bernie."

"Here I am," I agreed.

"I came by the store," he said, "and it was darker than the inside of a cow, and locked up just as tight, and I figured you had to be in back. So I called and the phone rang but you didn't pick up."

"I couldn't," I said, "because I wasn't there. I'm here."

"And where you are," he said, "is someplace noisier than any bookstore I ever been in. You in the subway, Bernie?"

"Close enough," I said.

"Well, hop on a train, will you? It took some doin', but I got everybody lined up, and at half past six they're all gonna start turnin' up at a certain bookstore we both know, and—"

"Carolyn has a key," I told him. "She'll help you open up. I may be a few minutes late."

It took a few more sentences to reassure him. I ended the call and retrieved my sixteen pound sphere of ebonite from the rack and resumed my original position.

That was easy enough. But could I get back in the Zone?

Three steps . . .

Release . . .

Impact . . . with my ball a little too flush on the head pin, the sort of placement that can leave the seven and ten pins standing in an unmakeable split.

But not this time. When you're in the Zone, the bowling

gods cut you some slack. Flush hit or no, all ten pins went flying.

Nice.

But for the evening's agenda, I'd have happily lingered at Bowl-Mor for hours—or as long as the Zone held me in its embrace. But I had people waiting, and more important concerns than strikes and spares. I paid up, put my own shoes on again, and walked to my store.

Where the whole world was waiting.

Well, not the whole world, but enough of its population to fill the available space. There was room for me behind the counter, but I paused on my way there to check out the crowd.

I saw Carolyn, of course, and Ray, and four police officers, two of them in uniform and the others no less identifiable for wearing plainclothes. I saw Orrin Vandenbrinck, bookended by his two bodyguards, the NBA-sized chap in the turban and his ninja-like companion. I recognized a florid-faced gentleman whom I'd never met, and a man who'd been wearing a Norfolk jacket the last time I'd seen him.

I saw Peter-Peter, and I saw two women who'd bought books from me, and—

Well, I saw a whole roomful of people.

I stopped at the counter, retrieved a thing or two from the shelf beneath it, found room for them in a pocket. I walked among my guests, bumping into this one and apologizing to that one, managing to keep a smile on my face, even for those souls who were glaring at me. I said things like "*Good to see you*" and "*Lovely evening*" and "*I had one grunch but the eggplant over there*," and it wasn't long before I was once again back behind the counter, seated on my stool.

Was I still smiling? Maybe, maybe not. What I do know is that my pocket was empty now.

Showtime.

A bell would have been nice. Or a wine glass, say, to tap with a spoon. Something to get their attention.

What I had was my Scotch Tape dispenser, and what I did was tap it against the side of my cash register. It wasn't quite the sound I might have wanted it to be, but it did the job. The conversations, none of them all that spirited, died in mid-sentence. Heads turned, and eyes met mine.

I didn't know what the hell to say to them. But I knew how to begin.

"Good evening," I said. "I suppose you're wondering why I summoned you all here."

36

And then I told them everything.

37

“If it wasn’t for the forty-seven things I gotta do,” Ray Kirschmann was saying, “what I’d do is take you an’ Shorty here over to Luger’s for a steak the size of a Cadillac hubcap and enough gin to float it. But—”

“But those forty-seven things take precedent.”

“It’s probably an even fifty, and I wish they didn’t, but they do. Next week for sure, Bernie. The best steak dinner in New York and it’s on me.”

I don’t know what the first item on his list might have been, but it probably involved escorting an unfortunate fellow down to Central Booking. Whatever it was, he went off to do it and left me and Carolyn otherwise unaccompanied.

She said, “Bern, did I hear that right? Did Ray Kirschmann actually offer to spring for dinner?”

“At Peter Luger’s,” I said.

“This is some universe. Did Ray ever pick up the tab for anything?”

“Not that I can recall.”

“I guess you really knocked his socks off, Bern, and I can understand why. You took all those people and all the crazy things that have happened and you made sense out of everything.”

“Sense,” I said.

"Although I have to admit I found some of it a little hard to follow."

"Some of it," I said.

"Yeah, you know. The details, and the way one thing led to another."

"Mostly," I said, "it didn't."

"Didn't what?"

"Lead to another. Most of the time, nothing led to anything."

"But—"

I took a breath. "In this universe," I said, "this brave new world of Bowl-Mor and SubwayCards, things don't make sense. They don't have to. There may be a certain logic that seems to operate, just as there is down the rabbit hole and on the other side of the looking glass, but there's nothing hard and fast about it."

"So when you laid it all out for them—"

"I was making it up as I went along. I'd laid the groundwork, that's what kept me so busy the past few days, and then when I said it, well, that made it true."

"It was true because you said it."

"Sort of true."

She thought it over, nodded slowly. "I think I get it," she said, "except for the part I don't. It's hard to wrap my mind around some of it."

"Probably impossible," I said. "It's hard for me, and I'm the one who made it up."

"But you'll explain it to me, Bern. At least you'll spell out what you told everybody."

"Sure," I said, "but maybe not right now."

"No, because right now I could possibly follow it. Even if there's nothing to follow. I mean—"

"I know what you mean."

"I'm glad one of us does. Bern, what do you want to do? And I hope it doesn't involve bowling."

"No more bowling."

"Do you want to go out for dinner? I'm not sure I'm hungry, but I could probably force myself. Though I'm definitely not up for a steak the size of a Cadillac hubcap."

"Neither am I."

"Is there something special about Cadillac hubcaps? Aren't all hubcaps the same size?"

"I think Ray just wanted to make it sound luxurious."

"What it sounds like to me," she said, "is way too much food. In fact any food at all sounds like too much food. Should we get a drink?"

"I suppose we could."

"At the Bum Rap? Or someplace fancier, to make it more of a celebration? Except I can't think of any place offhand, and the idea of the Bum Rap—"

"I know what you mean."

"So what do you think, Bern? What do you want to do?"

I looked into her eyes, and she looked into mine, and the question answered itself.

The cab driver not only knew where Arbor Court was. He also knew the quickest and most direct way to get there. There was, I had to admit, a thing or two I would miss about this new universe.

We were in a hurry, but not a mad adolescent frenzy. So

Archie and Ubi got fed, but they had to make do with dry food, because there was no time to waste opening cans.

Asterisk time.

* * *

"That was so . . ."

"Nice," I supplied.

"Okay. That fits. It was definitely nice." She laid a hand on my arm. "I was going to say sweet, and it was, but that wasn't the word I wanted."

"So many words."

"Bittersweet," she said.

"That'll work."

She propped herself up on an elbow. "I have the feeling," she said, "that we just did something for the very last time."

"I think you're right."

"When we wake up tomorrow morning, we'll be pumpkins."

"What's odd," I said, "is that I know what you mean. And yes, I think that's what's going to happen."

"Metrocards. Security cameras."

"Everything you'd find in the best of all possible worlds."

"You won't be able to go bowling."

"Or burgling. And you won't be able to go to Paula's."

"Or the Duchess, which I never did get inside of. And how many times did I go to Paula's? Once?"

"Really? Just the one time?"

"As if all I wanted to do was make sure it was there. And it was, but at the same time it wasn't. Do you know what I mean?"

"Um—"

"It's like someone commissioned a stage designer to recreate Paula's in her old spot on Greenwich Avenue," she said, "and the guy did a perfect job and got everything right, so that it looked real and felt real and even smelled real."

"But?"

"But the first thing you had to do was admire the guy's work, and if you're admiring it, well, that means you know it's a stage set."

"So it can't be real," I agreed. "This whole world's like that."

"It is, isn't it?"

"Probably not for the people who belong here. But we're just visitors, you and I."

"Strangers and afraid, in a world we never made. That's from a poem, isn't it?"

"More or less. But we're not exactly strangers."

"And not exactly afraid," she said. "And it's not a world we never made, because, duh, we're the ones who made it. Both of us, Bern."

I took a moment, nodded. "Paula's and the Duchess," I said.

"And Alice in Wonderland. Tweedledum and Tweedledee?"

"Oh, right."

"And Little Orphan Annie."

"Huh?"

"In the comics, Bern. And then on Broadway, the musical, but for me it was always the Harold Gray comic strip. Whenever I got my hands on the morning paper, that was the first thing I looked at. Sometimes the only thing. Don't tell me you don't remember Little Orphan Annie."

"Of course I do. Annie, who had empty circles for eyes."

"And?"

"And she used to say 'Leaping lizards,' and—"

"And her dog was Sandy, and do you remember what he said?"

"Arf."

"And?"

"And what? If he ever said anything but *Arf,* I must have missed it."

"Once you've said *Arf,*" she said, "you've pretty much said it all. Besides Sandy, Bern. Who else was in the strip?"

"Uh, I don't know. Daddy something. Daddy Warbucks?"

"Keep going, Bern."

"Keep going? Keep going where?"

"When you saw Daddy Warbucks, who else were you likely to see?"

"Oh."

"Well?"

"Punjab," I said.

"And?"

"And the Asp."

"There you go, Bern. Orrin Vandenbrinck started out with Dum and Dee for bodyguards, straight out of the Alice books, and when they got killed off who'd he replace them with? Punjab and the Asp, Daddy Warbucks's bodyguards for all those years."

I pictured the pair, the impossibly tall one in the turban, his silent and sinister companion.

"There's a definite resemblance," I allowed.

"A resemblance? You think that's all it is?"

"Well, the tall one's a Sikh," I said, "and there are a lot of tall Sikhs, and tall or short they all wear turbans—"

"And beards, Bern."

"And beards?"

"Check Wikipedia. That's what I did, a day or two ago when you were racing around town doing whatever you were doing. That's when it dawned on me that one of the ways I brought this world into being was by bringing Punjab and the Asp into it. Bern, hair is a big thing for a Sikh. If you want to be a Sikh in good standing, you never cut or shave any of your hair, not on your head or your face or your body."

"If you say so."

"But the dude in the turban who showed up at the Poodle Factory, and who was at Vandenbrinck's side a few hours ago at the bookstore—"

"Was clean-shaven."

"He could have stepped out of a Barbasol commercial. And if you happened to look at Punjab in a Little Orphan Annie comic strip—"

"You can do that online?"

"You can do anything online, Bern."

Anything that didn't involve Amazon or eBay. "And when Harold Gray drew Punjab—"

"No beard."

"You're positive?"

"Bern, I lived and breathed Little Orphan Annie. Trust me on this one."

I thought about it. "Okay," I said.

"Okay?"

"It would have to be your doing, that's all. I used to read the comic strip when I was a kid, but it never made that huge an impression on me. But we already established that you deserve credit for co-creating this universe."

"Credit or blame," she said. "Either way, this is a joint venture."

"Right."

"It took both of our imaginations to get us into this—"

"Mess?"

She gave me a look. "Situation," she said. "This joint venture. You made me take half the money, remember? From Abel?"

"Because we're partners."

"Sixteen thousand for you, sixteen thousand for me. And now there's just one thing more I need to make this partnership as even as Steven."

"What's that?"

"An explanation," she said. "You laid it all out for everybody at the bookshop, and most of them were quick enough to deny what you accused them of, but no one came up with the ultimate Alice objection."

"The ultimate Alice objection?"

"'*You're nothing but a pack of cards!*'"

"Oh."

"And I followed along, Bern, just like everybody else, and I don't know if you dazzled me with brilliance or baffled me with bullshit—"

"The latter, I suspect."

"—but either way the words got all wispy and floated away somewhere. Edgar Margate, for example."

"The jade collector."

""Rich Uncle Pennybags," she said. "That's who he looked like, the Monopoly Man. All he was missing was the monocle."

"And the bowler hat."

"He put his jade collection on display at the gallery on Lispenard, and arranged to have it stolen?"

"Right."

"But not by you."

"No."

"He wanted the insurance money, and he wanted to get it without giving up the jade figurines."

"Cash flow problems," I said. "Even a man who's the spitting image of Mr. Monopoly can have them. But what do you say we put this on Hold?"

"How's that, Bern?"

"I can explain," I said. "I can explain how Edgar Margate arranged to have his own collection stolen, and how the Kloppmann Diamond wound up in Peter-Peter's possession—"

"But it's not the real diamond, is it?"

"—and who killed Jason Philbert and Mason Dilbert—"

"Tweedledum and Tweedledee."

"—and everything else that's hard to understand. The reason it's hard to understand is it doesn't make any real sense, it's all Wonderland whimsy and Looking Glass logic, but I can explain it."

"I'm listening."

"But not tonight," I said. "Tonight I couldn't even put the words and thoughts together, and you couldn't take them in. But when we're back in our own universe—"

"The real world."

"Right."

"Although this world seems real enough," she said. "Except when it doesn't. And you think we'll be back where we started?"

"I think so."

"Tomorrow?"

"When we wake up," I said.

I was up and dressed at this point, and she sat on the edge of the bed and looked at me. "You're going somewhere," she said. "West End Avenue?"

"Right."

"You want to sleep in your own bed," she said, "in your own apartment."

"I think that would be the best way to handle it. This started when I finished *What Mad Universe* and dropped off to sleep." I patted my back pocket. "When I get home, I'll make myself a cup of chamomile tea and get in bed with *The Screaming Mimi*."

"Oh, you haven't finished it yet?"

"I've been kind of busy. And I decided I didn't want to finish, not just yet. So I've got a couple of pages to go."

"So you'll get in bed with the book."

"And the money," I said.

"The money?"

"The sixteen thousand from Abel. I don't know how it works when it comes to transporting something from one world to another, but I've been carrying around that wad of Benjamins all afternoon and evening, and I figure the best chance I'll have to hang on to them is if they're right there in the bed with me."

"Unless they turn into a Metrocard."

"As I said, I don't know how these things work, but I'll find out when I wake up. And you ought to do the same. Your share's in your stash, right?"

"Last I looked."

"Get it out," I said, "and sleep with it."

"Jesus, I'll feel like Scrooge McDuck. But okay, it's a good idea. I think."

"You'll know in the morning."

* * *

When I had one foot out the door, she asked if God was right.

"God's always right," I said. "It's part of his job description."

"In the book, Bern. *The Screaming Mimi.* Godfrey, the old drunk everybody calls God?"

"Oh."

"Didn't he maintain that if you want something badly enough you'll get it? Well, are you close enough to the end to know if he's right about that?"

"The deck's stacked in God's favor," I said, "because if you don't get it, then by definition you didn't want it badly enough. But there's a kicker."

"Wouldn't you know it?"

"If you want it badly enough," I said, "you'll get it. But it won't make you happy."

"Oh, wow. I'll have to think about that. Bern? Get home safe."

"I'll walk to the corner," I said, "and within twenty seconds a cab will pull up. I have to admit it, there are things about this universe I'm going to miss."

38

A shower, first.

Then a sandwich, peanut butter and jelly. And then, finally, chamomile tea and *The Screaming Mimi.* I turned the last page, read the last line, made sure the envelope and its $16,000 was tucked under my pillow, and reached to switch off the light.

And after all that, I told myself, *you won't be able to fall asleep.*

Shows what I know.

When I opened my eyes, I was eight hours older and surprisingly eager to meet the day. The first thing I checked was the envelope, still under the pillow and still stuffed full of hundred-dollar bills. The next thing I checked was my wallet, and what I found was what I'd expected to find—a Metrocard.

I didn't waste too much time examining it. It was a bright and brisk Friday morning, and a few miles to the south I had a store that needed to be open and a cat who needed to be fed. I put on fresh clothes, picked out a tie, slipped the envelope of cash into my blazer's inside pocket, and went out to greet the day.

In the elevator, I smiled at the camera. I was almost glad to see it.

*   *   *

A few hours later I was at the Poodle Factory, dishing out Laotian food. "I had this dream," I told Carolyn. "I was on a bus."

"That's how I got here this morning, Bern. The M10 crosstown."

"This one was in some other city. Possibly Tucson."

"Tucson?"

"It could have been Tucson. I'm sort of inferring, because I know that's where Fredric Brown spent his later years."

"Fredric Brown? Our Fredric Brown?"

"We were on the bus together."

"You and Fredric Brown."

"Right."

"On a bus in Tucson."

"When he was trying to work out a plot," I said, "he would ride buses all night, and thoughts would come to him."

"I'll bet they would. 'Why am I up so late? What am I doing on this broken-down rattletrap?'"

"Thoughts about the plot," I said. "Look, I read this somewhere years ago, I don't even know if it's true. Maybe it was just something he told some pest who asked him where he got his weird ideas. But it stuck in my mind, and there we were in the dream, up all night on the bus."

"In Tucson. Do they even have buses there?"

"They have buses everywhere, don't they?"

"But at that hour? Does a Tucson bus run all night long?"

"Doo-dah," I said. "We may have been the only two people on the bus, aside from the driver. And Brown did all the talking."

"What did he say?"

"I can't remember."

"That's great, Bern."

"It was a dream, dammit. Everything he said was interesting, but nothing would stick. He'd say the sentence and I'd take it in and then it would be gone."

"So you sat up all night with one of your all-time favorite writers and you can't remember a single thing he said?"

"There was one thing."

"Oh?"

"He stopped in mid-sentence," I remembered, "and took hold of my shoulder. He was this meek-looking little guy, but his eyes were very intense, and they bored into mine. And he said, 'There's just one thing I have to tell you, and if you forget everything else, make damn sure you remember this.'"

"And?"

"And then he just sighed, and shook his head, and moved his hand as if to wave the world away. 'Never mind,' he told me. 'It's not important.'"

"'Never mind?'"

"Right."

"'It's not important?'"

"Right."

We turned our attention back to what was on our plates. She said she didn't think much of my dream, and I admitted I wasn't proud of it myself.

"But it got me through the night," I said, "and we're here eating a tasty lunch from Two Guys."

"And the two guys are from Luang Prabang again."

"Oh, right. In the other world, the restaurant's ethnicity kept changing."

"It keeps changing here, too, Bern. But it takes a more reasonable amount of time to do it. I'm sure the clock's ticking for the two Laotian guys, but in the meantime we can have some good lunches."

"In this best of all possible worlds."

She nodded. "Bern? How come you're here?"

"Huh? I don't know. Wasn't it my turn to bring lunch?"

"I think it may have been mine."

"Oh."

"But I'm not talking about lunch and whose turn it was. Look, I got up this morning and I thought, well, time to head east for a long day of washing dogs."

"And here you are."

"And here I am. And you got up this morning and thought, well, time to feed the cat and drag the bargain table outside."

"Actually," I said, "what I thought was maybe it was time to retire the bargain table altogether. But I came down and opened up, and before I knew it I'd schlepped the thing out there. And just as well, because it was my only sale of the morning, and—"

"Bern."

"What?"

"We both did what we did because we knew what day it was."

"Thursday," I said.

"Right."

"So?"

"And last night was—?"

"Is there a point to this? Last night was . . ."

We looked at each other. You could have heard a chopstick drop.

"Oh," I said.

"Uh-huh."

"Last night was Saturday night, and I went to sleep and woke up on Thursday morning."

"Uh-huh."

"How is that possible?"

"I was hoping you could tell me, Bern."

We went on eating, and I thought about it, and we finished eating, and I went on thinking about it.

And eventually I said, "Okay, I see what happened."

"So do I, but I can't make sense out of it. We went to another world, and I don't know how much time we spent in it, but it was more than a week, and now we're back where we started and it's the same time it was when we left. There's probably a better way to put it—"

"There would almost have to be," I said, "but what you said will have to do for now. We stepped back into this world and found it unchanged. The neighborhood's the same, the security cameras are the same, and even the clocks and the calendars are the same."

She frowned. "This isn't some Alice in Wonderland crap, is it? If this all turns out to have been some horseshit dream—"

"No, it happened."

"But did it? I went to Paula's, you went bowling, we both went up to Abel's apartment—"

"It all happened."

I took the envelope from my jacket pocket.

"Oh."

"I put it under my pillow last night," I said.

"That's what I did with mine. Then I closed my eyes and thought about the Tooth Fairy, and the next thing I knew it was morning."

"And the Tooth Fairy—"

"Must have given me a pass," she said, "because I still had my envelope. And I checked, and it was chockful of hundreds."

"Just like mine," I said, "A person can dream about money, but if it's there when you wake up—"

"Then it wasn't a dream."

And so on. I'd figured on spending most of the lunch hour going over what I'd told to the assembled company in the bookstore, laying it out for Carolyn as best I could. But we never got there. About all we could do, besides admiring the culinary arts of Luang Prabang, was work at getting our minds around the fact that we'd gone to sleep on a Saturday night only to wake up nine or ten days earlier.

Nine or ten days, because I think our week away had had an extra Tuesday in it. I can't be absolutely certain of this, but—

Never mind.

Anyway, since no time had passed in what we found ourselves calling the real world, that explained why nothing had changed. How could it? It hadn't had time.

Even without an explanation of Edgar Margate's master plan and Peter-Peter's perfidy and all the other loose ends, lunch ran a little past its allotted hour. You'd have thought I might have had people lined up outside Barnegat Books, but I was back in the world of eBay and Amazon, and nobody was waiting. A few souls found their way in and out of the store during the course of the afternoon, but my only cash customer was Mowgli, who loaded up on poor old Jeffrey Farnol, including his 1931 novel, *A Jade of Destiny*.

39

"Talk about mixed emotions," I told Carolyn. "I didn't know whether to be glad to kiss it goodbye or sorry to see it go. It's amazing it was there to begin with. I had one woman buy me out of Jeffrey Farnol and then there was Katrina, dropping hints by scooping up everything with *jade* in the title."

"Katrina?"

"The closest she came to telling me her name," I said, "was when she said it was Jade, which seemed unlikely. It turns out her first name was Katrina and her last name was Beckwith, and you'll never guess where she worked."

"If you tell me, Bern, I won't have to."

"The Ginseng Gallery," I said, "on Lispenard Street."

"Where Edgar Margate put his jade collection on exhibit."

I started to say something, then broke it off when Maxine approached with our drinks. We were at the Bum Rap, you won't be surprised to learn, and this was our second round, and there was scotch in both of our glasses.

"Okay," she said. "You talk. I'll listen."

I said, "That's where they met, Edgar Margate and Katrina Beckwith. She'd come to New York to be an actress, and wound up as a sort of utility infielder on Lispenard Street. Margate dropped in one afternoon to see if anything caught his eye, and that's just what Katrina did. They had a meet-cute conversation out of a Nora Ephron screenplay, and he came back the next day and took her out to dinner, and she took him home to her apartment.

"Which doesn't sound like a big deal, because married businessmen like Margate and sweet young things like Beckwith fall into each other's arms all the time. Except Margate had been a faithful husband until he wound up in Beckwith's bed, and while she'd led a reasonably active life herself, she'd never fallen for anybody the way she fell for Margate.

"He wanted to stay married, and she was fine with that, and he also wanted to take care of her, and she was fine with that part as well. Margate wanted to move her to a nicer apartment, and he wanted to be able to take her places and buy her things, and he wanted to do all this without slighting his wife and kids. And there's a lot to be said for having your cake and eating it too, but it only works if you can afford to pay the baker.

"Or suppose you can find somebody else to cover the baker's bill? Like, say, an insurance company?

"Margate had put together an exceptional collection of jade figurines over the years, and had in fact bought one or two of them from Mr. Ginseng—and no, that's not the owner's name, which I've only heard from Ray Kirschmann, and he said it differently every time, like he was reading it off the menu at Shung Lee Dynasty.

"Never mind.

"The jade collection was a valuable asset of Margate's. He'd spent a fair amount of money on it, just under six figures. It was sort of covered by a rider on his homeowner's policy, but he wasn't really worried about theft and didn't want to pay a ton in premiums, so if the collection disappeared he'd be lucky to get half of what he'd paid for it, and he might have to go to court to realize that much.

"But if Margate put his jade on display at Ginseng Gallery, it would be covered by their insurance. And he could declare an inflated value, and the gallery would sign off on his estimate, because the higher the value the more people would want to come to the gallery to look at it. And the premium wouldn't bankrupt them, because the coverage they'd be paying for would be limited to the actual time the collection was in the gallery's possession, which would be what, a couple of weeks? Maybe a month?

"It wasn't difficult to arrange. The Edgar W. Margate jade collection went on display at Ginseng Gallery, officially valued for insurance purposes at an optimistic half million dollars. Its owner was already ahead of the game; the high valuation and the attendant publicity so positioned his collection that, if he had to sell it, he'd net two or three times what he could have expected a month ago.

"But why not grab the brass ring—or the jade bell-pull, if you prefer. Margate couldn't steal his own collection, and Beckwith couldn't steal it for him; they'd been circumspect about their affair, and there was no reason to think anyone at Ginseng Gallery knew about it, but they couldn't afford to take chances, not with a sky-high insurance payout on the line. What they needed to stage was a professional burglary, and that called for a professional burglar.

"Fortunately, Katrina Beckwith knew just where to turn."

"And that's where you came in, Bern. Right?"

"It's where I came in," I acknowledged, "but not where she turned. She didn't know me, not as a burglar and not even as a bookseller. The only burglar she knew was a courtly and well-mannered fellow named Byron Fleegler."

"That's an unusual name."

"And it took me a while to learn it. He never supplied it, or an alias either. The vacant apartment he sent me to had been occupied by a professor named Rubisham, but that wasn't our boy's name. Neither were Norfolk or Armagnac."

"He wore a belted Norfolk jacket," she remembered. "And he was going to pour you a glass of very old Armagnac."

"And this was supposed to happen when I met him to examine a library that didn't exist in an apartment that wasn't his. He was never a professor himself, although he'd played one once in an off-off-Broadway production of *If Winter Comes.* He was an actor, and he and Katrina ran into each other at auditions."

"And they had a romance?"

I shook my head. "Byron's gay."

"So am I, Bern. But in that universe people don't necessarily behave the way you'd expect them to."

"Byron and Katrina were friends," I said, "and that's all. And in the course of their friendship he let her in on his secret."

"He was a professor? No, because he wasn't. Oh, he told her he was a burglar?"

"That's how he made ends meet. He seemed both proud and ashamed of it, and she wasn't entirely sure whether to believe him, but it stuck in her mind, and when she and Margate needed a burglar, she gave Byron a call and met him for a drink."

"And he broke into the gallery and stole the Margate collection," she said. "Except he didn't."

"He never got the chance," I said. "I beat him to it."

* * *

Not that I remembered it. When I woke up in that alternate universe, I had everything that another Bernie Rhodenbarr had had—an apartment, a bookstore, a tailless cat. What I didn't possess were his memories. I might have a batch of jade carvings stowed in a secret compartment in my store's back room, but I couldn't have told you how they got there.

"I don't know how Margate's collection got my attention," I said, "or why I thought it would be better off in my hands than in Mr. Margate's. I don't suppose I'll ever know, and it hardly matters. Because, before Byron Fleegler got around to making his move, I evidently made mine.

"I wish I could remember it, because I was evidently impeccably professional about the whole thing. I got in and got out without drawing any attention or doing any damage. I took Margate's jade and left everything else in the gallery untouched. It would have been the kind of memory that would warm a burglar's heart in his old age, but all I can do is imagine it.

"And, ironically, I seem to have been the only person involved who didn't know the break-in and theft was my doing. Ray Kirschmann knew in a heartbeat, and Fleegler evidently came to the same conclusion; when Katrina congratulated him on pulling off the burglary, he had to tell her it wasn't him—but that he was pretty sure who deserved the blame.

"Or the credit. Margate was in a curious position. He was in line for an insurance payout that would amount to something like five or six times what he could have hoped to net from a Sotheby's auction. He'd eat the cake and make a good meal of it, but the downside was he wouldn't have it. And, remember, he really liked those carvings.

"Still, with half a million dollars he could find something else to collect. But that didn't mean he didn't have a problem. Because whoever the man was who'd actually stolen the collection hadn't done so in order to display them on his fireplace mantel. This opportunistic thief, this Rhodenbarr character, was evidently a pro. When he stole something, he wanted to turn it into cash."

"Unless it's the Mondrian painting he's got hanging on his wall."

I let that pass. "What, he had to wonder, was I going to do with his collection? It's not like gold or jewelry, you can't melt it down or break it up. If I wanted to sell it, where could I turn?"

"I don't know, Bern. Abel Crowe?"

"Abel would have admired the figures," I said, "and said complimentary things about the artisans who'd carved them, but he would have seen only one way to turn a profit on them, and he'd have probably suggested I cut out the middleman and do it myself."

"Do what?"

"Sell them back to the insurance company. That's tricky to negotiate, because an insurance company that deals with thieves is encouraging theft, and they all insist they'd never do that. But if you're in the business, and your choice is to pay half a million to the original owner or a tenth of that to a burglar—"

"Is that what you'd get, Bern? Fifty thousand?"

"I'd probably have to use a go-between," I said. "Probably an attorney, and not from a white-shoe firm. He'd have to be lucky to get fifty, and I'd be every bit as lucky to wind up with half of that. So call it twenty-five thousand dollars, and on the one hand you can say that's not bad for one night's work, but when you do the math you understand right away how come the insurance companies have those huge marble buildings in Hartford, and I live in a one-bedroom apartment on West End Avenue.

"And where would that leave Edgar Margate? Why, they'd tell him how lucky he was, that instead of having to settle for a cash payout he'd be getting his twenty-one carvings back.

"Once I made a deal with the insurers, he was screwed. But he had two other options, either of which might work. The simplest would be to buy the carvings directly from me. If Margate paid me, oh, say fifty thousand for everything, I'd net twice what I could expect from the insurance company, and he'd still have ninety percent of that half-million in his pocket.

"Enter Katrina, who came to my store and brought up the subject of jade without quite committing herself. I suppose her hints were pretty broad, but they sailed right over the head of the Bernie Rhodenbarr she encountered, because he wasn't privy to the memories of the Bernie Rhodenbarr who'd committed the burglary.

"So all she managed to do was buy a lot of books, and Margate didn't want to read about jade, he wanted to own it. Enter Katrina's friend, Byron Fleeger—"

"Mr. Norfolk Jacket."

"The very man. He's still a burglar, so why not set a thief to rob a thief? He's also an actor, and if he can find a way to guarantee my absence, maybe he can let himself into my bookstore and poke around until he finds the jade."

She was nodding along, and then she stopped. "Bern," she said, "it doesn't make sense."

"No kidding."

"Why lure you away? You never stay open past six. All he had to do was turn up in the middle of the night."

"I know. Maybe it was the actor in him, maybe he figured playing a fake professor would help him get an Equity card. But the whole thing's nuts, because you have to remember it took place in an irrational universe."

"Something you and I dreamed up."

"Right."

"Unwittingly."

"Very much so. But he did what he meant to do, luring me to an empty apartment on West Third Street. Then he showed up at Barnegat Books, but two other men got there ahead of him. One of them got in by vandalizing my gates and forcing my door, and was sitting in my desk chair when a second man used a glass cutter to follow in his footsteps. And by the time Byron got there—"

"Bern, I'm having trouble following this."

"Well, I should hope so."

"Bern, I think I'm getting a headache."

"I've already got one."

She'd raised a hand, and I thought she was going to scribble, letting Maxine know we were ready for the check. But instead she made the circular motion to summon up more scotch.

I said, "Really? You think we can handle another round?"

"I think we need it," she said, "whether we can handle it or not. What I know I can't handle is any more information, not tonight. We'll have one last round, and then I'm heading for the non-Euclidean intersection of West Twelfth Street and West Fourth Street."

"The Cubby Hole?"

"And I'm not sure I can handle that, either," she said, "but that's where I'm going. What's tomorrow?"

"If today's Thursday—"

"Then tomorrow could be just about anything, couldn't it?"

"I think the odds favor Friday."

"Assuming we wake up in the same world we go to sleep in."

"I'm pretty sure we will."

"Well, don't take any chances, okay? Go straight home. Don't stop to bowl a few frames."

"How could I? Bowl-Mor's gone."

"Well, don't try to find a way. And don't use your Metrocard, or whatever you've got in your wallet. Take a cab."

"If I can get one."

"You'll get one. And Bern? When you go to bed, just do me a favor, okay? Don't read anything."

40

"So I'm still a lesbian," Carolyn announced.

"Alert the media."

"What's that supposed to mean?"

"That your news flash isn't going to get anybody a Pulitzer. You never stopped being a lesbian. You made a point of declaring yourself as such several times a day."

"While you and I," she said, "were ducking each other's brains out."

"And the credit or blame for that," I said, "belongs to the world we were in at the time. But you never stopped being a lesbian, and I never stopped being your best friend."

She thought about this, nodded. It was something like twenty-two hours since she'd sent me home with instructions to avoid reading anything, and we'd each put in a full day's work and were back at the Bum Rap thanking God that it was Friday. She'd prefaced her earth-shattering news with an account of the previous evening, which had begun at the Cubby Hole and concluded in a suite at the Carlyle, with a woman whose half of a Silicon Valley software business was worth more than the Kloppmann Diamond.

And her husband owned the other half. They'd started the business together, and as it was becoming successful they got married, not exactly ignoring the fact that he liked boys and she liked girls, but deciding that was beside the point. And they had two kids in high school—"a boy and a girl, or maybe it's the other way around"—and they looked for all the world like a happily heterosexual couple, and he had his discreet same-sex affairs, and so did she.

And once or twice a year they'd leave the kids in Cupertino and fly somewhere, New York or London or Paris or Rio, and go discreetly crazy.

"So I had a good time," Carolyn said, "and confirmed my sexual identity. Not that it needed it, but still."

"Are you going to see her again?"

"What for?" She drank some scotch. "Bern, when I wasn't awash in Sapphic excess, I was thinking about Edgar Margate and Katrina Beckwith and Byron Fleegler."

"I can't believe you remembered all their names."

"I was paying attention," she said, "until I couldn't. And when I thought about it afterward, it sort of made sense. Except when it didn't."

"Oh?"

"Byron showed up at your store, and Mason or Jason was dead—"

"I think it was Mason."

"Like it matters. Mason was dead, and the person who killed him, whose name I can't remember—"

"I never gave it."

"Well, that explains it. Mason was dead and the killer was gone, and Byron poked around until he found Margate's jade carvings and carried them off with him."

"And took the time to tape the glass circle in place, establishing himself as the ultimate gentleman burglar."

"Right," she said. "But I thought you found the jade carvings untouched in your hiding place, where you must have stashed them after the burglary you don't remember committing."

"Ah," I said.

"But if Byron found them in your desk drawer, and took them with him when he left—"

"I made that part up."

"You made it up?"

"I made up all of it," I said, "but part of what I made up was what actually happened. But not all of it."

I explained. Byron Fleegler got close enough to my desk to see the dead man sitting there, and that was as much as he needed to see. He never opened a desk drawer, never found my $16,000, and never even looked for my hidey-hole. So he didn't come close to finding the carvings, and at that point his only real concern was getting away from a murder scene without doing anything that might implicate himself.

But by Saturday evening, when Ray and his helpers had filled my store with suspects and hangers-on, I'd been busy. I'd retrieved the carvings from where I'd stashed them, and I'd done a decent job of redistributing them.

"In Katrina's bedside table," I said, "and in Margate's office safe, and in the pocket of a belted jacket hanging in Byron Fleegler's closet. It was a hectic couple of days and nights, with a lot of locks to pick, and it would only have been possible in the universe we'd created."

"One without security cameras and pickproof locks?"

"That was a big part of it. Luck was another factor."

"Luck?"

"In that universe," I said, "I was just plain lucky. Like with cabs."

"You stepped to the curb and raised your hand, and a cab would appear."

"Every time. Well, I had a few days and nights where I took a lot of risks. And there were some close shaves, like ducking into a closet or a bathroom and holding my breath."

"That must have been scary."

"Exciting," I allowed, "but not all that scary. Because I somehow knew I was going to get away with it. And it worked. I put the carvings where they would do the most good."

"Saturday night," she said, "when you explained it all, Edgar Margate said it was all nonsense, and any carvings that turned up in any of those places had obviously been planted to frame him."

"He wasn't entirely wrong."

"But then Ray asked him to turn out his pockets, and Margate put his hand in his pocket, and his eyes bulged."

"They did, didn't they? Poor old Mr. Pennybags, with his eyes halfway out of his head."

"And he took his hand out of his pocket, and he couldn't believe what he was holding."

"A little green squirrel," I recalled, "with both his paws clutching a nut."

"You must have planted it on him. When you walked through the crowd, being the genial host."

"A little sleight of hand," I said.

"If he'd felt anything—"

"But he didn't."

"Or if he'd just idly put his hand in his pocket. But he didn't do that either, did he?"

"No," I said. "And when everybody saw him standing there holding the squirrel, it didn't help him make the case that he'd been framed. And he had, of course, but he'd been framed for something he'd actually done."

"And that's true of everybody, right? Not just Margate and Katrina and Byron, but all of the others?"

"Ah," I said, and reached for my own drink. "Not exactly."

"There were two other big questions," I said. "Who killed the Tweedle twins, Jason and Mason? And who wound up with the Kloppmann Diamond?"

"Abel Crowe wound up with the diamond, Bern. We sold it to him. But that's not how you explained it."

"While you and I were riding up to the twenty-ninth floor," I said, "with the admittedly felonious intention of burgling the apartment of the absent Istvan Horvath—"

"There was nothing there to steal."

"If we'd known as much, we could have stayed home. But we rode up to Twenty-Nine, and Peter Tompkins saw an opportunity."

"Peter-Peter?"

"He'd met Istvan Horvath, he knew I wasn't Istvan Horvath, and if I was there under false colors I was probably looking to commit a crime. He watched the floor indicator and saw that we got off at Horvath's floor, so we were probably looking to burgle Horvath or one of his neighbors, so that meant I was on the premises and available to take the fall for anything that might get stolen that night from anybody in the Innisfree."

"Like Orrin Vandenbrinck."

"The man himself," I agreed. "Peter knew he was away, he'd watched the whole party pile into the limousine on their way to the theater. He'd have to leave the lobby unattended for a few minutes, but the building was mostly unoccupied and non-resident visitors were few and far between. The risk seemed minimal.

"The hard part was proving the publisher wrong and actually being able to put down a Lee Child novel. The rest was easy, because Peter's master key would let him use the private penthouse elevator. He rode it to its only destination, the Vandenbrinck penthouse, and he stepped out of it and into the living room."

"And just down the hall the television set was making a racket, and two men were having an argument, and—"

"No such thing," I said. "All was quiet, and some unerring instinct led him to the master bedroom, where he opened the right drawer and found what could only be the Kloppmann Diamond."

"How was that possible, Bern?"

"It wasn't."

"Oh. But you just said—"

"I made all this up," I said. "When did anybody ever voluntarily stop reading one of the Reacher novels? He stayed at the desk, eyes glued to the page, and he was right there when we left, and as far as he was concerned I was Istvan Horvath coming and going."

"Oh."

"Now do you want to hear—"

"Yes, of course. I'll try not to interrupt."

I drew a breath. "He found the diamond," I said, "and immediately headed for the elevator. But when he passed what I guess was the den, something got his attention. Maybe he smelled gunpowder, maybe the TV was on, maybe the door was ajar and something caught his eye. He took a moment to investigate, and what he saw was one of the bodyguards. Evidently only one of them had accompanied Vandenbrinck to the theater. The other had stayed behind, and someone had kept him company and shot him dead."

"So Peter—"

"Kept a cool head, and went back to the desk, determined to finish his shift. He was there when the first cops showed up, and he escorted them upstairs to the penthouse and let them discover the body for themselves. And when Ray Kirschmann came around to ask questions, he remembered the self-designated Istvan Horvath and gave Ray my description.

"Then his shift ended, finally, and he went home to his studio apartment in the Bronx. He probably took a little time to admire the Kloppmann Diamond, and to try to work out what the hell he was going to do with it, but the first order of business was to tuck it away, and he did so in a reasonably inventive manner. He rolled it up in a pair of socks and let it keep company with the other pairs in his sock drawer.

"And that's right where Ray found it."

"He knew where to look?"

"Someone may have given Ray the idea," I said. "Someone may have remarked idly that the first place an amateur hides something is where he keeps his socks."

"Someone may have said that?"

"It wouldn't surprise me."

Long silence.

"Bern? That's the scenario, right? The way you laid it out the other night."

"Right."

"But Peter-Peter didn't go to the penthouse. He went there when the cops came, he took them up there, but until then—"

"Unless he had to pee, which is certainly possible, I'd say he never left the desk."

"You found out where he lived."

"Which wasn't terribly hard, actually. What with Google and social media. He lives just a few blocks from Arthur Avenue, and wouldn't you know he posts pictures of his food?"

"You went there," she said, "and rolled up the diamond in his socks."

"Just like an amateur," I said.

"But how did you get your hands on a fake diamond, one that could pass itself off as the Kloppmann stone? It's not like a Mondrian, you couldn't sit down and paint it yourself."

"No."

"Then—"

"It wasn't a fake."

"It was a real diamond?"

"It was the genuine article," I said. "A diamond, and not just any diamond. The Kloppmann Diamond."

"Abel gave it to you?"

"Abel was already in his stateroom, on his way to one exotic port of call after another."

She looked at me. "I don't believe it," she said.

"Okay."

"Except I do. You actually broke into your friend Abel's apartment."

"There wasn't really any breaking involved," I said. "I couldn't have opened the locks any more gently if I'd had his keys."

"You picked his locks. You cracked his safe."

"Again, cracking's not exactly *le mot juste*. It's true that I opened the safe, but there was no force involved. Just, you know, a certain amount of ingenuity and innate skill, polished by years of experience, and—"

"Our good friend Abel bought the diamond from us, and you stole it back."

"You know," I said, "when you put it that way—"

"When I put it that way," she said, "it sounds terrible, but what other way is there to put it? You did business with the only receiver of stolen goods who happens to be decent and honorable—"

"The only one I know. There could be others."

"You sold him a priceless diamond, Bern, and then you stole it back."

"I took it back."

"Without permission. I think that counts as stealing."

"If he hadn't already left on his cruise," I said, "I could have gone to him and explained the situation, and he'd have given me the diamond. But he wasn't where I could reach him, so I had to take his consent for granted."

"If you'd explained it to him—"

"He'd have understood, and cooperated."

"'Ve vill chust undo our deal, Bernard. You are velcome to ze diamond.'"

"Something like that, but the accent's a little heavy."

"'And of course you vill return ze money I paid you, you and ze beautiful Carolyn.'"

"Oh."

"But you didn't, did you, Bern?"

"No."

"So do you want to explain to me how it wasn't stealing? Keeping the money and taking back the diamond?"

"Half the money was yours. I didn't have the right—"

"I'd have given it back to you in a heartbeat, Bern. You had to talk me into taking it in the first place, remember?"

"I thought about returning the money," I admitted.

"So what stopped you?"

"It was just a thought. My next thought was that I might have a need for the money, and that Abel wouldn't."

"Why not?"

"He'll take that cruise," I said, "and he'll go from one cruise ship to another, and eventually he'll get what he's decided he wants."

It took her a minute. "Oh," she said at length.

"Right."

"Burial at sea."

"When he talked about it," I said, "he made it sound as though it was something he found very appealing."

"That's so sad, Bern."

"Is it? What happened to Abel in this universe is what's sad. He was brutally murdered by a podiatrist, and that was a lot of years ago. In the universe where we sold him the Kloppmann Diamond, he got the chance to go on living, and to an overripe old age at that. He survived a concentration camp, remember?"

"He must have been—"

"He was around thirty in 1945 when the war ended. You want to do the math?"

She did, and her eyes widened.

"That universe we conjured up has been good to Abel," I said. "He gets to be well over a hundred, and his health is okay and he still has all his marbles. And, right up until they're ready to play the bagpipes for him and put him overboard, he'll be able to pride himself in owning the most famous gemstone in the world."

41

"Dum," she said. "And Dee."

"Oh, right."

"Jason and Mason. Bern, unless I'm missing something, they were the only two actual casualties. Both shot dead, one in the Innisfree penthouse while we were swiping the Kloppmann and the other in your store."

"Right."

"Jason and Mason, and it's apparently impossible for me to remember which is which."

"Well, they're both dead," I said, "and while we laid eyes on them from a distance we never really met either of them, and those weren't their right names anyway, so why bother?"

"In other words, don't worry my pretty little head about it?"

"There you go."

"Who killed them, Bern?"

"Beats me."

"You don't know?"

I shook my head. "Haven't got a clue."

"How is that possible?"

"Ignorance is always possible," I said, "and there's no end to the things I don't know."

She thought about it. "When you explained it, you sort of

implied that Peter-Peter might have taken a gun along when he went up to the penthouse."

"I'm pretty sure what I said was that there was no evidence he had anything to do with the bodyguard's death."

"No evidence."

"None whatsoever."

"In other words, we can't prove it but we know he did it."

"Someone may have come away with that impression," I said airily, "but there'll be no murder charges brought against Peter Tompkins."

"And you don't think he did it."

"Not for a moment," I said. "How could he? He never went up to the penthouse."

"Oh, right. That was just something you invented."

"And it seemed credible," I said, "given that they found the Kloppmann rolled up in his socks."

"Where you put it, after you got it back from Abel's safe. So Peter-Peter didn't lure the other Tweedle to your store, or follow him there."

"Certainly not."

"But the same person must have killed both of them, Bern. Right?"

"You think?"

"Come on," she said. "Both shot dead, both killed the same way. Was it the same gun both times?"

"It could have been. Ray was still waiting for a ballistics report."

"So who could have done it? Who was responsible for the Croatian Cessation?"

"They weren't Croatian."

"They weren't?"

"They were Transnistrian."

"I don't even know what that is."

"Natives of Transnistria."

"There's no such place."

"There certainly is."

"Not in this universe, Bern."

"In this universe," I said, "and also in the one we just got back from. It's a breakaway province of Moldova." And I explained just how Transnistria had asserted its own independence after the breakup of the USSR, and how a war had ensued, and how it turned out, and it was all news to Carolyn. I won't go through it here, but you could look it up.

Or not.

"Transnistrian," she said, when I'd finished. "Did I say it right?"

"Close enough."

"That's interesting," she said. "Sort of. But it doesn't explain who killed them, or why."

"I think it's safe to say that they did some bad things in Transnistria, and wherever else they lingered in the course of the odyssey that ultimately brought them to New York."

"Bad things," she said. "Well, I wouldn't put it past them."

"Let's say, for the sake of argument—"

"What's the point of arguing?"

"—that the Tweedles killed a man in Transnistria, or somewhere else in Eastern Europe."

"But not Croatia."

"And let's say the man's son wanted vengeance."

"Oh, he had a son?"

"No," I said. "You know what? It's better if it's a daughter.

The daughter adored her father and swears she'll avenge him, and she turns up in New York and finds the men responsible."

"Jason and Mason."

"She manages to meet one of them in a bar."

"What bar, Bern?"

"Well, it probably wasn't the Oak Room at the Plaza. She strikes up a conversation in his native language—"

"Transnistrian?"

"Whatever. Next thing you know it's time for the boss to catch Gillian Fremont's opening at the Delorean, but somebody has to hang back and guard the Kloppmann Diamond. So Jason or Mason—"

"I'm pretty sure it was Jason, Bern."

"—magnanimously volunteers to stay home, and takes the opportunity to smuggle the most beautiful woman in Tiraspol up to the penthouse."

"Tiraspol's in Transnistria?"

"It's the capital."

"And she's a real beauty, huh? But you didn't ever meet her, did you, Bern?"

"I didn't have to," I said. "I made her up. I don't know what happened, or who managed to be up there with Mason—"

"Jason, Bern."

"Fine, Jason. Whatever. He had somebody in the den with him, somebody who put three bullets in him, so why wouldn't it be a Transnistrian daughter out for revenge?"

"And why wouldn't she be gorgeous?"

"Exactly," I said.

"And then, after she shot him—"

"She found some way to get out of there."

"Okay. I won't ask you how."

"Good."

"And then I guess she found a way to keep an eye on people coming and going from the Innisfree, and when the surviving Transnistrian went to your bookstore, she followed him there." She frowned. "But what would give him the idea to go there?"

"You tell me."

I wasn't the only one who could make things up. "Peter-Peter described the two of us to Ray," she said, "and Ray didn't need more than half a minute to ID us. When he did his interrogations, he'd have tried to find out if anybody knew you. And it would be natural enough for him to mention your name."

"That's how Vandenbrinck found out I was involved," I said, "and knew to turn up with Punjab and the Asp."

"And hire you to get his diamond back."

"Right."

"Which you did, Bern."

"Did I?"

"At the moment it's probably in an evidence locker," she said, "but it won't stay there forever. He's the legal owner, he's got title to it, and it won't be too long before he gets to put it back in the drawer of his bedside table."

"Unless he decides on a safer place for it."

"First he'll have to let his actress girlfriend try it on. Gillian? I want to say Freebie."

"Fremont."

"That's better. He hired you and you delivered, but did he pay you anything?"

"Not a penny," I said. "It never occurred to me to ask for anything. The way it must have looked to Vandenbrinck, all I did was hold court at the store and spin some incomprehensible story of what had happened. As far as recovering the Kloppmann, well, it was Ray who found it in Peter's sock drawer."

We talked back and forth, and at some point another round of drinks appeared as if by magic, and disappeared every bit as magically. The conversation wandered here and there, as it will do, especially when drinks keep appearing and reappearing. I don't know that either of us got drunk, but it was probably just as well neither of us was going to be called upon to drive or operate machinery.

There were, Carolyn kept saying, a few things she didn't entirely understand. Like where the killer went, the vengeful daughter who'd done in both of the Tweedles. And how the second Tweedle had pulled off the break-in, and what he'd done with whatever he used to wreck my window gates.

"Look," I said at length, "you're trying to make sense of all of this, and it's not possible. Right now, you and I live in a rational universe."

"We do?"

"More or less. Things happen for a reason, even if sometimes it's a stupid reason, or an incomprehensible one. But the universe we conjured into existence made things up as it went along, and they didn't have to make sense. I don't know who killed the Tweedles. The woman I fabricated seems like as good an explanation as any, but she's just somebody I made up."

"I think I get it."

"In fact," I said, "one way or another, we made all of it up. From the SubwayCards and Bowl-Mor to Punjab and the Asp, we made it up."

"Then it didn't happen, Bern?"

"Oh, it happened."

"So it was real," she said, "*and* we made it up."

"Right."

"And I don't really have to understand it, do I?"

"Nope."

"Now that," she said, "is a good thing."

I walked her most of the way home.

"October," she said. "Don't you love October, Bern? I've got to say it's New York's best month."

"And this year there's more of it than usual."

"Because we had our little vacation in another world, and here we are, right back where we started."

"Right back *when* we started."

"Oh, that reminds me," she said. "I'll be tied up tomorrow night."

"Really? I didn't know you were into that sort of thing."

That earned me an eye roll. "Two friends of mine, they've been together for three months. That's the longest relationship either of them has ever had, so they're throwing a party to celebrate."

"Sounds like fun."

"To you, maybe. I just hope they're still together at the end of the evening. The last time I saw them they were trying to kill each other."

"Really?"

"Well, verbally. The C word turned up in just about every sentence. But that was at Paula's, so who knows if anything like it ever happened?"

"Maybe they worked it out in that other universe," I suggested, "and everything will be fine tomorrow."

"Maybe. So that's tomorrow, but maybe I'll see you Sunday."

I shook my head. "Come Sunday," I said, "I've got a date. You'll never guess who called."

"You're right."

"How's that?"

"Like you said, Bern. I'll never guess."

"So I'll tell you. It was Katie."

"Katie?"

"Katie Huang."

"Juneau Lock," she said. "Your Taiwanese flutist. Or is it flautist?"

"It's whichever you want."

"She's back in town?"

"She will be. At Carnegie Hall, performing Mozart's Double Concerto for Flute and Harp with the Bratislava Symphony Orchestra. There'll be a ticket for me at the box office, and afterward I'll be taking her out for a very nice dinner."

"And who knows," she said, "what might happen after dinner."

42

At lunch time Monday, Carolyn showed up at the bookstore with bento boxes from a sushi joint we'd been meaning to try. There are high-end sushi restaurants that charge the earth, and maybe they're worth it, but I'll never know. I figure sushi is either all right or it's not, and if it's not you go to the emergency room.

Monday's sushi was fine. Carolyn reported on the three-month anniversary party, which had been happily uneventful, and I reported on my evening with Katie, which had not.

"I really like her," I said. "You know how it is when you get together with someone you haven't seen in months? With most people you have to catch up, but with some you don't. You're both just there."

"You had a good time."

"A very good time."

"Will she be around for a while, Bern?"

"This morning," I said, "we had omelets at my usual breakfast place, and finished up just as her Uber showed up to take her to the airport. Right now she's somewhere between here and Amsterdam."

"Wow."

"That's a good word for it."

"It sounds as though the two of you really get along, Bern.

If she was back in New York full-time, or even most of the time—"

"What would probably happen," I said, "is things would run their course, because they always do."

"For you and me both," she said.

"Right."

"I'll meet somebody, and I'll think *Hey, maybe this'll work out,* and then it crashes and burns."

"That's what happens, all right."

"And then I think, *Shit, I really thought maybe that would work out.*"

"Uh-huh."

"And then I think, *You dimwit, it just did. This is how it worked out.*"

"There you go."

"There we both go," she said, "time and time again. I guess that's okay, isn't it?"

"I'd say so."

"Sooner or later," she said, "Katie and her flute will be back in New York for longer than a day or two, and you'll get together. And it'll last until it doesn't."

"The way things do," I said, "until they don't."

"And you never know who might pop into your store, and what might come of it."

"Just the other day," I said, "two great-looking women came by, one after the other. And there was a certain chemistry in the air, I have to say, and it wasn't just my imagination, because each of them made a point of giving me her phone number."

"Really? How come you never told me?"

"I told you. How come you don't remember?"

She looked puzzled, and then light dawned. "That was in—"

"Another world," I said. "Their names, you may recall, were Mallory Eckhart and Gretchen Kimmel, and they both bought plenty of books, too, which shows you what a different world it was."

"And gave you their numbers, and didn't you tell me you copied them into your phone? Bern, what would happen if you called their numbers?"

"Nothing," I said.

"Nothing? How can you be sure? Bern, it seems to me it's worth trying."

"It seemed that way to me, too," I said. "Saturday night, while you were partying and the *Law & Order* rerun was failing to hold my interest. I called both their numbers, and both were in service, but not in the service of Mallory Eckhart or Gretchen Kimmel, not in this world. I got a man who spoke a language I couldn't identify, let alone speak, and a machine that told me I'd reached the offices of some generic-sounding firm, but that my call was very important to them, and the last thing I should do was hang up."

"But I'll bet you did, didn't you?"

"I did," I said, "and then I made one more call."

"Oh?"

"I still remembered Abel's original number. And the last time I dialed it—"

"He answered, and we wound up eating Girl Scout Cookies."

"And I told myself that world was closed to us now, but I called the number anyway, and some woman answered. She told me I had the wrong number, and I said I was sorry, and we were both telling the truth."

After a long moment she said, “Bern, we don’t get to find out what happens in that other universe, do we?”

“I’m afraid not.”

“Will anybody wind up going to jail?”

“Probably not. The Tweedles were the only victims, and I don’t have a clue who killed them, and neither does anybody else.”

“That daughter from Transnistria, out to avenge her father.”

“Edgar Margate got his collection back,” I said, “and the worst case scenario is he’ll have to reimburse the insurance company. My guess is it won’t get that far, because he and Ray will work something out to their mutual advantage.”

“Whatever world he’s in, Ray’s pretty good at coming out ahead.”

“I don’t know if Mr. Pennybags and Katrina Beckwith will have a future together,” I said, “but they’ll have to sort that out themselves. And Byron Fleegler doesn’t have to worry about going to jail, and neither does Peter-Peter.”

“So it all works out,” she said, “but then I guess it always does, doesn’t it? One thing keeps on leading to another. Something happens, and you sell a book and I wash a dog, and life goes on. We keep on keeping on, don’t we?”

I thought of the proverbial lady who fell off the observation deck of the Empire State Building. I said what she said as she passed the thirty-fourth floor: “So far so good.”

“And that’s good enough, Bern. Somehow we survive. Even when we have the bad luck to get what we want. What’s the matter? Where are you going? Did I say something?”

“I keep forgetting to give you this.”

“*The Screaming Mimi.* By our old friend Fredric Brown. I

don't know, Bern. Are you sure it's safe for me to read this? I won't wake up in a world where parallel lines meet?"

"Like at the Cubby Hole? At the corner of West Fourth and West Twelfth?"

"Bern—"

"I think you're safe," I said. "You can read anything you want. We're back in this universe for keeps."

"I hope so." She weighed the book in her hand. "*If you want something badly enough, you'll get it.* That's the book's message, right?"

"Half of it. The other half is that once you get it, you won't want it anymore."

"I guess we both already know that, don't we? But I'll read it anyway, and after that I think I'm gonna have another go at *Candide.* I read it in school, but all I remember is that this is the best of all possible worlds, and I have to say I see that a little more clearly in the light of recent events."

"I know what you mean."

She didn't say anything, and neither did I, and the silence stretched a bit, and then our eyes met and locked.

She said, "I never knew I wanted it, but I guess I must have. And you must have wanted it, too, whether you knew it or not."

"I guess."

"I swear I never knew I wanted to sleep with you, Bern. I've known I was a lesbian since before I even knew there was such a thing. And then my Metrocard turned into a SubwayCard and took me places I never dreamed I wanted to go."

"I know."

"And all of a sudden," she said, "you were the only person in the world I wanted to go to bed with. I never stopped being a lesbian, but it was sort of beside the point."

"I know what you mean."

"And it was just wonderful, but at the same time it scared the living crap out of me. Because what would it do to our friendship?"

"I was going through the same thing," I told her. "Our friendship's the best thing in my life—"

"Mine too, Bern."

"—and could we ever go back to being the way we were?"

"Well?"

"I think we're fine," I said. "I think I feel exactly the same way about you as I did before."

"Me too."

"Except with one slight difference."

"Oh?"

"Well, we've had the experience," I said. "And it's not like it happened in an alcoholic blackout and we don't remember it."

"I certainly remember it," she said.

"Me too."

"Vividly."

I nodded. "And fondly."

"Uh-huh."

"So for years we were best friends who had this unconscious and unacknowledged itch—"

"And now it's been scratched."

"Right."

"And scratching it turned out to be very satisfying, and now it doesn't itch anymore. Bern? I'm glad it happened."

"So am I."

"Genuinely glad. And I'm glad we're back the way we were before."

"Me too."

"Right where we belong, living our lives in the best of all possible worlds. It really is, isn't it, Bern? The best of all possible worlds."

"There are a lot more possible worlds than I ever imagined," I said, "and God knows there's a lot wrong with this one, but when all is said and done, yeah, I have to say he was right."

"The best of all possible worlds. Aren't we lucky to be in it?"

"Very lucky."

"A straight man and a gay woman, and on some level there was some sexual tension between them, even if they never suspected it. And they slipped off to another universe and dealt with it, and now they never have to do it again, do they?"

"It's been handled."

"It has," she agreed, and something came into her eyes. "On the other hand—"

"On what other hand?"

"Well, life's never a hundred percent predictable, is it? And who's to say what might happen some night after a few drinks, with Patsy singing "Faded Love," or Ron Carter playing bass behind Ethan Iverson. I mean, you never know what could happen, do you?"

"No," I said, "guess you don't."

"What'll probably happen," she said, "is nothing, and that's fine. But if something does, well, I just want you to know I'll be okay with it. Because as long as we're in it together, this'll still be the best of all possible worlds."

MY NEWSLETTER: I get out an email newsletter at unpredictable intervals, but rarely more often than every other week. I'll be happy to add you to the distribution list. A blank email to lawbloc@gmail.com with "newsletter" in the subject line will get you on the list, and a click of the "Unsubscribe" link will get you off it, should you ultimately decide you're happier without it.

LAWRENCE BLOCK is a Mystery Writers of America Grand Master. His work over the past half century has earned him multiple Edgar Allan Poe and Shamus awards, the U.K. Diamond Dagger for lifetime achievement, and recognition in Germany, France, Taiwan, and Japan. His latest novel is *Dead Girl Blues*; other recent fiction includes *A Time to Scatter Stones, Keller's Fedora*, and *The Burglar in Short Order*. In addition to novels and short fiction, he has written episodic television (*Tilt!*) and the Wong Kar-wai film, *My Blueberry Nights*.

Block contributed a fiction column in Writer's Digest for fourteen years, and has published several books for writers, including the classic *Telling Lies for Fun & Profit* and the updated and expanded *Writing the Novel from Plot to Print to Pixel.* His nonfiction has been collected in *The Crime of Our Lives* (about mystery fiction) and *Hunting Buffalo with Bent Nails* (about everything else). Most recently, his collection of columns about stamp collecting, *Generally Speaking*, has found a substantial audience throughout and far beyond the philatelic community.

Lawrence Block has lately found a new career as an anthologist (*At Home in the Dark*; *From Sea to Stormy Sea*) and recently held the position of writer-in-residence at South Carolina's Newberry College. He is a modest and humble fellow, although you would never guess as much from this biographical note.

Email: lawbloc@gmail.com
Twitter: @LawrenceBlock
Facebook: lawrence.block
Website: lawrenceblock.com

CPSIA information can be obtained
at www.ICGtesting.com
Printed in the USA
LVHW021422151122
733197LV00007B/225

9 781954 762206